BOOKS BY SUZA KATES

The Savannah Coven Series
Whisper of a Witch
Conviction of a Witch
Binding of a Witch
Haunting of a Witch
Possession of a Witch
Deception of a Witch
Suffering of a Witch
Vengeance of a Witch
Sacrifice of a Witch

Watchtower Maidens
Return of a Witch

The Sisters' Grimoire Trilogy
The Sisters' Grimoire
Winter Fae
Chosen Blood
Brit
Rising Storm

Single Titles
Hallowed Eve
The Penance Stone
She Who is Hidden

DISCOVERY OF A WITCH
A WATCHTOWER MAIDENS NOVEL

SUZA KATES

ICASM PRESS

SAVANNAH

Published by Icasm Publishing LLC
5710 Ogeechee Rd. Suite 200 #278, Savannah, GA 31405
www.icasmpress.com

Library of Congress Cataloging-in-Publication Data

Kates, Suza
Discovery of a Witch / Suza Kates
    p. cm.

ISBN-13:978-1-942318-54-5
ISBN-13:978-1-942318-55-2(ebook)
I. Title

Printed and bound in the United States of America

10 9 8 7 6 5 4 3 2 1

1

Most of her dreams had come true in Savannah.

Lina Chastain stole a quick glimpse of the town she loved, glancing through the windows of her French café on Factors Walk. Green-painted trim framed ancient live oaks, their limbs filtering sunlight into dappled patterns.

Spring owned the city today. Azaleas bloomed pink, trolleys rolled by, and birds flitted everywhere. This was absolutely her favorite time of year, when the earth flourished with renewed life and gave historic buildings a colorful facelift.

She noticed a woman meandering, her face lifted to the sun. Lina envied her the simple pleasure but, for her, relaxing *me-time* would have to wait. Right now, work was calling. Rather, it was signaling, as a woman near the front held up her coffee cup and gave it a jiggle.

With a smile and a chin-notch to let her know she'd been seen, Lina turned to pick up a small round tray.

So she didn't see when he walked past the windows. She didn't know he'd returned.

But Bex had.

"Hey, look who's here." Sidling up next to Lina, Bex lowered her voice to whisper, "Cade is back."

Clenching the tray, Lina exhaled slowly through pursed lips. *Cade.*

Pretending she hadn't been affected by Bex's announcement, she tilted her head and said with all innocence, "Who?"

"Ha. I know you know who." Bex wiggled her brows, a glint bouncing off the tiny gemstone at the end of one black arch. A student at the Savannah College of Art and Design, Bex worked alongside her most days of the week. She was flamboyant, energetic, headstrong—and positively the best server Lina had ever hired.

Still playing ignorant, she handed the tray to Bex. "Here. I believe the couple at table two would like more cappuccinos. I'll start the drinks while you clear the dirties."

"Your avoidance tactics don't work on me, you know." Squinting one eye, Bex tossed a strand of hair from her face— one of many sea-green streaks in the raven black. "But since I value customer service, I will go clear." She gave Lina a mock salute and headed off, breezing by to check on another table as she made her way to the cappuccino-couple.

Suppressing a grin, Lina shook her head and watched the younger woman work her charm. Intentionally *not* watching Cade as he walked to a table.

For months he'd been a regular, just another customer for her to serve. Then along the way, they'd become friendly, enough that he'd shared his excitement with her on the day his first book released. That was the day she'd learned his full name was James Kincade, and the writing he did in her café was far more than a hobby.

She couldn't say exactly when attraction had bloomed. But it had—bigger and brighter than magnolias in May.

Now just the mention of his name made her stomach flip.

As he took a seat, Lina busied herself with palmiers and decided the arrangement of cookies looked fine. Then she gave in, sliding a look toward the corner.

She planned to be discreet. She planned to be quick. Just one fleeting glance and . . . he caught her.

Trapped, she locked her gaze with his, with those piercing gray eyes. And pleasure shivered through her chest.

The smile that flitted to her lips felt wobbly, so she tossed a small wave and turned to occupy herself with the espresso machine. *Keep working. Keep busy. And get a hold of yourself.*

A sigh burst from her lungs, so she hit the grinder to cover the sound.

Yes, most of her dreams had come true in Savannah, but she still had one or two left—the *big ones*.

But because they were the big ones—love, family, future—they required careful consideration and couldn't be based on emotion alone. Even if picturing it all with Cade filled her with a sparkling warmth.

Hard work. Practicality. These were the foundation for all good things. To Lina's way of thinking, that included relationships. Especially, she thought, tapping the basket of grounds, when the man chased practicality right out of her head.

Like he was doing now.

She mentally chided herself and returned her focus to making drinks. She locked the basket in place, ran hot water through, and let daydreams drift away on the scent of espresso.

Her parents had put their trust in her, allowing her to take over the business. So that meant business came first. She'd worked tirelessly the last several years, proving to her parents—and herself—that she was ready and willing to be in charge. To handle the planning and ordering and hiring and firing. All the behind-the-scenes details that kept the café running.

And running at a profit.

Everything rested in her hands now, while her parents took a much-deserved break. At least six months they'd be in France, renovating the château that had been her mother's childhood home.

And nothing would cause her to let them down. Nothing. Nothing. Nothing.

A trio of young women arrived at the counter, rescuing Lina from her own troubled mind. She flashed them a welcoming smile and went about steaming milk into foam, giving them time to discuss pastries and who-was-having-what.

Bex zipped past, headed to the kitchen with dirty cups. Just as quickly, she popped back out and beelined straight for the women, who now seemed ready to order. "I've got this," she tossed to Lina. "Why don't you deliver those drinks?"

With a troublemaker's chuckle, she paused and said, "Oh, and you'll need to greet tall, dark, and handsome, because I forgot." She gave a fake shrug of regret. "Oops." Then she launched into answering the women's questions, leaving Lina to handle tables.

Including Cade's.

Like I've done a thousand times before. Okay, maybe not *that* many, but still, there was no reason to be nervous. Feeling ridiculous, she gave one sharp, affirmative nod and loaded the cappuccinos on a tray.

First, she served the couple their drinks and, when they claimed they needed nothing else, she eased over to greet Cade.

He wore a dark gray T-shirt and faded jeans, laptop already open on the table. Probably working on his next book.

She did her best not to notice his well-developed arms or thick brown hair setting off his wintry gray eyes. The intensity of his gaze was distracting on its own. But paired with his intelligence, that *body*, and the sharp wit Lina knew he possessed . . .

Oh. There went that shiver again.

She pressed a hand to her stomach and put on her friendliest face. "Cade, how are you?"

"Lina, hey," he said, his tone easy and casual. "Busy day. I'm surprised I was able to get my table."

"You got lucky." Did her voice sound breathless? She cleared her throat and gestured to the view outside. "Weather like this always brings people in."

"I'll bet." He studied the people passing by for a moment, which gave her time to appreciate his strong profile, the straight nose and clean-shaven—

Stop that. She curled her fingers into her palm, her nails giving tiny stabs.

"The usual?" she asked him.

Settling back against his chair, he nodded. "Black coffee and a Parisien on a—"

"Croissant," she finished. "And you'll wait to decide on dessert later."

"Am I that predictable?"

She gave a soft laugh, feeling more at ease as they fell into their normal banter. "I get the sense *predictable* is not the best word to describe you."

He gave her a half-cocked grin. "Some might agree."

"So no, not predictable. I just know you too well."

As soon as the words left her lips, she felt a change, a soft current of electricity that snapped between them. His stare held hers for a moment. And another. Neither of them seemed able to break the connection.

Or neither of them wanted to.

Instinct tickled in Lina's gut. And just like that, she knew. The attraction was mutual.

Her pulse escalated and throbbed in her ears. As if she'd skipped the espresso and gone straight for the beans. "Ah . . . I." As her tongue stumbled over itself, she stepped back. "I'll just go start your order."

Maintaining a slow, steady pace, she weaved her way through the tables and didn't stop until she reached the kitchen. There, she finally released a mortified groan.

Bex trailed in after her, a hound who'd caught a scent. "Whoa. Are you blushing? What happened? Did he ask you out?"

"No." Lina put her fingers to her temples and shut her eyes.

"No one asked anything. I just made a fool of myself. I bolted from his table like a girl with a crush." Her eyes popped open and she looked at Bex. "Did I just say that out loud?"

"Yes, you did." Bex danced in place. "You're crushing on him. I knew it. I knew it!"

"Oh, please. A crush?" Lina scoffed and crossed her arms. "What grown woman even says that?"

"Apparently, you do." This from Manny, the cook, as he layered ham and Swiss on a croissant.

Lina would have cast him a scalding glare, but Bex was pulling on her elbow. "Now listen to me. You have to get back out there, take him his drink, and notch up what you've already been doing."

"No, I—" Lina waved her hand. "Wait. What have I been doing?"

"You know." Bex did a bad imitation of a hip-sway. "The shyness, the laughter, the lowered lashes." She batted her own in demonstration.

When Lina only stared at her, she said, "Hello. You *flirt* with him."

"I do not."

"Yeah, you do," Bex and Manny said as one.

Lina arched a blonde brow. "This feels like mutiny."

Bex pretended not to hear her and carried on, rubbing her hands together. "He flirts with you, too. It's just different. A subtle, dry kind of *cool-guy* flirting. You have to pay close attention or you'll miss it."

Manny snorted. "Cool-guy flirting."

"Shush," Bex said from the corner of her mouth. "This is important."

"No." Lina wagged a finger at her employee. "What's important is serving brunch to the people who keep us all employed."

"Yes, and we will. But you like him, Lina, and he makes you

nervous. Men *never* make you nervous."

Lina stiffened, the truth in Bex's words sending tension rippling down her back. "Alright, enough. We can't spend any more time on this. Besides," she lifted a dismissive shoulder, "he's really not my type."

"Yes, he is," Manny chimed in again, bobbing his bald head in affirmation.

"Yeah, boss. He is definitely your type." Softening her tone, Bex laid a hand on Lina's shoulder. "Even if you don't think he should be."

Bex was pitching like a pro today, all of her balls firing straight over home plate. And Lina didn't have it in her to swing away.

Because Bex was right. Despite Lina's physical reaction to Cade, something lurked just beneath his surface, something that gave her pause.

Staring up at the ceiling, Lina sighed before baring her truth, her misgivings. "I don't know. Sometimes he gets those thousand-yard stares and seems so serious, so *broody*—lost in all the darkness he puts in his books."

"He's a *writer*," Bex said, like that made everything obvious. "Aren't they supposed to be broody?"

"Maybe," Lina said, still wondering what cast the long shadows behind his eyes.

Bex continued to watch her. "I can see you're considering it."

Lina straightened her spine and lifted her chin. "I'm considering the raspberry macarons. They're running low."

"Alright, alright." Bex rolled her eyes all the way to Atlanta. "I'll take care of it." She pursed her lips. "And I'll make sure the macaron flavors are equal ratios."

"It's important the colors—" Lina began.

"I know. Presentation matters." To balance her quick response, Bex blew out a breath, gave Lina a quick hug, and stepped back. "But I really hope you change your mind. You work hard enough, and you *are* entitled to a little fun. What's the danger in one date?"

"I just don't have time. I have . . . responsibilities."

"Which you always make sure are taken care of." Still facing Lina, Bex retreated from the kitchen. "You know I love you, Lina, and I only want you to be happy."

"I—"

"Just remember," Bex said, cutting her off again. "There's no such thing as the perfect man, and what you think you want, may not be what you actually *need*."

With that, she pivoted and was gone, leaving Lina to stare at the empty doorway for a moment longer.

"Ahem." Manny tapped the stainless-steel counter and burst the fragile bubble of her thoughts. "Mr. Kincade's Parisien is up. You want to take it out?" His question sounded weighted with double-meaning.

"Of course," she answered breezily. "Can't keep the customers waiting."

"Mm-hmm." Manny winked and went back to smearing pesto on a baguette for a Provence sandwich.

Suddenly wavering, Lina frowned. Picking up Cade's order, she stared at the homemade potato chips. As if they held all the answers.

Maybe Bex was right. What harm could come from having dinner with a man she already knew and liked? Or just coffee? They should keep it simple. Make it casual.

In fact, she decided with a roll of her shoulders, she might even ask *him* out. Why not? If Bex could wear green hair—No, if Bex could *rock* green hair, then surely Lina could find the courage for a single date.

A date with Cade.

And maybe a kiss.

With the image in her head, Lina bit her lower lip. Feeling warm and shivery all at once.

~~~

So much for carefully laid plans.

Cade stared at the far wall and the framed cover of *Paris Match*, his finger tapping on the keyboard—*m-m-m-m*—until he noticed what he was doing. With a grunt, he deleted the letters and rested his hand on the table.

He'd almost burst out and asked Lina to have dinner with him, right in the middle of her morning rush. And precisely *not* the way he'd intended.

Still, he would ask her. Today. But at the right moment, when neither of them would feel hurried or uncomfortable. Cade didn't fool himself, and he knew his limitations, like the fact that he sucked at reading the emotions of others.

But Lina was different. From the start, he'd felt a certain connection with her, a tug—strong and instantaneous—that he couldn't ignore. And didn't want to deny.

Oh, she'd taken a little longer to get to the same place he was, but over weeks and months, he'd sensed the change. Lingering looks, fluttery smiles. And now he felt confident the time had come. Today was the day.

He caught motion in his peripheral vision, but it was only Bex exiting the kitchen.

Then Lina appeared, and his breath caught. It often did when she entered the room, like a sunbeam breaking through the clouds.

Her blonde hair was tied up in a messy knot, leaving a few tendrils loose around her face. If he were describing her in a book, he might call the color champagne.

But she wasn't a character, wasn't made of words. And to him, she held the mystery of starlight.

Tearing his eyes away from Lina, Cade focused on the computer and the blank page that taunted. How was he supposed to write about murder and the macabre with quixotic words floating in his head? Sunbeam. Tendrils. Starlight.

Cade swallowed hard. *Damn.* He was in trouble.

And wouldn't his father have something to say about that? Cade could imagine the words he would use, the jibes he'd sling at his only son. Romantic. Foolish. Worthless.

Weak.

Irritation flared in his chest, but he quickly doused the flame with ice-cold logic. His father's opinion didn't matter anymore. Cade had made sure of that.

These days, he made his own decisions, his own choices, and his choice was to pursue Lina. She all but radiated kindness and joy, the type of person others naturally gravitated to.

There was just something about her that made Cade want to bring her flowers. A gesture that would be a first for him.

But not roses, he thought, studying her as she flitted back and forth behind the counter. Roses were too cliché. Too stuffy. Not daisies either, as they weren't quite serious enough.

But tulips . . . yes. Bright and cheerful elegance. Just like her.

Cade made a mental note to check out local florists because, one day, he would bring her tulips. He wanted to know her better and to have her in his life, in this new life he'd created for himself.

Lina ducked into the kitchen and then, like she'd heard his very thoughts, followed a straight line to his table, a mug in one hand and a plate in the other.

"Here you go." Her lips kicked up in an open smile and her eyes danced, the green as dark and deep as an endless forest. "When you're ready for dessert, just let me know." Hands now empty, she pinched the gold pendant she wore between her fingers.

"Thanks, Lina." Taking the opportunity, he gestured to the necklace. "I've always wanted to ask you about that."

"This?" She held up the golden disc. "It's a coin. Been in my family for generations." A lilt entered her voice. "One of my ancestors drilled a hole in it, back when it wasn't worth much more than face value."

"And now?" Intrigued, Cade focused on the pendant. He was keeping her from work again, but this was just one more facet of who she was. And he was fascinated. "What's it worth today?"

"Well, there *is* a hole in it," she said, a sly hesitation telling him she debated over how much to reveal. "You're used to doing research, so I'll get you started. It's called Ecu d'Or au Soleil, circa . . ."

She narrowed her eyes and cocked her head. "Promise you won't tell anyone I walk around with this hanging from my neck?"

Charmed, Cade laughed and crossed his heart. "A solemn oath."

"Okay, two hints then. Louis the eleventh, and the year fourteen-seventy-five."

That was enough information to make Cade minimize the window with his manuscript and open a search bar.

Lina chuckled at his enthusiasm and said, "Don't forget to eat."

He glanced up, but she was already moving away to help someone else. Content to bide his time, he settled in to enjoy the Parisien and learn more about the coin.

Before long, he gave a low whistle. With or without the hole, she put a lot of trust in the box chain holding the heirloom. And no, he'd tell no one how much the coin was actually worth.

Curiosity satisfied, he turned his mind to the current chapter and finished off his coffee. After an hour, he'd drunk two more cups and written two-hundred words. Terrible words. Unimaginative words. Distracted-by-Lina words.

His thoughts were like spilled BBs, scattered all over and hard to catch. Eventually, he gave up and started searching online. Losing himself jumping from one obscure topic to the next, making notes of anything he might one day use.

By the time he closed his laptop, the crowd had dwindled. Only three tables remained and no one was waiting in line. Lina worked alone at the counter, using the lull in customers to organize and straighten.

His moment had arrived, and nerves made a bid to climb from his gut. So he drowned them with a final gulp of coffee.

On some level, his hesitation amused him. He'd spent his childhood avoiding flying fists and deflecting harsh words.

Yet pretty Lina Chastain made him feel clumsy and incapable.

Rubbing his palms down his thighs, he stood up and approached the counter. Lina was stacking dessert plates in the service area but turned around when he said her name.

"Hi." She moved to the display case. "Ready for dessert?"

"Sure. But first," Cade ignored the ripple of doubt in the back of his mind, "there's something I want to ask you."

Her movements quieted, and she looked at him with the barest hint of a grin. She seemed at ease, so he surged ahead. "I'd like to take you to dinner sometime."

There it was. Plain, simple, and unavoidable. Whatever her answer, at least he would know.

Lina's smile spread. Her eyes warmed. She drew a breath, and—

Her gaze darted over his shoulder to something behind him, and a slight wrinkle marred her brow.

Shifting, Cade tracked her line of sight to a petite brunette marching through the open doors. Agitation shouted from her tight, rigid posture.

By the time the woman drew near, Lina's happy expression had vanished, replaced by a frown. "Bryn," she said, her stare sharp with worry, "what's wrong?"

2

Lina studied Bryn, taking quick note of the purple semi-circles under her eyes and the tight set of her lips. Anxiety pulsed from her in waves.

A mental alarm sounded, and she clasped Bryn's hand resting atop the display case. "Are you okay?"

Releasing a short, windy laugh, Bryn squeezed Lina's fingers in assurance and then let go. "It's that obvious?"

"It is to me." Friends since the first grade, Lina could catalog all of Bryn's expressions, and distress was not a look she wore often.

"It's nothing." Bryn scratched her cheek and dropped her gaze to the sweets beneath the glass. "Just some crazy family stuff." She looked back up, caught Lina's frown, and quickly diverted by angling toward Cade. "Sorry, I didn't mean to interrupt."

"No, we were just talking . . ." Cade glanced at Lina, "about dessert." He took a step back, giving the two women some space.

"Cade," Lina said, not wanting him to leave yet, "I'd like you to meet Bryn Scott, a good friend of mine."

He inclined his head. "Nice to meet you."

"Likewise." Bryn worked up a grin before tapping the glass. "Since we're talking dessert, I think I'll take a chocolate croissant to go, and a coffee."

"And a croque monsieur." Lina lifted one brow, telling Bryn

not to argue. Bryn could never resist the hot, cheesy goodness, and she looked as if she could use some nourishment. Other than caffeine and sugar.

Bryn drew a long, deep breath, paused, and then, "Yeah. Sounds good."

"Cade?" Lina sent him a questioning glance. "What for you?" She intended to finish their discussion. And *not* the one about food.

She'd done a sharp, surprising pivot from indecision to certainty. Now she found herself desperately wanting to tell him . . . *yes*. So she waited for his reply, hope a fragile bubble ready to burst.

At last, he relaxed his stance. "One of those croissants for me, too."

"All right." Lina plated his pastry and put Bryn's in a bag, then she turned to fill a coffee to go.

As Lina worked, Bryn filled the silence. "I haven't had a chance to tell you that my Aunt Rae is back."

Capping the coffee, Lina set it on the counter. "You told me she was in town for someone's wedding."

"Yes, but now she's *really* back. She's going to stay." Despite the violet tint that spoke of exhaustion, Bryn's eyes lit up. "She's staying for good."

"Bryn, that's great." Lina beamed, truly happy for her friend. "I know how much you've missed her."

"Yeah. I have." The sound of Zen chimes suddenly jangled from Bryn's pocket. She pulled out her phone to see who was calling. "Speak of the devil."

When she turned away to answer, Lina explained to Cade, "Her aunt is a photographer and has spent most of her time traveling. Maybe you've heard of—"

"What?" Bryn asked, the alarm in her voice stopping Lina mid-sentence. "You've got to be kidding me. No. No. Just go. I'll meet you there." Bryn shoved the cell back in her pocket.

"Sorry, I can't wait for the sandwich."

"Bryn, you've got me worried." Lina tried to lighten the comment with a chuckle. "I've never seen you like this."

"I've never seen me like this either," Bryn mumbled, rubbing her hand across the back of her neck. "It's complicated. We'll talk later. But I . . ." She edged away, bag and coffee in hand. "I just have to go." She hurried from the café and out into the sunshine.

Lina and Cade both stared after her.

"I hope she's okay," he said.

"So do I." But Lina knew her friend was far from okay and was already formulating a way to leave work early. Bex could handle the café for an hour until the other server arrived.

Cade stared at Lina, scrutinizing. "On second thought, I'll settle up and take that croissant to go." He tilted his head meaningfully. "Maybe you should take off, too."

The strain she felt eased a bit, and she sent him a look of gratitude. "It's like you read my mind. And I will. But first," she said, pushing a flaxen strand from her face, "I believe you mentioned something about dinner?"

His handsome mouth hitched up on one side. "Is tomorrow night too soon?" Deep and rich, the timbre of his voice slid through her system and curled up beneath her heart.

Despite the lovely chaos inside of her, Lina smiled and spoke in a remarkably calm voice. "Tomorrow night is perfect."

~~~

Once Bex assured her she'd be fine handling the cafe on her own, Lina did a quick inventory of baked goods, jotted out a prep list for the following morning, and packed up the croque monsieur she'd asked Manny to prepare.

She left through the front door and crossed a bridge spanning the sunken alley below. Treading carefully on the deep stone steps built ages ago, she walked down to where she'd parked her white MINI Cooper.

Even with the influx of spring tourists, the drive to Monterey Square would be short. She took Bull Street, crossing the shopping district on Broughton, then slowed to a crawl behind an orange and green trolley car on Chippewa Square, where "Forrest Gump's bench" used to sit.

Lina knew the route by heart and enjoyed her slow-roll in the afternoon sun. She had her window down, appreciating the pleasing warmth while it lasted. Sweltering heat would soon cloak the city, persisting through summer and deep into the fall.

Soon she stopped at the curb in front of the Scott home. The ivory-hued Italianate house showcased nineteenth-century grandeur—high windows with ornate, gilded frames and a sweeping staircase leading up to a four-columned portico.

Bag in hand, Lina scurried up the steps and rang the doorbell. She didn't have to wait long before Bryn's grandfather opened the door. Over six-feet tall with a touch of silver in his dark hair, he was the picture of a distinguished gentleman.

Until his voice boomed through a brilliant smile, "Lina, what a nice surprise." His brows shot up in question. "You're not working?"

"I am. Well, I was. I left a little early today."

He slapped a hand to his heart, feigning shock at the revelation.

Chuckling, she shook her head. "I take time off once in a while. Every blue moon or so."

"As you should."

"Bryn stopped by a little while ago but rushed off before she could eat. I decided to play delivery girl." She reached inside the bag, casting him a sideways glance of mischief. "And since I'm here," she retrieved a box and offered it to him, "these are for you."

Peering through the clear plastic on top, he accepted the gift with obvious relish. "Macarons. You know these are my weakness. Just a minute. Do I see pistachio?"

Again, laughter bubbled from Lina's throat. "You do." The reaction Mr. Scott always had to her macarons was just another reason she brought them whenever she could. That, and the fact she adored him like a second father.

"Thank you." He patted the box and winked. "But I'm afraid Bryn isn't here. She's gone with Rae."

"Oh." Disappointment dropped the word like a stone.

"But they're at Arik's. I'm sure they wouldn't mind you stopping by."

"Arik?" Lina rolled the name around in her head, tabbing through memory files until she landed on the right one. "Wait. *Arik*? The same one who—"

"The very same." A slight furrow creased his forehead. As a father, he likely held a perpetual grudge for the man who'd broken his daughter's heart. "I know. I know. I'm still getting used to the idea myself." He huffed. "But they were both very young when they fell out, and Rae is happier now than I've seen her in a long time, so. . . ."

He gave her a shrug that asked *What can you do?* "Now. Directions. Do you know Hall Street, off of Forsyth Park?"

"Yes."

"Just follow Hall until you get to a red stone mansion on the corner. I doubt you'll have any trouble, but call Bryn if you do."

"Thanks, and sorry to bother you."

"For your macarons? I'd open the door to Sherman's army." He winked and gestured with the box. "Good to see you," he said, and then paused to add, "and good to see you taking a little time for yourself."

After he'd shut the door, she made her way down the steps, wondering why everyone seemed to think she worked too hard.

She fired up her car and returned to the scenic drive. Forsyth

Park bloomed with spring flowers and happy people. The huge expanse of grass hosted a variety of activities—students working in sketchbooks, a couple tossing a ball to a chocolate Lab, and a fierce frisbee tournament between bare-chested males. With a mostly female audience.

The pleasant scenes might have cheered her on any other day, but worry for Bryn kept slipping through, tiny whispers in her mind that something terrible had come into her friend's life.

Driving around the south end of the park, she hooked a right on Hall Street and slowed, in search of the house Bryn's grandfather had described. This wasn't the first time she'd been down this way, but she'd never had reason to stop and visit any of the palaces.

For that's surely what they were, with lot sizes and square footage four times the downtown average. The architecture here proclaimed a long history of elegance, and giant oaks spread their crooked arms high above the road, proof they had held firm through centuries. As had some of the houses.

Lina spotted Bryn's car and pulled over to park. Lips parted in awe, she exited her own vehicle and took halting steps down a paver walkway, scanning every detail of the mansion. The home was built of brick but whispered of *castle,* with a domed turret and lion's-head seals of red stone.

The steps led her up and through a wide arch to a large covered entrance where the lion-head motif continued with the doorbell. Musing over the dignified whimsy—was there such a thing?—she pressed the button and heard answering chimes from inside.

Soon the door opened, revealing a tall, fair-haired man whose smile didn't quite reach his dark brown eyes. "Can I help you?"

"Hi, sorry to bother you." Lina tightened her hold on the café bag. "I'm looking for Bryn. Her father directed me here."

"Oh, of course," the man said, his features relaxing, becoming more amiable. "Please come in." Still, he tossed a glance over his shoulder before stepping aside.

"If this is a bad time . . ."

"Lina." Bryn appeared, walking toward them with brisk steps. "Why are you here?"

Taken aback, Lina moved her mouth but no sound came out. The edginess was so unlike Bryn. Bryn who grinned during a Karate fight, baby-talked to dogs, and always knew a good joke.

Finally, Lina found her voice. "I wanted to bring your croque monsieur, though I'm sure the cheese is cold by now." The laugh she attempted came out forced and brittle.

"Oh, thanks." Bryn rushed forward and took the bag. "I mean it, thanks. I'd ask you in, but we're kind of in the middle of—"

"Bryn?" Another voice carried from beyond a set of French-paned doors that stood open to a long corridor. "Who is it?" Wheeling herself in a chair, an older blonde woman studied Lina with interest.

"It's just a friend with my lunch," Bryn called back. "Thanks again," she said, taking Lina's arm to steer her back over the threshold.

"I'm sorry, but I had to come," Lina whispered quickly. "Are you okay?"

Before Bryn could answer, the woman spoke, her tone mild yet steely with command. "Invite her in."

Bryn froze in place, an unrecognizable flurry of emotions crossing her features.

"Bryn?" Lina took her friend's hand. "Now you're scaring me. I feel like I should go, but I don't want to leave you."

"I'm okay. Honestly. I just . . ." Bryn exhaled and squeezed Lina's fingers. "I was going to tell you anyway, so you might as well come meet everyone."

"Everyone?"

"For starters, this is Arik." Bryn indicated the man. He

nodded in return.

"It's nice to meet you," Lina said. "I've heard your name over the years." Recalling how those discussions had gone, she quickly clamped her mouth shut.

Arik chuckled, breaking some of the tension that hovered in the air like sheets of glass. "I'm sure it was usually accompanied by some inventive curses."

"And plenty of them were mine." Bryn gently shoved his shoulder, but stress lines still framed her deep brown eyes.

"I'm sorry to show up like this," Lina said.

"Nonsense." Arik waved away her apology and gestured to the bag Bryn held. "Would you like me to take that to the kitchen?"

"Oh, sure." Bryn handed it over.

"I'll meet you back there," he said before asking, "can I bring either of you something to drink?"

"No, thank you. I'm fine." Lina didn't want to impose any more than she already had.

Bryn shook her head in the negative, and Arik left. His departure gave Lina a chance for a more in-depth perusal of the vestibule, a space large enough to hold the entire kitchen of her café. Twice.

A giant medieval-style tapestry covered one wall, depicting a scene with sword-bearing knights and ladies in a garden. Rich embroidery invited Lina to pick a ripe, red apple.

Beneath the tapestry sat an antique choosing table, a crystal vase of lilies atop its gleaming wood. Their floral scent mingled with faint traces of lemon, and Lina took a deep, indulgent whiff—she couldn't help herself—then spun in a slow circle.

She came to a stop face-to-face with Bryn, who quirked her mouth to the side. "It's okay to gape. I did the first time I came here."

"It's amazing." Lina crossed her hands on her chest. "It's . . . magical."

Bryn's smile faltered and she grunted. "That's one way to put it."

Now that they were alone, Lina decided it was time to find out what kept putting that troubled look on her friend's face. She moved closer. "Bryn, seriously, what is going on?"

"Follow me and all shall be revealed." The teasing fell flat, and Bryn grimaced. "I'm sorry, Lina." Bryn's sigh could have blown out the sun. "The last few days have turned my life upside down. Normally you would have been my first call, my first shoulder to lean on, but . . ."

"But what?" Lina coaxed, placing a comforting hand on Bryn's shoulder. "Whatever it is, you can tell me."

"I know, and that means so much to me, especially now. But this story, it's not only mine to tell. I'll take you to Rae and introduce you to Arik's mother."

"The lady in the wheelchair?" Lina glanced down the hallway, but the mysterious woman had vanished.

"Yes, and that's part of the story, too."

Lina jerked her eyes back to Bryn's. A frozen needle stitched a seam down her spine. "Her being in the wheelchair is part of the story?"

"Yes."

Suddenly afraid to have her answers, Lina remained silent, and when Bryn walked away, she quietly followed. They went beneath a staircase that wound up from a side passage and through the open doors. Familiar with the layout, Bryn continued to guide her, easily navigating wood-paneled corridors.

To Lina, the place was a labyrinth.

She tried not to stare into the rooms they passed, each fabulous in its own way. Behind every door she glimpsed silk-papered walls, wainscoting, Persian rugs, antiques. Her head was buzzing from the sheer scale of luxury when they arrived at another wide doorway and stepped inside.

This time, she didn't just gape—she sucked in a breath, slapped her chest, and released a small cry of wonder.

Tiles covered the expansive floor in a Gothic pattern, and diamond-paned windows lined the far walls. A behemoth fireplace sat between them in the corner, a glory of carved marble, behind an elaborate yet masculine desk. In the center of the room, a crimson couch anchored a seating area replete with exotic end tables and more than one Tiffany lamp.

Magnificent. The word popped into Lina's head, not only in reaction to the lavishness, but also because of the books. Shelves, walls, *floors* of books.

Her astonished gaze roamed around the library and up to a mezzanine where walkways allowed access to more of the collection. "Wow," the word out on a breath. "Sorry. I just . . . wow." And, since she couldn't form a coherent sentence, Lina chose to simply shut up.

"Don't feel bad. I made it halfway up the stairs before I caught myself."

Lina knew that voice, velvety smooth yet matter-of-fact. She scanned the room until her gaze landed on a woman in an upholstered wingback chair. "Cassidy?" Lina pulled her head back in surprise. "What are you doing here?"

Ice-blue eyes snapped with frozen flames. "Nothing good." Swirling brown liquor in a tumbler, Cassidy tossed back her hair. The midnight-black fell straight as a razor to just past her shoulders.

She owned a bookstore on Factors Walk not far from the café, but her presence and strange manner gave Lina a bad vibe, like she'd interrupted some clandestine meeting.

Perplexed, Lina cast a look around the room, encompassing all those gathered in the library—Cassidy, Bryn, her Aunt Rae, and Arik's mother, who had parked her chair on the other side of the desk, near an ancient-looking globe in a wooden stand. She stared at Lina, not unkindly, but in appraisal.

Bryn slapped her palms together, startling Lina. "So you already know Cassidy," she said, "and this is Mrs. Mansur."

"Please, call me Marit," the older woman told Lina. "I'm very pleased to make your acquaintance." She exchanged a knowing glance with Rae who stood near the windows.

"I told Lina I'd explain everything." Bryn kept changing her stance while her words popped like bullets from an errant machine gun. "I'd end up telling her anyway, because we're close. And she's here, so I might as well."

Then she did a full pivot. "But maybe now's not the time. Maybe we shouldn't involve her."

"Bryn." Rae stared at her niece. "You know it's probably no coincidence that she's here."

"Who?" Lina asked. "Me?" But no one was listening.

"She's *here*," Bryn stressed, leaning forward, "because she thought I'd like some lunch." Hands on her hips, her posture grew defiant.

"Bryn," Rae said again. Sun slanted through the leaded glass to fall across her face, a face hauntingly serene compared to Bryn's mounting emotion. "Everything will be fine."

"But—"

"You know what has to happen."

Bryn clenched her fists. "No," the single word a sniper's shot.

"We can't control the choosing." This from Marit, who also radiated calm. She folded her hands in her lap and turned to stare at the globe. "Forces are bringing you all together now, and they will not be stopped."

Lina's chest gathered in on itself, dread doubling up with confusion. "Are you still talking about me?"

No one answered, not even Bryn.

"We have to do this." Rae still spoke to her niece as she slowly crossed the room. "It will be better if we just get it over with."

Bryn pressed her fists together, jaw clenched.

But then her arms dropped, her shoulders sagged. "I know,"

she whispered and looked at Lina.

Cassidy leaped to her feet. "Wait," she called to Rae, "at least prepare her first. More than you did for me."

But Rae ignored her and advanced, closing in on Lina.

Instinctively, Lina took a step backward, barely resisting the primal instinct screaming at her to get out. *To run.* "Bryn?" Her voice wavered.

Rae eased closer. "We have to find out."

"Find out?" Lina's entire body trembled now, but she couldn't move, frozen in place by a strange mixture of horror and curiosity.

"Everything's going to be okay." Rae spoke softly, golden stare holding fast as she lifted her hand.

And reached for Lina.

3

Rae's hand landed gently on her arm, and a sharp burn flared to life on Lina's neck.

She gasped, clamping her hand just below and behind her left ear. The pain was instant and intense, conjuring a picture of a hot, glowing brand.

But then, just as quickly, the burn released.

Lina rubbed her skin but felt no sensitivity, no tenderness. Like it had never happened at all.

Though the pain had been brief, stark fear remained—terror sliding through her veins and into her gut, where it lodged like a block of ice.

Rae removed her hand, but points of electricity still danced where she'd touched Lina's arm.

"What did you do to me?" Lina heard the break in her voice, her palm still pressed to her neck as if she could contain whatever spell Rae had cast.

Bryn's family history had never been a secret, and now past conversations returned to her, filling her head with things she couldn't comprehend, things she wouldn't accept.

Images of ritual.

Murmurs of magick.

"Bryn?" Lina said, her eyes begging for explanation.

Bryn was at her side in an instant, her arm encircling Lina's shoulders. Then Cassidy came to her as well, both women flanking her, providing a sense of comfort. Of solidarity.

"I'm so sorry." Bryn touched her head to Lina's. "I didn't want this for you."

"It's not your fault." Rae still stood there, hovering too close for Lina's comfort. "You didn't ask for this. None of us did."

Cassidy's voice was low but scathing. "No, we didn't."

Lina turned, her gaze flying to the other woman's neck. In answer, Cassidy pushed her black hair aside, revealing a scar or—Lina leaned closer—a symbol of some kind. Pale in color, the mark wouldn't be visible to a passing glance, but as she stared, an image formed.

Three curvy lines. They ran horizontally with several smaller circles floating above one end.

"What is it?" Lina whispered.

"I haven't found out yet." Cassidy narrowed her eyes, the arctic blue growing colder by the second. "I was waiting for an explanation when you arrived."

The look she gave Lina echoed the resolve in her voice. "Now it seems we both need answers."

"It's not Rae's fault, either," Bryn said. "We didn't choose to be part of this, but . . . we've come to accept the responsibility." She angled her left side toward Lina and Cassidy and brushed back her hair.

"Responsibility?" Cassidy echoed, peering at Bryn's neck.

Lina studied Bryn's mark as well. The circle was in the same place as Cassidy's, but inside Bryn's, there were five wavy, vertical lines.

Bryn drew a deep breath, the way one did before diving from a cliff. "It's an ancient symbol for air." Her gaze shifted to Cassidy. "Hers is water."

"Elemental symbols?" Only when Lina curled her fingers in fear did she realize she was still holding her own neck. Without hesitation, she dropped her hand and demanded, "Do I have one?" Though she already knew.

Bryn squinted as she examined Lina's skin. "Yes. I can't be

certain but . . ."

"Just tell me," Lina snapped. Fear and frustration combusted, shattering what remained of her calm, practical nature. "Tell me what is happening!"

"Ah, something tells me I'm too late."

All heads turned toward the sound of Arik's smooth voice. He stood in the doorway holding a tray with dainty cups and a matching teapot. For all the upset he showed, he may as well have been serving a ladies' luncheon.

Cassidy's nostrils flared. "This is funny to you?"

"No. Absolutely not, and I apologize if I sounded flippant." He moved to a long mahogany table with carved legs and set down the tray. "Gallows humor, I suppose. My entire life has been affected by this family legacy, so things that seem unbelievable to you are simply part of my daily routine. But I assure you, I take what's happening very seriously."

With the slightest furrow in his brow, he glanced to Rae, Bryn, and finally, his mother. "Three of the women I care most about in the world are involved, and others I know have been hurt, simply due to proximity."

"Arik." Rae frowned at him.

"I'm only being honest. They deserve that much." He shrugged and looked back to Lina and Cassidy. "I'm not trying to frighten you, but sugar-coating will do you no favors."

"Bryn," Marit said, diverting everyone's attention, "describe Lina's symbol to me." She spoke in a soft and steady cadence, and Lina got the impression she was trying to maintain a sense of order.

Bryn sent Lina a look of apology and studied her neck again. "Lines like Cassidy's, flowing side-to-side, a few tiny circles underneath. And rising from above . . . it looks like a seedling that's about to open."

Marit's gaze landed on Lina's and held. "So now we have the power of earth."

"Power?" Lina squeaked. "No, I don't . . ." Picturing the thing on her neck, Lina wiped at her flesh with erratic strokes. "I don't want it. Take it off."

"I don't want mine either," Cassidy said. "Whatever this is, you need to pick someone else." She glared at Rae. "Remove it. Now."

"Rae doesn't decide who receives the mark." Marit folded her hands in her lap. "She is merely the conduit, channeling the gift that you were always meant to have."

"Gift? But how can —" Cassidy stepped away from Lina and made a halting motion with both hands. "Look, I consider myself an open-minded person, enjoy a good philosophical debate, and read everything from true romance to ancient aliens. Hell, I've been on more than one ghost walk in this town, trying to snap pictures of the elusive blue orbs. But whoever or . . . *whatever* makes the decisions, they've made a huge mistake. So, no. Sorry. I'm out."

She turned on her heels and strode toward the door.

"You can't just leave," Bryn called.

But Arik was the one who stepped in front of her. "Please, just stay and let us explain. Your life is books, so I'm guessing you're a seeker of knowledge. You can't deny that a sigil has spontaneously appeared on your skin, and I know you want to understand why. So," he spread his hands and stepped aside, "if for no other reason . . ."

Silence smothered the room as Cassidy stared at him, wrestling with her choices. Finally, she scowled again at Rae, then returned to her chair near a section of bookshelves and plopped down. "I don't know why I would accept any of this. I don't know you people."

"But you do know Lina," Marit pointed out, rolling forward. "Lina is friends with Bryn, and Bryn is related to Rae. You already have connections, and these bonds will only continue to strengthen."

Without responding, Cassidy picked up her tumbler again. She didn't drink the liquor, only swirled, swirled, swirled.

Lina turned from watching Cassidy to look at Bryn. Yes, they were friends, the very best of friends.

If nothing else, she trusted Bryn implicitly. "I don't know what to do or what to think," she took that trusted hand in her own, "but I'm listening."

Bryn's eyes became liquid brown pools of unshed tears. "I'm with you every step of the way, Lina. I *know* what you're feeling, and I understand the fear."

"We both do." Rae reached up to lightly trace a finger down her own neck. "My symbol represents the power of spirit, or ether." Wearing a long ponytail, she had only to turn her head for Lina to see the mark. Concentric circles, very different from the symbols the rest of them had.

"I've never heard of the power of spirit." Sighing, Lina relented and walked to the ruby-red couch. She sank down to the plush fabric, and when Bryn sat with her, a small knot of anxiety loosened.

Which left another fifty or so still tight in her stomach.

"Some say spirit is the fifth element." Cassidy continued to stare into her glass. "And that the five elements are represented by the points of a pentacle."

"Yes," Rae said. "Legends revolving around the five elements of nature go back farther than I'd ever imagined. Or cared to look."

Now that they were all listening, Rae drew a deep breath and began. "I've always practiced magick to a certain degree, but my symbol and the power that comes with it are both new to me. The sigil on my neck is also known as the mark of the Akasha. The Akasha is the first of the Watchtower Maidens and is able to activate the other four."

"The what?" Cassidy turned around in her chair, clearly interested.

"Are we supposed to be these four . . . who?" Lina reached up to rub her pendant. The connection to her family gave her something familiar to cling to in the midst of the unknown.

"Watchtower Maidens," Bryn said.

"But why us?" Lina glanced aside to her. "Why now?"

"Because I found—" Rae gestured to Marit and Arik, "*we* found a medallion." She went to the massive desk, opened a drawer, and held up a golden disc for inspection. "This unlocks the globe." She pointed to the antique next to Marit. "And once we opened the globe, the magick of the Akasha was released."

"Wait, a gold medallion that unlocks a relic. Mysterious symbols." Cassidy stood and took a few steps closer before stopping and tossing up her hands. "And magick? *Real* magick? I just . . . I just can't."

"I appreciate your skepticism," Arik said, crossing the room to deliver two cups and saucers to the table in front of Lina and Bryn. "And we wouldn't expect you to simply take our word. Not for something of this magnitude."

A soothing lavender aroma wafted from the tea, and Lina surprised herself by taking a cup to sip. Still reeling, she didn't mind a creature comfort. Nor did she mind letting Cassidy voice the fear and doubt for both of them.

But Arik's easy-going manner seemed to quell Cassidy's resistance, enough for her to join them in the sitting area. Once she took a seat, Arik brought her a cup of tea. She accepted, but the smile she gave him looked more like a grimace.

Arik spoke to Marit. "Mom, why don't you start at the beginning?"

4

Marit rolled her chair back and gazed at the antique sphere resting in a stand of brass and wood. "The power of the Akasha wasn't the only thing locked inside this globe. Rae," she said, "would you do the honors?"

Medallion still in hand, Rae walked over and slid the golden disc underneath the globe. A small *click* whispered in the air, and the sphere opened like a flower in bloom.

"The history of the Watchtower Maidens is inscribed on the walls of the interior." Marit made a circle with her finger, indicating the five separate pieces. "The writing is a secret language, one known only to those who were with the Maidens in the beginning. A code passed down to their descendants."

Now Marit turned her attention to Lina and Cassidy. "The first thing you need to understand is that there have always been dark forces in our world, but in the earliest of days, before mankind, these forces ruled the earth. They thrived in the darkness and chaos, unchallenged for thousands upon thousands of years.

"Eventually," she continued, "humans came into being. Over centuries, they developed skills and harnessed the powers of the earth. Societies developed and religions rose, creating unity and faith. The will of people to advance and to live worthy lives became a force of its own and unbalanced the natural power of the creatures who'd reigned for so long."

"And of course, the monsters fought back." Cassidy shrugged

and set her empty teacup aside. "What good is a story without an antagonist?"

"Yes, the darkness fought back, but by now there were also people who'd discovered the energies of the elements."

"They'd learned to do magick," Lina said, filling in the blanks as Cassidy had done.

"Exactly." With a small nod, Marit brushed her short blonde hair back from her face. "And while some mastered magick, others studied the enemy. Approximately 500 BC, a tribe of warrior scribes came into existence. They learned the aethyrical language, the language of spirits." Marit paused and sat up straighter. "Some called it *demonspeak*."

Lina rattled her cup in its saucer and decided to put it down before she broke the fragile china. This time, no one asked questions or offered insight.

"These warrior scribes became known as the Huktai. As a descendant, my husband was a Huktai." Marit's attention shifted to Arik. "And so is my son." Her expression softened, a mother gazing fondly at her child.

She cleared her throat and said to the women, "The Huktai have always protected the Maidens. And they will continue to do so for as long as necessary."

"Protect them from what, exactly?" Cassidy asked in a low voice, hands gripping the armrests of her chair.

"The scribes learned the name of the entities who lived here, the strongest of them collectively known as *DoSaa preSyajana*. Servants of darkness."

Marit paused, furrowing her brow. "Humanity used their new knowledge and continued to wage war on the evil creatures. In the face of their enemy's growing strength, the dark beasts grew weaker."

"Unbalanced power." Cassidy nodded to herself. "Like you said before."

"Yes," Marit said. "The DoSaa had no choice but to flee to a place of safety, a place where they could rest and restore their forces. A netherworld. They built a gate, a portal if you will, and made their escape."

"What they didn't expect," Arik said, jumping in, "was the joining of the Huktai's knowledge with the magick of others." His eyes gleamed with pride as he spoke to Rae. "Enter the Watchtower Maidens."

Rae gave him a conspiratorial smile in return, and for a moment—just a moment—Lina felt excitement stir in her belly.

"The five original Maidens possessed great talent, masters of an ancient craft known as Draconi Magick." Marit pressed her palms together and interlocked her fingers. "They used their power to call upon the four corners of the earth, the four elements of nature, all bound together by the power of spirit, of ether. The aethyrical power previously controlled by the dark."

"They created a seal." Arik spread his hands, clearly enthusiastic about the subject. "An enchanted seal that would lock the gate, thereby trapping the DoSaa in whatever hellish dimension they'd run to."

He raised a finger, a professor to his pupils. "And here is where the story turns ugly."

"Oh," Cassidy laughed, "*now* it turns ugly?"

Arik met her gaze. "Well, what's worse than fighting an enemy you know?"

Cassidy rubbed her chin as she mused over the question. "*Hmm*, an enemy you don't expect." She looked up at him again. "Betrayal."

Arik pointed that finger at her and grinned. "Yes."

Rae skirted around the desk and sat on a corner closer to the others. "Some of the Huktai feared the Maidens and the extent of their power. So they turned their weapons on the five women who had helped protect all of humanity." Her expression darkened. "They murdered the Maidens in their sleep."

"And fled like cowards," Arik added.

Lina scooted to the edge of the couch, interest in the story overriding concern. "What about the remaining Huktai? What did they do?" Caught up in the tale, she almost forgot the central role she now played.

Marit took over the telling again. "They broke the seal into four pieces, the aethyrical texts, and gave them to different Huktai to keep hidden in various locations. This way, the spell inscribed on the seal couldn't be used to re-open the gate and allow the DoSaa to return. As with many enchantments, it can be reversed by one who speaks the language and has the right ability."

She shifted in her wheelchair. "But the original gate vanished long ago, swallowed by the ground. Or so they say."

Marit lowered her gaze, now heavy with sadness. "My husband, Arik's father, spent his life searching for more pieces to the puzzle, and he believed firmly that another gate had been constructed." She pressed her lips together and lifted her head. "And that it had been built here in Savannah."

"Who would have built it?" Lina propped her elbows on her knees and leaned forward. "Do you know where it is?"

"We don't know who built it, if it even exists." Arik notched his chin toward a particular bookshelf. "My mother and I are working to translate my father's journals. There's no telling how much we have left to learn."

He edged over to stand next to Rae. "If there is a gate, we aren't certain where it is, but—"

"We have a pretty good idea," Rae finished for him. "If there is one, that brings us back to the priority. The four pieces of the original seal. The texts. The writing inside the globe describes them as stone fragments, and we have to find them first. We can't allow another gate to be opened."

Cassidy tapped her foot and tilted her head, thinking. "You're placing a lot of faith in an old story that may just be a parable. Where did this magick globe come from in the first place?"

"You're right. I do have faith." Rae held out her hand. "It's hard to deny magick once you've seen and felt it for yourself." A kind of mist began rising from her palm, the color of violets with a hint of sparkle.

A kind of cool breeze blew straight through Lina, leaving her in a state of shock. For once, neither she nor Cassidy spoke but simply stared with mouths open.

"The creation of the globe is another sad story," Rae said, continuing calmly, as if she hadn't just shaken them to the core. "And it's written inside as well. Both the globe and the medallion were created by the last Akasha to wield power. In the sixteenth century, during the witch trials in France, she was hunted down, taken prisoner, and eventually killed. Likely by those who would see the Watchtower Maidens fail."

"Why would anyone want that?" Lina asked.

Rae pursed her lips. "Unfortunately, there have always been people easily tempted by the promises that evil makes. Wealth, power, immortality. And yet some just enjoy doing wicked deeds."

She inhaled and continued. "But before the Akasha was captured, she and her husband, also a Huktai, created the globe and inscribed the history for those who came later. She then cast a spell to lock her magick inside."

"The last Akasha's husband spirited the globe away for safekeeping," Arik said, "along with the medallion and a piece of the seal. His family had long been guardians of a text. Hopefully, one of his descendants still has it, but since the globe and medallion were eventually separated, we can't be certain."

"I have a question," Lina broke in, her mind spinning to process the information. "Rae is the Akasha now, but there hasn't been another since the witch in France?"

"Well . . ." Rae trailed off and sent a wary glance to Marit. "There have been Akashas since then, but none ever had the globe and medallion at the same time. Therefore, they couldn't unlock it to receive the power inside or the ability to locate the other Maidens."

"Mom?" Arik lifted a brow and looked at his mother. "No sugar-coating."

"I second that." This from Cassidy.

Lina steeled herself for whatever was coming and, at this point, almost preferred a thick, sweet layer of confection.

Because the acrid taste of fear had returned.

"Actually," Marit put her hands on her thighs, "I was the Akasha before Rae. You see, the symbol transfers when an Akasha dies or becomes unable to fulfill her duties."

Lina couldn't stop herself from glancing down at Marit's wheelchair. Bryn had told her it was part of the story. What could have happened?

When she looked back up, she found Marit watching her.

"I'm sorry," Lina whispered, feeling rude and insensitive.

"It's fine." Rather than appearing offended, Marit tilted her head and smiled. "But no, the symbol didn't pass because I was injured. In fact, I'm getting better every day and hope to be walking again soon. You see, I had the mark of the Akasha most of my life, but then it was . . . suppressed."

"By a curse," Arik clarified, his staunch no-sugar policy clearly in effect.

"A what?" Lina flinched. And felt all those knots in her stomach tighten again.

"As I said before, my husband dedicated his life to researching, and a little over ten years ago, he came across a clue to the medallion's location. Together, we went in search of it and, in the process, we were attacked."

Marit swallowed, the pain she still bore etched into her features. "My husband was killed, and I was cursed. The curse left me in a vegetative state until recently, when Rae and some of her friends set me free."

Arik moved to his mother and put a hand on her shoulder.

"You see, the curse kept the symbol bound within her. And as long as she remained alive, it wouldn't pass to the next Akasha."

"Wait, wait." Lina's head grew heavy and static filled her ears. "You said this happened only ten years ago?" She and Cassidy exchanged looks of shock. "But that means . . ."

"Yes," Bryn said from beside her, her somber look confirming Lina's fear. "It means we have enemies here in Savannah. And they will do anything to stop us."

5

Great towering oaks grew on each side of the road, creating an allée that led to the old plantation house. In the creeping gloom of twilight, Searenn drove down the lane in her Jaguar. Sleek. Silver. Straight off the lot.

And for the low, low price of one major mind fuck.

Remembering the salesman's confused expression, she laughed savagely, deciding the ability to influence others might be her favorite post-resurrection skill.

And hadn't she earned it? Her newfound gifts were the least of what she deserved after fighting her way from a putrid pit of sludge and enduring the most unimaginable torture. The masters had designed such brutal cruelties, punishments and tests fashioned just for her. For the one destined to be sent back.

Despite the pain she'd suffered, she wouldn't change a thing. Because here she was, the newer version. Searenn 2.0. Stronger. Harder.

And meaner than the snakes she'd killed with her bare teeth.

Her knuckles tightened on the steering wheel as she punched the gas, gravel kicking and crunching beneath the tires. Golden fields stretched all around before bumping up to marshlands and their wide-open skies. She'd been down this particular road before, too often to count. This time, everything looked brand new.

No pun intended, she thought, grinning as she considered

her new body, stolen just recently from a weak, mortal woman. And damn—Searenn licked her lips—she had put this body to good use, enjoying as many men and depravities as she pleased.

Even with her new status, the pleasures of hard men still served her well.

Pulling to a stop in front of the house, she took her mind away from sex and perused the historic building, already half-consumed by runaway weeds and vines. She couldn't wait to have the plant life cut back, to contain the wildness. Wildness the previous owner had so enjoyed.

She exited the car and spat on the ground. Ronja was dead and gone, an immortal witch no longer. And in her place a new queen. The queen of death.

She liked the image the words evoked. For hadn't she ruled over death? Hadn't she returned to the land of the living? She exulted in her rebirth, and in the knowledge that her power was far greater than Ronja's had ever been.

And in place of Ronja's lone demon, Searenn was backed by the most ancient malevolence the world had ever known.

This world of man with its simple, meaningless, mewling existence. Her revival had not only given her new skills, but had also charged her with a mission. And if she were to succeed, she'd need a home base, preferably one befitting her position.

The previous mansion of the Amara would fill that need. Though the steps groaned beneath her weight, there were reasons she'd returned to the plantation house.

The isolation was certainly a plus, but she needed things that could only be found here. Some of her own personal belongings . . . and Ronja's pit.

A deep recess dug into the earth, positioned over an energetic marker, and already aligned with powers of the dark.

One look in the lawyer's eyes, and Searenn took over his mind. And with it, the entirety of Ronja's estate.

She didn't need the keys to open the door but used them

anyway, as an act of possession. Outside, twilight was giving way to night, the horizon turning the color of a bruise, so she flipped a switch to cast some light.

Nothing had changed. Nothing was new. Except for the layer of dust now covering every surface.

Deciding to worry about food later, she made her way upstairs, scraping her nails across the black and silver wallpaper. Ronja's gaudy statement of evil. Soon, she'd hire people to renovate the house.

Or would she? Did she even need to pay? How long could her persuasive spells last?

After all, if a vampire could have thralls, why not the queen of eternal damnation? The idea made her laugh, a deep, vicious sound in the gloom of night.

She embraced the shadows now, having suffered darkness like no other. Still, for practicality's sake, she turned on a hallway lamp—this time with a mere wave of her hand—and proceeded to her old bedroom.

The door still creaked when pushed open, and her sturdy gray blanket still covered the bed. But she didn't give a shit about sentimentality.

Intent on her purpose, she crossed the room and opened the closet. Lowering to one knee, she ran her fingers along the back edge of the floor until she felt a board wobble. She jerked out the plank and tossed it aside, no longer concerned with hiding her stash. No longer worried about keeping her secrets.

Reaching in and under, she stretched until she felt canvas, an Army bag folded over itself to protect what was inside. Her family heirlooms, and most prized possessions.

Rising, she exited the plain bedroom and headed for the master, already eager to test-run the huge tub and expensive mattress. Here the door didn't make a sound as she eased inside, and she'd swear the scent of fancy bath potions lingered. She'd love to have a long, hot soak and pile up in the luxurious bed.

But . . . first things first.

She moved to the chest of drawers and set down the bag, unfolding the thick material before undoing buckles and snaps. Finally, she extricated the books and papers passed down from her mother.

Few things in Searenn's previous life had held much value, but she'd bought only the best to safeguard her family records. The special artifact box had metal corners for stability, and inside the wrappings were no average plastic or paper, but polyethylene archival bags.

Without a glance at the first word, she knew she'd be able to understand the writings—scribbles and inscriptions that had long eluded her comprehension. Since her return, she'd held a new breadth of knowledge, an awareness gifted to her by the dark masters.

Her previous captors, the *DoSaa preSyajana*.

She ran a hand across the protective material and began to step away from the dresser. Then she stopped. Ripping off her hoodie, she studied her reflection in the large mirror. The blood, flesh, and bone had belonged to another, but Searenn's spirit had taken over.

Tattoos decorated her skin once more, covering almost every inch of her body. Except for her hands and face, the visible areas that might give her away.

Droehks had long been forced to conceal their ink, the markings of their strength, their ability to summon and control demons. Her kind had been driven into hiding, hunted by the humans who'd almost stamped them out of existence.

But no more.

Searenn dropped the hoodie and kicked it to the corner. Let them see her for who she was. Let them come and try to do her harm.

Teeth bared and muscles flexed, she stared into her own eyes—one black and one pale blue—and gave a proud toss of her hair, the same wicked black as her ink. *Just let them come.*

With renewed urgency, she picked up the ancient documents and took them to Ronja's desk. "No." She curled her lip and sat in the brocade chair. "*My* desk."

Despite the rage spitting and hissing like hellcats in her veins, she slid the books and folders out gently and set them aside. All but one particular tome.

Bound in animal hide mottled blackish-brown with age, the book held the truth of her people. A story so ageless the original language had been forgotten, even by the surviving Droehks.

Another flick of her hand, and lamps flared to life. She caressed the cover, opened to the first page, and delved in.

Her mind devoured the stores of information, the previously indecipherable words now as simple as a grade-school primer. She pored through the pages, feeling both pride and awe as she learned of her heritage.

Droehks had always wielded power over demons. Now, she understood why. The earliest, oldest monsters had mated with humans, thus creating a half-breed species. One that had evolved into her clan. Her family.

With fervor she read of the great treachery, of how mortals and magicians had taken over the earth, eventually forcing out the dark entities. And then locking them away forever.

Or so they'd thought.

For another hour she scoured the documents, finally landing on an unexpected gift. She opened a slim book with strange writing on the front.

She instantly recognized the symbols as Tamil, a five-thousand-year-old language. Was she proficient in every tongue now?

Another thrill rushed through her, a burst of unrestrained conceit.

In a blink, the markings translated for her. *Geneologies.* Curious, she looked inside. Her ancestors had kept meticulous records of their own lineage, their own births and burials. But that wasn't all.

They'd also tracked those of their enemies.

Those called the Huktai featured most prominently, the legacy of their family history documented from father to son. Searenn trailed her gaze down each page, reading and remembering.

Until she stilled, fingers splayed beneath two names with an additional notation.

Her stolen heart pounded and blood pumped through her system, awakening each cell with its own sweet poison.

They had one of the texts.

One of the four stone artifacts she had to have in order to open the *Dakhma*. The gate built by those who'd come before. Her ancestors.

Using her finger, she traced from the two names, following their family line to its very last entry, written in pen only forty years ago. While her family had been unable to read the archaic books, they'd always known to monitor the Huktai, especially those entrusted with the aethyrical texts. Over centuries, they'd done their job.

And Searenn now had a path to follow.

"I need a computer." Glancing around, she searched the room, then recalled how Ronja had disliked electronics in the bedroom. But there had to be at least one laptop somewhere. She just needed to—

A distant thumping interrupted the plan forming in her head, and it took her a moment to recognize the sound. Someone was knocking on her door.

"Who the hell?" She stood abruptly, flipping the elegant chair on its side with a *whump*!

Irritated by the distraction and invasion of her privacy, she stomped downstairs and yanked open the front door. She paused, unspeaking, and took in the two individuals standing on her porch.

At first glance, they looked almost identical, both with short hair as black as her own but with pure white framing their faces. A dye job? And both exactly the same?

But one was a female, shorter and wearing an ebony minidress with stockings and clunky shoes of the same dark color.

Before Searenn could kick their asses off her property—or do something more creative—the girl moved her perfect pink lips. "Your grace," she said, bowing her head, "we are happy this auspicious time has finally arrived and have traveled far to be at your command."

Her words carried a foreign accent, something heavy and exotic.

"Don't call me that," Searenn snapped. "You make me sound like a fucking princess." She studied the male, also dressed in the color of death. He had the same pale skin, the same soulless black stare. "You two are brother and sister."

"Twins," the girl acknowledged. "We are followers of the dark lord Asmodai, ruler of the earthbound. Those who did not escape. Our kind have been here in this country only a few generations, but long have we been waiting for you." She tipped her head again. "And only you."

"So . . . you've come to serve." Considering, Searenn gave them another onceover and crossed her arms. "I'll need some people, but . . . you both look a little *frail.*"

The brother smiled then, and the menace in his depthless eyes made him seem far older than she'd originally guessed.

"Looks can be deceiving." He held Searenn's stare, a sensation of corrupt magick rolling from him in a current.

"We'll see," Searenn said, reassessing the two strangers. She noticed baggage sitting in the gravel drive. "Looks like you came to stay. Fine. I'll see if you're worth my time." She scrunched her brow. "What are your names?"

"Dacia." The girl placed a hand to her sternum before

indicating her brother. "And Alexandru."

"Then come in, Dacia and Dru. You're just in time." Searenn turned away, tossing over her shoulder, "I'll be taking a trip."

6

"What do you think, Mr. Remi?" Lina spoke to the cat's image in the mirror. Hearing his name, the old yellow tom paused in licking his paw, sent her a blasé look, and gave his full attention to claws that apparently needed trimming.

"I agree. It's just right." Studying her full-length reflection, she modeled her emergency little-black-dress the way she might a gown tailored for a royal ball.

She pressed a hand to her stomach, blew a long, slow breath through pursed lips, and slipped into carefully chosen heels. "It's just a date," she told herself.

For the hundredth time that day.

"It's just dinner."

Actually, she reminded herself, swinging by Remi to scratch behind his ears before leaving her bedroom, it was going to be dinner and *a surprise*. Or so Cade had said when he'd called earlier, asking if she minded eating a little earlier than planned.

Considering she'd allowed extra prep time, she didn't mind at all. In fact, she couldn't wait to see him again and had spent the day balancing between excitement and pre-date jitters.

She took cautious steps down the stairs and, against her will, recalled the *other* feelings she'd been having all day. Fear, disbelief, anger—all unwelcome emotions she'd ruthlessly shoved into a mental lockbox.

The compartmentalizing was a kind of denial. She knew this.

And she didn't care.

Why should her life be interrupted by something she'd never asked for and hadn't agreed to? Her days were busy enough with the café and now, she thought, raising her chin stubbornly, she might be adding romance to the mix.

The fact she'd been resistant to that romance only yesterday didn't play into her logic, because whether or not she went on a date with Cade was up to her. It was *her choice*.

The incomprehensible Watchtower Maidens notion—not to mention the *brand* on her skin—had been foisted upon her against her will.

So no, she wouldn't waste her time. Her life was structured and orderly, as she preferred. She kept two separate day-planners for Pete's sake, and nowhere had she penciled in "find ancient stones before demons do."

Downstairs now, she grabbed her beaded handbag off a table and tried to take five deep breaths like her mother often suggested. If only Lina had inherited her mom's laid-back spirit along with her father's pragmatism.

She had never been very good at channeling Zen. Her usual way of dealing with problems was to break them down and tackle them head-on. Just get it done.

But how was she supposed to do that with things she couldn't even wrap her head around? Magick. Witches. Elemental powers. What category did she file them under?

"Nope. I won't think about this tonight." She gave a single decisive nod. "I'll think about it tomorrow." And with images of Scarlett O'Hara whirling in her mind, she snickered and stole a glance at the grandfather clock. Ten 'til six. Cade should—

The doorbell chimed in answer.

So the man had good looks, intelligence, *and* punctuality. A trait she greatly admired.

Another breath to steady her nerves and Lina opened the door. "Cade." She filled his name and her smile with more confidence than she was feeling. "Right on time."

"A bad habit of mine," he said. "Do you need a few more minutes?"

"No, no. I just need to make sure the back door is locked." And take the minute it required to walk there to get her wanton instincts under control. In a suit the color of charcoal with a crisp white shirt—no tie and unbuttoned at the collar—Cade's look might be called casually formal.

But to Lina's mind . . . he was just *hot*.

"Please, come in. I'll just be a sec." Leaving him there, she quickly checked the doors to the courtyard and returned to find him reaching through the stair rails.

"Someone's come to check me out." He sent her a sidelong grin as he continued scratching beneath Remi's orange chin. The cat allowed the petting but kept his eyes open, evaluating the stranger who'd entered his domain.

"Careful, or he'll let you do that for an hour," Lina joked. "And then you'll be picking orange hairs off of your suit for the rest of the night."

"Small price for making a new friend." Pulling his hand back through the rails, Cade gave her a subtle onceover, careful not to let his gaze linger too long. "You look great," he said, "and the dress is perfect."

"Thank you."

He moved to her side, putting his hand lightly on her back to walk her out. The contact sent a frisson of heat straight to her belly just as his crisp male scent teased her nose.

"You *smell* great," she whispered. And froze. Had she said that out loud?

One side of his mouth kicked up.

Yep. She'd said it. And he'd heard it.

"What's it called?" she asked, trying to normalize. "Your cologne?"

"Uh . . . I think it has Blue in the name." He stared down at her, his hand still on her back. "It's only aftershave."

His gaze penetrated hers, his palm scorched right through her. As he leaned in, going for the kiss.

But he stopped abruptly, his jaw tightening. Then he gestured toward the door and visibly relaxed. "Ready?"

"Yes." The word all but burst free, but she put on a mask of calm and tried to ignore the dip of disappointment. And tingle of anticipation.

Because now she'd be thinking about kissing him all through dinner.

Firmly back in his courteous role, Cade escorted her down the brick steps and held open the car door until she slid in and got comfortable. Lina considered herself an independent woman, but his effortless chivalry called to a secret part of her, the feminine part of her that enjoyed feeling cherished.

As they pulled away to glide down Jones Street, he said, "Your townhouse is great. I noticed the plaque beside the door. Built in 1806?"

"Yes, I love that about Savannah. The way houses brag about how long they've been here." Lina luxuriated in the car's leather seats and masculine scent. "Truthfully, it belongs to my parents. They purchased the property when I was little, intending to rehab and sell for a profit, as they'd done with others in the city."

"Your parents seem to have good heads for business." He turned on Abercorn. "You must come by it naturally."

"I guess I do." Staring straight ahead, she added, "My mother said when they were finished, she couldn't bear to put it on the market. She'd put more of her heart into the townhome than anywhere else, and without realizing it, had picked all her favorite colors and styles. She'd been designing the home of her heart."

"Well, I'd say she's definitely got a talent for it."

"That's nice of you. And I happen to agree. Which is why

it's no hardship to have the place all to myself while they're in France."

"That's right." Cade sent her a glance before refocusing on the road. "You said they'd be there for a while, fixing up your mother's childhood home."

"Yes." As they passed beneath a streetlight, she studied his face. "You remember."

He nodded in the dim light, his lips curving. "I remember."

They cruised past Colonial Cemetery with its huge arched entrance and then slowed to round Columbia Square. Lina had her first inkling of where they were going, a hunch Cade confirmed when he parked near Reynold's Square.

Lina almost got out of the car but caught herself and waited for him to come around and open the door. In an easy and mutual silence, they cut through the square, her heels tapping on bricks near the statue of John Wesley.

"I hope you like this restaurant." Cade notched his chin to a two-story building the color of a Catalina rose. The doors stood open at the top of the steps, emitting a golden glow from inside the Olde Pink House, one of Savannah's finer restaurants.

"I do," Lina said. "Although, I haven't been here since I graduated high school. The danger of living in such a spectacular city is that you forget to take full advantage of its charms."

"Then you're due for another visit."

Cade confirmed their reservation with the hostess and followed the woman to one of the more private dining rooms. Here the brick walls had been painted ivory, a stylish contrast to the exposed beam ceiling of dark brown. Flames flickered inside hurricane lamps, and trees sheltered the windows of the second floor, creating a space both elegant and cozy.

"It's so romantic," she said, slipping into the high-backed chair. "I mean . . ."

"I'm glad you think so." Cade sat opposite her. "But I'm

afraid you've found me out, discovered my secret plan."

Lina put her napkin in her lap. "Which is?"

"To make sure you stop seeing me as one of your customers."

Her eyes met the wintry gray of his. She felt a pinch, a sigh. Then something popped inside her like a champagne cork.

The spreading fizzle told her it was joy.

A server approached and broke the spell. And with her head and heart still fuzzy with thrill, Lina could only listen as he described the evening's specials. She didn't bother to open her menu. She'd never be able to focus.

After he'd finished, she remembered at least one item that sounded good. "I'll bet that pasta is delicious," she told Cade.

"I was thinking the same. And if you like wine, they have an amazing Tuscan Chianti."

"*Mmm.* Sounds exactly right."

Once the server had taken the menus and gone, Cade waited a beat, considering her from across the table with an expression that warmed her all over. "I'm glad you're here with me, Lina."

The warmth turned to heat and rolled through her, soft and pleasing. "I'm glad you're not my customer, Cade."

He gave her that crooked grin of his. "I was afraid you might cancel." When she frowned, he added, "If things had turned out badly yesterday. With your friend."

Cade saw tension slip across her features and spread down to her shoulders. "I'm sorry. I shouldn't have brought it up."

"No, it's fine."

She sipped from her water glass, the hurried movement telling him things were not as fine as she'd like him to believe.

"She was given some unexpected responsibilities," Lina said. "They've added a lot of stress. That's all."

"It's good she has a friend like you. One she can count on." Cade had meant to be reassuring, but he would swear her face paled.

The server returned to open the wine and pour for them

both, preventing him from saying more. But he spoke as soon as he was alone with Lina again. "Well, she definitely gave the impression of one who's capable, ready to handle whatever is thrown her way."

"She is." Lina nodded but seemed lost in thought. "She's always been strong. And strong-willed. I've been lucky to have her in my life. Through grade school, high school, and then we even went to college together."

"I'm trying to form a mental picture of that." Cade wanted to lighten the mood. He wanted to see her smile again. "Meticulous Lina and strong-willed friend."

When she laughed, he laughed with her.

"It wasn't too crazy," she admitted, loosening up again. "At least not all the time. We had our fun, of course, but we both had our eyes on the future. I studied business, having decided to stay with the café, and Bryn majored in finance."

"Now that, I did not expect."

"That's Bryn for you," Lina said, trailing her finger up and down the stem of her glass. "Full of surprises."

The food arrived then, bringing the aroma of caramelized onions and pecans. Cade took advantage of the distraction and allowed Lina to do the same. Whatever she'd discovered about Bryn was still troubling her, so he'd avoid any further mention of her friend.

She stabbed a ravioli with her fork but focused on him before eating. "I've told you some about my friends and family." Her lips curved. "Now it's your turn."

Gluing his gaze to his bowl, Cade thought of the carefully structured facts he kept ready for these situations. Over the years, he'd learned how to skirt the truth, without actually lying.

But the thought of being deceitful with Lina—in any way—filled his mouth with the taste of ash.

And it must have shown.

"I'm sorry," Lina said, her fork still hovering over the shiny white bowl. "You don't have to—"

Cade lifted his hand casually. "It's just that my parentage probably isn't my best selling point." He shrugged and lightened his tone. "But that's what first dates are for, right? Finding out what the other person brings to the table, and what you might be getting yourself into?"

"Maybe." She angled her head to the side. "But don't think I didn't notice how you let the subject of Bryn drop. I'm willing to return the favor."

Considerate yet straightforward, Cade thought, and so like her. Another reason to return her honesty with some of his own. But what would she think if she knew the whole story? Would it change the way she looked at him?

"I can tell you my family isn't like yours," he said, reducing the stark comparison with a laugh. "We had our traditions, plenty of structure, rules, and discipline. Just less of the affection than the average parent-child relationship."

Sympathy flashed in Lina's green gaze, but that was exactly what he didn't want. Tonight wasn't the time for sad stories.

"We may have lacked the normalcy of your typical American family but, on the plus side, things could never be called boring. One time," he said, waggling his fork and chuckling as he spoke, "my father sent me to a monastery in the mountains."

"He what?" Lina's eyes widened and she froze, wine glass halfway to her lips. "Why would he send you . . . Where?"

Amused by her reaction, Cade speared a ravioli and stuck it in his mouth. He grinned at her as he chewed.

"Come on, you can't drop a line like that and then leave me in suspense." She set her glass down and waited.

"I'm not allowed to disclose the location, but—" His own laughter cut him off when her jaw dropped. "I swear I'm telling the truth." He'd never imagined he'd enjoy this particular story, but sharing with Lina somehow cast things in a different light.

"He sent me for training—martial arts, focus, patience, wisdom—your basic coming-of-age movie. At least, that's how he saw it."

"Did it work?" Her lips quirked in a teasing expression. "Did it make you wiser?"

"It made me thinner," he said. "Vegetarian diet." As if rebelling from the memory, he ate another meat-filled pasta.

After a moment, he went on. "It wasn't that bad, really. The monks spent a lot of time on reflection and meditation, not to mention the chores of everyday life. I would do my part of the work fast and then make myself scarce, escaping into books every chance I got."

"How old were you?"

"Fourteen." That was the truth.

"How long were you there?"

"A few months." And that wasn't.

When he caught himself distorting facts, Cade decided to hit fast-forward. "Basically, my father had a plan for me. I had my own. Luckily, he wanted me to go to college, so I left. And I never went back."

"And now you're an author." Lina used her wine glass to make a toasting gesture. "With a second book releasing next month on the eighteenth."

Cade paused. Apparently, he wasn't the only one who'd tucked away details from their conversations. "You remembered."

Lina simply grinned over the top of her glass before taking a drink. Then she returned her attention to her plate. "So how about a preview of what's to come in book two?" In a playful whisper she added, "I promise not to tell."

The lighthearted banter came easily and continued throughout the meal. Cade couldn't remember ever enjoying a woman's company the way he did Lina's.

When his cheeks and stomach ached, he knew he'd never laughed as much either.

At last, the bowls were cleared and a dessert menu delivered. Pursing her lips, Lina perused the offerings. "It all sounds very decadent. And rich." She laid down the laminated card. "I think I'll have to pass."

"I can't fail on our first date, and it seems wrong to skip dessert completely." Resting his arms on the table, Cade leaned forward. "Do you like pralines and fudge?"

She mimicked his pose. "Am I breathing?"

"I'll take that as a yes. Good." He signaled for the check. "This offers the perfect segue."

"Segue to what?"

"To the surprise."

7

Sunset was almost a memory by the time they walked down the sidewalk of Bay Street. Between two of the buildings comprising Factors Walk, Lina caught sight of a yacht gliding down the river.

Taking her hand, Cade guided her into making a turn. They passed beneath an arbor, thick with vines and bursts of tiny white flowers.

But as they crossed the walking bridge, Lina felt a flutter of unease. Most of the shops had *Closed* signs in their windows, lights low and locked up tight. Only one place still burned bright within.

Cassidy's bookstore.

The anxiety she'd felt at Arik's house rushed back, rising up like a black wall. She stuttered to a halt. "Cade, what are we doing here?"

He pointed to a poster displayed outside the door. "Karen Arlington is here tonight. She's doing a reading and then signing books."

"Karen Arlington?" Lina's voice sounded distant to her own ears. Was it mere coincidence he'd brought her to Cassidy's place of business? "She's one of my favorite authors."

Revelation hit, and she jerked her head toward Cade. "That's the surprise." Relief poured through her in a calming flood. He knew nothing of her connection to Cassidy or what Bryn and Rae had revealed the day before.

"I had no idea she'd be here." She wrinkled her brow, now more confused than afraid. "How did I not know that?"

"If I had to guess," Cade said, starting forward, "I'd say it's because you work too much." He opened the door, engulfing them in the welcoming scent of coffee and something sweet.

"You're the third person to say something like that in the past two days." Lina huffed in resignation. "Maybe I should start listening."

But later, she decided. Reassessing her work schedule would have to wait. Right now she was too enthralled by the idea of meeting Karen Arlington. *Karen Arlington!* Stepping inside, she tracked the store in search of the author, gawking with hands clasped, having herself a true fan-girl moment.

Chairs sat in rows before a podium, and a table had been positioned in one corner next to a banner advertising the writer's latest book. Exhilarated, she whirled to Cade. "Now I see why you wanted to eat early. So we'd be here in time for the reading."

"And don't forget about the pralines and fudge." He indicated another setup with coffee urns and trays of the promised desserts.

Glancing over, Lina made the connection. "Just like in the book, when the mother is teaching her daughter . . . Oh, that's so . . . " She put a hand to her heart and felt the sting of emotion in her eyes.

With a shake of her head, she laughed at herself. "Now I'm embarrassed."

"Don't be." Cade's expression softened. "Misty-eyed is a good look on you."

On impulse, Lina took his hand in hers. "Cade, this is so thoughtful. So considerate."

"And a little selfish on my part, if I'm being honest." He caressed her fingers. "I confess, I like seeing you happy."

Another moment, and he cleared his throat, glancing past

her, as if surprised by his own admission. He inclined his head toward the refreshments. "Coffee?"

Though everything inside her felt lighter, she managed to sound normal when she said, "I'd love some."

Cade filled two cups while Lina made a plate of sweets for them to share. As she did, she peeked at him from beneath her lashes. *He* was turning out to be the real surprise, putting such effort into making sure this night would be memorable.

Anyone could have taken her to an expensive restaurant, but bringing her here showed he cared about who she was, her likes and dislikes. A sweet gesture, designed just for her.

So, selfish? No. That word couldn't be applied to Cade.

Shame rode up the back of her neck, guilt over how she'd misjudged him. She'd worried something lurked beneath the surface, telling Bex he had shadows in his eyes.

Turns out, she'd doubted the wrong person. She was the one battling shadows.

A familiar voice called for everyone's attention and jarred Lina back to the present. She turned to find Cassidy beside the assembled chairs. "Ms. Arlington will join us shortly, so please gather in or near the seating area. Thank you."

Her gaze landed on Lina, and they exchanged nods of greeting. If Cassidy was curious or troubled about her presence, she revealed nothing.

Moving with the other attendees, Lina and Cade took two of the seats still available in the back. Karen Arlington appeared at the podium to a polite but enthusiastic applause and, before long, Lina forgot her own worries, swept away by the story of one of her favorite characters, a story of courage, of love and loss. She paid rapt attention as the author read.

Until Cade's thigh brushed hers and shook her with a sensual jolt.

She held her breath and pretended not to notice, concentrating instead on the words being spoken. The reading soon captivated her again, but she remained aware of his nearness and the heat transferring from his body to hers.

When the author finished, Lina scooted to the edge of her seat to applaud, standing as the others around her did. "That was wonderful," she said, facing Cade. "Of course, now I have to read the book all over again."

They eased out of the rows of chairs. "But," she continued, "because I was impatient and bought the e-book as soon as it dropped, I need a print copy. And I can't pass up one that's been signed. Would you like one? I'd be happy to—"

"Already taken care of," he said, touching her arm. "Karen's assistant put a couple aside for us. If you don't mind waiting until afterwards, I'll introduce you."

"Who? Me and Karen Arlington?"

He chuckled. "That was the plan."

Delighted, Lina beamed at him. "Oh, Mr. Kincade. You have earned many points tonight. Many, many points." In lieu of a happy dance, she squeezed her arms to her sides. "But seriously," she said, "I can't tell you how much I've enjoyed this evening."

He lifted his hands. "Then my work here is done."

"Oh, I hope not." The comment flew from her mouth before she could think better of it.

But he simply stared at her, his gaze burning into hers as he gave her that slow, signature smile. "Well then, Ms. Chastain, I'll have to see what I can think of next."

Just the idea made Lina's stomach flutter.

While they waited, they refilled their coffees and found a spot by a back window. The river glimmered black in the night, sparkling where the water reflected lights on the bridge, boats, and docks.

When the crowd started to thin and mostly staff remained, Cade made good on his promise and introduced her to Karen Arlington. Lina spoke with the author for several minutes, managing not to stutter or babble—which she considered a great accomplishment.

As they said their goodbyes and walked away, Cassidy approached from the side. "Hello, again. I wanted to catch you before you left, since I haven't spoken to you yet."

Lina gave her a don't-worry wave of the hand. "That's understandable, considering how busy you've been."

"A little bit." Cassidy laughed and extended her hand to Cade. "Cassidy Thorson," she said, "And you . . ." she angled her head to the side, squinting a little, "look very familiar."

"Cassidy," Lina said, "I'd like you to meet Cade."

"That's it." Cassidy snapped her fingers. "James Kincade. Thrillers. We carry your book."

He rocked back. "Impressive recall." And shook her offered hand. "It's a pleasure to meet you, and thank you. You have a great place here, and it's nice to see some still believe in bricks and mortar."

"Thank you, and the pleasure is mine. I have a weakness for the scary and suspenseful." She glanced over when a young man called out to ask if he could start taking up the extra seats. "That'd be great. Thanks, Daniel."

"Tonight was well done," Cade said. "I've been to a few readings and know they're not as easy to host as one might think."

"Cassidy's a pro," Lina offered with a wink for her friend. She may not have known her that well before, but being drafted into a war of witches and demons tended to form a bond.

"I appreciate that." Cassidy glanced between Lina and Cade and seemed to make a decision. "If you're ever interested in doing a signing, I'd love to have you here."

"Thanks. An event in town would be good." Cade turned to Lina. "I didn't realize you two knew each other."

"We met a while ago at a meeting for Business After Hours," she said. "Sort of a cocktail gathering for local proprietors."

"Yes." Cassidy's voice took on a distracted quality. "And we found out we have a lot more in common than we ever realized." Absently, she rubbed her neck, drawing Lina's gaze to the symbol, in plain sight with her black tresses tied back.

Eyes flaring with awareness, Cassidy quickly dropped her arm.

Lina reached for her own neck, instinctively wanting to hide the sigil. But the move would draw attention instead, so she switched directions to cover a feigned yawn.

Cade frowned. "We should probably go. Do you have your usual early morning tomorrow?"

"Yes," Lina said, feeling like she'd been caught in the act. And she almost had been. Cade hadn't noticed, but the call had been too close. How would she have explained she and Cassidy having such similar marks?

She should thank every deity for the good sense to wear her hair down tonight.

But if they continued to date, he'd see the symbol eventually. What then? Would she create a lie or tell the truth?

Both options made her stomach drop through the floor.

"It *is* getting late," she said to Cassidy. "For me anyway," she added in a weak voice. "It's been good to see you again." But Lina dodged the other woman's gaze as Cade said his goodbyes.

Outside the moon had risen, but pewter clouds had ridden in to hide most of its light. Lina and Cade chatted about Karen Arlington and his own potential signing at the store, but somehow the small talk rang hollow.

Lina told herself it was her imagination, that seeing Cassidy's symbol had dampened her mood. The mark served as an unwelcome reminder, a literal sign Lina couldn't deny.

Still, the short drive to her house brimmed with silence, and she only hoped her sense of foreboding didn't spill over to Cade.

At the townhome, he parked and came around to open the door for her again. This time, he took her hand to help her out.

And as they walked up the steps, he didn't let go.

She expected the usual niceties about lovely evenings and doing it again sometime. But when they reached the door, he moved in, his hand cupping her cheek as he lowered his lips to hers.

She felt the warmth and need, barely restrained, and didn't resist when he deepened the kiss. He went slow, and not too deep—but enough to draw a sigh of longing from her when he pulled away.

"Good night, Lina." He stroked his thumb along her jaw before releasing her and starting down to his car.

When his taillights disappeared, she was still standing outside the door. In wonder, she touched her lips. And realized she'd never said goodbye.

~~~

Cade barely stayed within the confines of the speed limit. He carried Lina's sweetness on his lips as he drove, but along the way, her flavor was ruined, polluted by the tang of adrenaline.

The taste of fear.

Arriving at his home, he couldn't get out of the car fast enough. He pictured her smile as he ran up the steps, heard her laugh as he unlocked the door. Trying to tamp down on panic, he rushed to the room he'd made his office and zeroed in on a particular set of shelves.

He skimmed a finger along book spines, scanning titles. *Where is it? Where did I put it? It should be . . . here.* He stilled when he found the book, his hand hovering, almost as if he were afraid to open it. Afraid to find his answer.

He'd seen the mark on Cassidy's neck. A unique symbol that triggered a memory.

He kept all of the books he'd ever loved or used for research, and the thick maroon volume had once graced the bedroom of his youth. Written in gold, Gothic-style letters embossed the cover. *Myths and Legend of the Arcane.*

Reading the name after so many years caused a hybrid response, pulling both nostalgia and dread from deep within his gut.

They're only stories. Nothing but fairy tales. He needed to believe that. Especially now.

Lina hadn't revealed her neck, but her hand had skimmed upward, a mirror image of what Cassidy had done. Just after she'd spoken of what she and Lina had in common.

Standing in place, Cade didn't bother to sit or find a table, only flipped through the book to a specific chapter. He found the heading and slowed, turning pages one by one. At last, he found a group of drawings, an illustration of five symbols.

And there it was.

"No. It can't be possible." His head ached, suddenly packed with incredible ideas.

And terrible ramifications.

With a heavy chest, he closed the book, staring blankly at the shelves. "Lina, what have you gotten yourself into?"

8

Searenn descended into the earth, a wave of midnight satin trailing behind her down the steps. The robe had once belonged to Ronja and bore little resemblance to Searenn's hoodies and jeans.

But tonight she would use the pit, an occasion that called for something fierce and elegant.

At the bottom, she followed a short passage to a solid stone wall. Or so it appeared. To remove the enchantment, Ronja had needed to speak a charm.

Searenn required a single thought. *Open*. An arched entrance appeared, its curved edges wavering and blurred, for it was not of this world.

From behind her, she heard a gasp of wonder. The darkheart twins—as she'd come to think of them—had been allowed to accompany her below. To the area beneath the plantation home, where an entire dungeon had been gouged from bedrock.

Formed by ancient power, the layer of stone sat atop a sacred place, a gateway to the primeval world.

Waving her hand, Searenn lit the torches along the wall. Flamelight flickered on crimson-stained rock, the sight of past injury stirring an odd arousal in her belly.

She wanted to taste some of that. Some fresh, hot life, spilled by her own hands.

Another time, she thought, continuing on, stepping through an opening in the far wall. The smell of loam overwhelmed as her bare feet found warm earth. The pit lay before her, black and deep.

Like the souls of the ones she'd come to call.

Easing forward, she spoke over her shoulder. "The book."

Dacia hurried to place a heavy tome in Searenn's hands.

The twins had come bearing gifts, and one of their presents had been this book, a compendium of evil creatures, all still slithering in the shadows of humans.

Every manner of fiend had been recorded, the stealthy, wicked beasts of the world. The ones unable to escape through the original gate. Some even Searenn had never heard of.

A scarlet ribbon marked the page she wanted, and she opened to lines scratched by hand eons ago. A conjuring.

Beside her, Dacia all but quivered with glee. "A fine choice, your grace."

"I told you not to call me that."

The girl bowed her head, her pitch-black hair gleaming in the firelight. Her brother Dru stood off to the side, a warrior ever-ready to defend.

Leisurely, Searenn neared the altar on the edge of the pit. Created from lava stone, the slab bore a mosaic of crystals, teeth, and fragments of bone. Blood had been used to cement the mixture, and also to strengthen the conduit.

The link to the Onderdâark.

The underworld where she'd been imprisoned existed in another realm, but with the right tools, doors could be opened. She would crack one open now and send a message.

She would ask to awaken the *malkora*. The Hunters of Man.

Though she'd memorized the words after a single pass, Searenn held the book aloft as an act of ritual. "*Noth rakee gûl.*" A frozen wind rushed from the pit, rising up to caress her cheeks.

"*Maî sharat thraki-yayn.*" She spoke to her masters far beneath. And through them she raised the darkness. "*Du bish šlaga neî må."*

The ground quaked beneath her. The wind whistled and shrieked.

With her hair blowing back, Searenn raised her voice. *"Durbae. Durbae ish thrakkaa!"*

All around her, shadows began to move, the beasts hidden within responding to her summons. Writhing and moaning, they clamored for freedom, for the life denied them so many long years.

Cloaked in black, they remained unseen to the human eye. But not to Searenn. Her new vision spanned all the realms.

The monsters elongated, stretching upward. Oily sinew composed their tall, thin forms, fleshless and exposed, like corpses well into rot. They stood on two hooved feet, their huge horns curling into lethal points.

Here, at last, were the first of her soldiers. Beasts born of the Onderdâark, but trapped in this dimension.

For millennia they'd been here, alone and powerless. But now as they awoke, Searenn felt their craving for revenge, their hunger for blood and bone.

As the arctic breeze died, Searenn lowered her arms. She closed the book and spoke to the shadows. "You know why I've awakened you. The time of reckoning is finally here."

Her gaze scanned the subterranean chamber, each hidden corner crawling with energy. "But our fight has only just begun. The witches of old have been reborn, and even now they gather."

A wave of fury rolled from the blackness, its force threatening to extinguish the torches.

Searenn gave a smile, a reaper's sickle. "I share your anger. I know your hate." She stretched out her arm and felt an icy touch. Caresses from her banished Watchers, her risen children.

"Remember what they did to you, these women known as

the Watchtower Maidens. Dig deep and embrace your wrath."
She held out her hands and let the dark haze immerse her, the
tendrils stroking with the tenderness of lovers.

"Go now," she said, basking in their adoration. "Seek out the
ones who would have your death. Find them, watch them, but
do not hunt. Do not feed." She hardened her voice daring any
to break her command. "That time will come."

9

After a quick change of clothes, Lina hurried out of the townhome, jumped into her car, and drove toward Drayton Street. One of the main roads, it was the fastest route back to Factors Walk.

She just hoped she'd be in time to catch Cassidy.

With guilt riding her shoulders, she focused on the road and tried not to think of Cade. Or the incredible first kiss they'd just shared. She had no right to think of him this way, no right to see him again. At least not now.

When her whole life was descending into chaos.

She pushed down on the gas and sped back toward the river, overcome by a desperate need to talk to Cassidy. The only other person who would understand.

Luckily, she found an empty spot close to the bookstore. Lights still warmed the interior with a muted glow, not the bright overheads that had lit the space before. Rushing across the bridge, she grabbed the door handle and tugged.

Locked.

Not ready to give up, she rapped her knuckles on the glass. Cassidy lived above the store, having turned the loft space into an apartment.

Lina knocked again, a little louder, but Cassidy must have heard her the first time. She appeared from behind the rows of bookshelves, a curious look on her face.

Opening the door, she shook her head, bemused. "You know,

I think I've been expecting you."

"You have?" Lina stepped inside and exhaled, comforted by the open and unconditional welcome.

"Yep. When I saw you earlier at the signing, I got a wild urge to kick everybody out so we could talk." She chuckled. "Of course, common sense prevailed. No matter what's going on in my personal life, I never let it affect business."

"I hear that," Lina said, surprised that she could still laugh so easily.

"Since you're here," Cassidy asked, "you want some coffee?"

"Actually, yes." Lina followed her toward the counter and leaned against the shiny mahogany. The historic building still held much of its original character. "I don't think I'll be sleeping much anyway."

"No. Me either," Cassidy said. Yet she yawned. "I spent last night researching, and then reading everything I could get my hands on. By the way," she said, pointing to the espresso machine, "I'm making the good stuff, so what's your preference?"

Lina considered her options, since none of them were bad. She had to admit, she enjoyed letting someone else prepare drinks for a change. "I'll just take an Americano."

Cassidy sent her a wry look. "I'm having a macchiato, so the milk steamer will get dirty anyway."

"In that case," Lina said on a laugh, "I'll take a cappuccino."

"As I thought."

Cassidy made quick work of the drinks, then suggested they find a more comfortable place to chat. She led Lina to the spread of windows overlooking the river. The dark stretch of water remained calm and soothing, but Lina could hear voices from farther up River Street, the first sounds of a Friday-night-free-for-all.

Big comfy chairs sat together, a small round table between them. Cassidy dropped into one and heaved a sigh. "What. A. Day." She blew out again. "Actually, make that *two* days."

There was no need to explain. Awareness of the new Watchtower-Maiden status needled at Lina constantly. Exhausting and irritating, like a thorn stuck inside her shirt that she just couldn't find.

"So," Cassidy said at last, "James Kincade." She didn't have to wiggle her brows lasciviously. Her tone of voice did it for her.

Lina grinned, but then it slipped away. "Maybe. I don't know."

"Are you kidding?" Cassidy plopped a hand on the table between them. "What's not to know? He's a gorgeous, brilliant, sophisticated hunk of manly man. And those, my friend, do *not* grow on trees."

Though the teasing had meant to lighten the mood, the truth of her words made Lina feel worse.

"You're right about that. He's one in a million." Lina rubbed her thumb around the rim of her mug, staring at the foam and wishing she could turn back time, just long enough to avoid Rae Scott and her Akasha's touch.

"I didn't do any reading last night, not like you." She raised her gaze to meet Cassidy's. "Instead, I've been pretending none of it ever happened. Or at least, I've been trying to."

Cassidy nodded but didn't speak.

"Cade and this . . . this *madness*, both happened on the same day. The exact same day." She stared out at the river, at the twinkling lights in all their innocence. "But how can I start something with him knowing what I'm involved in now?"

Cassidy tilted her head back and forth, then centered to sip her macchiato. "I see what you're saying, and I don't envy your situation."

"He really is amazing," Lina said, her voice growing soft and plaintive. "Even more than I realized, and I've known him for months, on a friendly level."

"Some of the best relationships start out that way, because you get to know someone beforehand."

Lina only nodded.

"I understand why you'd rather avoid reality, but if it's any consolation, my approach hasn't helped much either. I thought if I could learn about what we're dealing with, if I could understand it, I might be able to make it fit with who I am." Cassidy's voice took on an edge. "But, no. It still feels wrong."

"Exactly." Lina leap-frogged on the other woman's resistance. "If we were destined to be the Maidens, shouldn't we have some instinctual recognition? Shouldn't some innate part of us want to accept?"

"I don't know." Cassidy sank lower into her seat, stretching her legs out in front of her and crossing at the ankles. "All I really want to do is dive deep, deep into a pool of denial. Unfortunately, I've come around to seeing that's just not possible. Not anymore."

"I know. *Ugh.* I know." Lina rubbed her neck, a new habit of hers. One she detested. "Especially with these brands on our skin, as if we've been marked as property." She slapped her hand on the chair, frustration simmering, threatening to spill. "And you know what? I'm angry. I am super pissed off. I mean, I just feel so . . . *violated.*"

"Sing it, sister." Cassidy flipped up her hand but moved nothing else.

"Why me?" Lina continued. "I don't have a single micron of magick."

Cassidy chuckled, sliding her gaze over. "Really? Not even a micron?"

"Stop." In spite of herself, Lina laughed with her. "You know what I mean."

"I do exactly, because I've never even considered trying to work magick or do any spells. Well, except for that packet I bought during a bachelorette party in New Orleans. But that doesn't count, since it's still shoved in my closet somewhere. Never even opened."

Cassidy sat up and stared at Lina. "So we agree that you and I couldn't conjure a flame between us."

"Nope. And I did use a Ouija board once, with absolutely no results. So there." Lina raised her cappuccino to emphasize the point. "I have no power."

"Or at least," Cassidy leaned toward her, "you *didn't*."

When Lina only wrinkled her forehead, Cassidy pressed. "Come on. Be honest. Haven't you felt a little different since yesterday?"

"No." Lina felt and heard the force in her denial. "Dammit. No." She huffed, her fingers tightening on the coffee cup. "And if I keep saying no, maybe one of us will start to believe it."

"It's sort of a low-grade sensation, like a whisper deep inside." Cassidy closed her eyes, as if trying to listen to the sound she described. "And maybe I do recognize it." Her lids popped open. "I just don't know why."

Cassidy raised her hands. "Still, as weird as it all is, there's no denying it's happening to me." She pointed at Lina. "And to you. If even a fraction of what I've read is true, this is big. *Huge*. With an end-of-the-world kind of significance."

"Huktai. Draconi magick. Demons." Lina pressed her hands to the sides of her head. "Cassidy, it's insanity."

"I know." Cassidy blew out a breath. "But Lina, crazy as it seems, the question isn't whether or not any of this is real. It's obviously real enough to put symbols on our bodies. And even if we didn't ask for this, even if we don't want it, if half of what Rae and Marit said is true . . ."

"Then people are in danger," Lina finished.

Cassidy's lips thinned. "Looks like our minds have been circling around the same track. I'm afraid. Hell, I'm terrified. But if we turn away from this and someone gets hurt . . . Well, I'm not sure I can live with that."

"Me either." An odd tranquility stole over Lina. She locked her gaze with Cassidy's. "Maybe *that's* why we were chosen."

"Lucky us," Cassidy scoffed. "Born at the right time, and too conscientious for our own good." Then she cracked a smile. "Or born at the wrong time, depending on how you look at it."

"Regardless, the moving parts all seem to be coming together, here and now—Rae opening the globe, discovering magick, the possibility of a gate."

"And now us." Cassidy tapped the point of her finger on the table. "The final piece, and one that's been missing for centuries." Her voice took on an ominous quality. "Looks like the gang's all here."

Silence weighed heavily in the room as they both absorbed, as they both, finally, accepted.

Cassidy spoke into the stillness. "Here's another thing that'll rock your world."

"Like I need any more of that."

After a huff of laughter, Cassidy said, "You know in movies when they show witches standing in a circle, saying things like, 'Hail to the Guardians of the East?'"

Casually, Lina lifted her shoulder. "Yeah, I've seen something like that."

"That's when they're calling the four corners. They're calling the *Watchtowers*."

Lina blinked once. Then again. "They're calling us." A chill spread across her back. "Holy shit."

The two of them were staring at each other when a low *thump* sounded somewhere in the store.

The chill on Lina's back changed to an icy blade. The sharp edge sliced down her spine.

Cautiously, they turned, both rigid and alert.

Still unmoving, Cassidy stared down an aisle, a dark path leading to the far side of the store. "Lina," she whispered, "did you hear that?"

10

"Did it come from inside?" Lina asked, holding her breath so she could listen.

"Yes." Cassidy eased up from her chair, her gaze focused on the long aisle between bookracks. "Too loud to have come from outside. Sounds like someone's in my office or the storage rooms."

Sluggishly, as if her legs refused to work, Lina stood as well. Fear pumped through her veins, hot and painful. "We should get out." Her whisper sounded frantic. "Call the police."

Cassidy nodded and reached to grab Lina's arm. "But what if—"

"It doesn't matter," Lina cut her off, certain the other woman's instincts had led her to the same terrible conclusion. Someone breaking into the bookstore a day after they'd received their symbols? That was no coincidence.

They'd been introduced to the most ancient of evils.

And now it was here.

"Whoever or *whatever* is back there, we can't stay." Lina shook Cassidy's arm, forcing her to listen. "We have to get *out*."

Cassidy's pupils had gone wide with fear, leaving only a rim of pale blue. "Yes. The front door."

Another *thump!* and they both jumped, Lina clamping a hand to her mouth to stifle her cry.

The sound thrust Cassidy into action. Still holding on to Lina, she began edging toward the front.

Lina couldn't tear her gaze away from the aisles. Every rack they passed blocked her sight and ramped up the adrenaline buzzing through her system. Every corner they rounded held potential threat. She kept expecting to see something.

And then she did.

Stopping abruptly, she slipped from Cassidy's grasp.

Darkness cloaked the far end of the room. And within the darkness, something moved.

Deep inside, Lina knew she should run, but terror held her feet in place, a rush of fear so strong it pinned her to the floor like a surge of electricity. Hairs lifted on her arms and pricked the back of her neck.

"Do you see it?" she asked, hoping Cassidy was still beside her but too afraid to turn and look. "Back there. In the shadows."

"Let's go." Cassidy's words rasped, riding on panicked breaths. "We have to go."

Another movement, and a silhouette took shape—tall, looming. Lina couldn't make out its face or eyes. But she knew . . . it was staring at her.

"Lina, now!" Cassidy shouted.

The thing in the shadows lunged forward.

Lina broke into a run behind the other woman, the primitive drive for survival finally kicking in. She shoved her way out, thankful the door was unlocked, and stayed right on Cassidy's heels.

"This way!" Cassidy called back, sprinting down the cement walk toward a set of metal stairs. "We have to get to my car!"

Below and on the opposite side of the buildings, River Street overflowed with people. But here, they raced through the night alone, only wind whispering in the huge Live Oaks. Cars breezed by on Bay Street, but they were too far away.

Lina heard the door burst open again, and then footsteps thudding on concrete. Whatever she'd seen had given chase. And it was right behind them.

She rushed after Cassidy, their own steps pinging on metal as they ran down to the sunken alley. At the bottom, Cassidy reversed directions, huffing out, "I'm parked at the end of the building."

They squeezed between the front bumper of a car and the base of tree, then sprinted downhill on the cobblestone drive. Lina prayed she didn't twist an ankle or fall on the uneven rocks, but she didn't dare slow down.

Ahead of her, Cassidy was digging in her pocket. For her keys? *Please. Please.* If not, they would have to run all the way around to River Street.

Dark caverns loomed to her left, underground hollows known as the Cluskey Vaults. Built in the eighteen-hundreds, the bricked-in cavities were part of the retaining wall and had once served as storage areas. Now they held only historical plaques, and vast empty spaces reaching beneath the city streets.

A sudden awareness drew Lina's attention to the second vault. A figure emerged.

Cassidy reacted, veering away from the man just as his arm swung out. The blow whizzed past Cassidy's head, but she lost her footing, staggering to one side.

Lina couldn't stop in time. She was running too fast.

The man squared off, ready to intercept her with his arm pulled back. Wisps of haze, black and glistening, rose from a crescent shape clutched in his hand.

Lina screamed, lifting her arm in defense. Then she tripped, going down hard on the cobblestones as the hulking figure struck out with a grunt.

The fall saved her, and momentum rolled her another few feet. But he was practically on top of her.

She scrambled back, imagining his weapon arcing down. Another scream built in her chest and climbed for her throat.

She was still scooting along the ground when light exploded, glaring in her face. The sound of pounding bass filled the alley as a car rounded the corner, its headlights blazing like sweet salvation.

Wasting no time, Lina lurched up and ran to Cassidy. Together they bolted down the hill, Cassidy pointing to the silver SUV as she unlocked the doors with her key fob.

"Who was that?" Lina shrieked, her mind a mass of confusion. "Was that a man? I mean, a real person? I thought . . ." She didn't know what she'd seen in the store, but she'd sensed the presence of something . . . *other*.

"No fucking idea." Cassidy screeched backwards out of the parking spot. Hands white-knuckling the wheel, she paused, staring back up into the alley. "Here they come."

Lina followed her line of sight to see two huge men advancing on the car. "River Street!" She gestured wildly with both hands. "Go! Go!"

Jerking the steering wheel to the left, Cassidy sped toward the cobbled road lined with streetcar rails and packed with tourists. She eased through the pedestrians, going as fast as safety allowed.

Lina spun around in her seat, looking back for the men. "I don't see them," she said, only now noticing the heavy throbbing of her pulse in her ears, the same tempo of her heart knocking against her ribs.

Her breaths sucked in and rushed back out as she kept her gaze glued to the road behind them. Nothing . . . nothing . . .

A big black vehicle nosed its way out onto the street.

"There's a car," Lina said, "but I can't tell if it's them." Panicked, she scanned the area. "Maybe we should pull over and go inside a restaurant or a bar . . . any place with a crowd."

Cassidy glanced out. "Maybe."

Lina studied the people strolling by, so happy and excited for a night out in the city. "No. What am I thinking?" A couple and two little tow-headed girls were staring in a shop window. "We can't put others at risk."

A gang of young men spilled into the road, and Cassidy jerked to a halt. "Come on. Come on!" Her eyes shot to the rearview mirror. "Can you tell yet? Can you see?"

"No." Lina watched the other car in the side mirror but couldn't make out the driver. "I'm not sure it's them. Maybe they gave up."

The way cleared, and Cassidy pushed forward. So did the suspicious vehicle. Finally, it rolled beneath the lights of the sweet shop.

Lina spotted the man from the alley, his expression intent. "It's them." She swung back to the front again. "They're following us."

"We'll be out of this swarm in a minute." Cassidy drummed impatient fingers on the steering wheel. "But so will they. Should we drive to the police station?"

Dread rolled over Lina's shoulders, heavy and oily. "No. They're after us, and we both know why." She turned to Cassidy. "There's only one place we can go."

Cassidy shot her a sidelong look and nodded.

"I'll call Bryn." Lina patted her pockets. "No. I don't have my phone."

Cassidy started to shake her head, but then snapped her fingers. "Wait. I have mine." She opened a compartment between the seats. "I had to run out for last-minute supplies for the signing and left it in here."

She handed the phone to Lina and stepped on the gas, taking advantage of an opening in the mob. At the corner, she swung a hard right onto an access road.

The SUV rumbled uphill over rough stones, taking them to the front of Factors Walk again. At the top, Cassidy barely slowed to glance both ways before barreling through the stop sign. The angry blast of a horn followed them as they screeched away.

"I'll take Abercorn," she said. The main artery of Savannah, it was a straight shot to the historic housing district.

Lina punched in Bryn's number, glad she knew it by heart. Her friend answered almost immediately. "Lina, hey—"

"Someone's after us," she spit out, then drew a deep breath to add, "I'm with Cassidy. We were at the bookstore. Two men tried to . . . I don't know, to kill us."

"Where are you now?" Bryn asked before calling for Rae in the background.

"We're on—Hey!" She slammed into the door when Cassidy made another sharp turn.

"They're back," Cassidy said. "And they're gaining on us."

"Hold on," Lina told Bryn. "We're heading toward Arik's house. They're behind us again. Maybe we should—"

"No," Bryn snapped. "Come straight to Arik's. We'll be waiting for you outside. And Lina," she said, "Do. Not. Stop."

"We won't." The engine revved, and they made another turn. Lina gripped the door handle to steady herself.

"Don't hang up," Bryn told her. "We're going outside now. How far are you?"

"Uh . . ." She scanned the buildings for a landmark. "There's the Amethyst Inn. We're coming up Habersham."

Bryn repeated the information on her end.

"I don't see them anymore." Cassidy darted her focus between the mirror and the road ahead. "Lina, can you look?"

She turned to stare out the back window. "No. Nothing. Maybe we lost them?"

"Doubtful." Cassidy wore a grim expression. "Did they turn on the other street? Maybe they're trying to head us off."

"We're almost to Arik's now. Make this right." Lina exhaled and felt a little of the aching panic seep from her chest.

Cassidy made the turn and sped the final block to Arik's. "I can't believe this is happening."

Lina swallowed, her throat tight and dry. "Neither can I."

Their headlights slashed down the road, illuminating Bryn

and Rae standing out in the street. Waiting. Just as promised.

Lina hardly had time to feel relief before the sound of an engine cut through the night. "Cassidy," she began, but the other woman didn't seem to hear.

And she didn't seem to notice the motorcycle speeding toward the intersection.

"They don't have a stop sign, Cassidy. The bike!" Lina screamed.

Cassidy finally hit the brakes, sending them fishtailing toward the corner of Arik's yard.

The motorcycle swerved in the opposite direction, attempting to skirt around their tail end. They might just miss him.

But at the last moment, the cyclist's back tire clipped Cassidy's rear bumper, the impact shuddering through the SUV. Metal clanged and thudded as the bike tumbled over pavement.

"Oh, my God!" Cassidy yelled. Her mouth fell open as the car came to a stop, angled across the intersection. "I hit him! I hit him!" She pawed at her door, trying to get out, Lina doing the same on her side.

The two of them piled out, joining Bryn and Rae in their rush to the fallen rider. He'd ended up farther down the street, lying on his back with arms and legs splayed across the concrete.

A low moan seeped from his black and red helmet.

"I'm sorry. I'm so sorry." Cassidy's voice broke on a sob. "We need to call for help." She took her phone from Lina, but her shaking hands almost dropped it.

Lina moved to her side, putting a consoling arm around her shoulders. "It's okay. We'll get help."

Another groan from the motorist drew their attention. He started to lift his head.

"No, don't move." Bryn hurried over and dropped to her knees.

Pausing in her attempts to dial for help, Cassidy moved

closer.

"Just stay still." Rae kneeled as well. Brow furrowed in concern, she reached out and gently touched the cyclist's shoulder.

A muffled cry came from inside the helmet, and Rae jerked her hand back.

The rider reached up with one leather-clad arm, pushing at the helmet.

"Don't," Bryn said, but too late. The biker shoved it off.

And released a cascade of bright red hair. "What's going on?" she asked. She reached upward with her hand, only to have it drop to the pavement as her eyes fluttered shut.

Rae pressed her palm to her chest, looking to each of the women gathered there in the road. Awareness lit her whiskey-brown gaze, and in that instant, Lina knew.

They had just found fire.

11

The sound of a car screeching to a stop registered in Lina's mind. She turned to see Arik leaping from a black car and racing toward them. "What happened?"

Rae blinked and stared up at him. Then she stood quickly, as if snapping out of a trance. "We have to get her inside," she told him, holding out her hand. "Do you have your phone?"

Without question, he passed it over and kneeled to pick up the biker. She'd passed out, and her head lolled against his shoulder.

Panic spread like a fracture in Lina's chest. "Maybe we shouldn't move her."

Bryn came over and took Lina's hand, then reached out for Cassidy's. "It will be okay, but you have to trust us."

Lina blew out a breath and nodded blankly. What else could she do? So much of this situation was beyond the norm, and typical behavior simply didn't apply.

Rae spoke into the phone, "That's good. Thank you." She fell into step behind Arik as he crossed the yard to his house. "Help is on the way," she called over her shoulder.

Lina started to follow Rae but realized Cassidy was standing still, her face as white as the moonlight shining down. "Let's go inside," Lina said softly, hooking her arm through Cassidy's to steer her toward the house.

They passed Cassidy's SUV just as Bryn jumped into the driver's seat. She cranked it up and pulled to the curb.

By the time Lina and Cassidy made it to the front steps, Arik was rushing back out. "They're in the ladies' parlor. Take the hallway to the right."

Still holding on to her shell-shocked friend, Lina led her down the corridor, heading toward a brightly lit doorway at the end. A Tiffany-style lamp illuminated one corner, and she had the impression of light-colored decor against the dark paneling of the Victorian-era home.

Inside, they found Rae standing beside a powder-blue fainting couch, fingers steepled beneath her chin. The injured woman lay motionless, the spill of her hair like flames against ice.

She still wore the black jacket typical of bikers with an orange T-shirt that read *Santa Fe Trading Company* on the front. One hand bore abrasions from her fall, from her skid across pavement, and one of her black boots was badly scuffed.

Holding hands now, Lina and Cassidy moved to stand behind the couch. They held silent vigil. Waiting. Tension stretched, nearing the breaking point with every precious minute that passed.

"Help will be here soon," Rae's voice rasped, holding her gaze on the unconscious woman, as if watching to make sure she breathed.

It wasn't long before headlights flashed past the windows and tires screeched to a halt. Lina heard car doors slamming and then Arik's voice. But where were the sirens?

Seconds later, Arik burst back into the parlor just ahead of a blonde woman who cut straight to the couch.

Lina wrinkled her brow as she took in the woman's dress and heels. "Paramedics?" she asked, watching as the stranger laid gentle hands on the biker.

"She's a healer," Rae explained, clasping her hands together. "Her name is Willyn."

Unsure what to make of the strange turn of events, Lina

studied Willyn. She had no medical bag. She had no supplies. She didn't seem to be doing anything at all.

"Shouldn't we call an ambulance?" Lina said at last, unable to keep her fears to herself any longer. "What if she has internal bleeding?"

"She does," Willyn said without looking up.

"Oh, my God. But how—"

Cassidy squeezed Lina's hand. *Hard.* She stared down at the unconscious woman but remained silent, her usual dry wit snuffed out by shock.

"The bleeding is here," Willyn said, her hands near the biker's right collarbone. "A tear in her subclavian artery. Traumatic rupture."

The healer seemed to be talking more to herself than the rest of them, but her words slapped Lina in the face. "Artery? That's not good."

"No, but I can fix it faster than the surgery she'd need if we took her to the hospital. And without making incisions." Willyn spared Lina a glance, radiating pure kindness from her soft gaze. "I promise, letting me help her is the best thing you can do."

Lips tight with concentration, she returned her focus to her patient.

Lina glanced at Rae again, and then to Bryn who stood a few feet behind her. They'd chosen to call Willyn instead of 911 and seemed to have complete faith in her abilities.

So, Lina decided, drawing a breath, she would have complete faith in them.

Still, she tensed, sucking in a breath as Willyn pressed her palms to the woman's body.

The room fell into a swollen silence. But soon, ripples emanated from beneath Willyn's hands.

Lina blinked to clear her eyes, but the distortion remained, the kind of blurriness that rose from hot desert highways.

Willyn eventually glided her palms to the shoulder joint, mumbling something about soft tissue damage.

Minutes passed, and then she traced her fingertips up and over the woman's scalp. "Just double-checking," she explained, since she'd given her patient a full body "scan" as soon as she'd arrived.

At last, the healer stood. "Okay, now we let her rest. You did the right thing by calling me," she told Rae. "Considering what you're dealing with, it's better to keep things in-house, so to speak."

"How is she?" A second woman peeked into the room, a sleek fall of ebony down to the middle of her back.

"Sleeping. But she'll recover." Willyn held out a hand, gesturing to Lina and Cassidy. "You two haven't met Shauni, have you?"

"No," Lina said.

Cassidy shook her head, a bit more color in her cheeks after being assured the woman she'd hit would be okay.

"I'm sorry we had to meet like this." Shauni stepped closer, her gaze moving between Lina and Cassidy.

"Okay to come in?" a man asked from the doorway. Tall and tawny-haired, he hovered just outside in the hallway, another man right behind him.

Shauni smiled and waved them in. She held out her hand to the blond man with glasses stuck in the front pocket of his shirt. "This is my husband, Michael." She nodded toward the second man—attractive in a dark and dangerous way. "And Willyn's husband, Dare."

"We were all leaving a restaurant when we got Rae's call," Willyn said, "so we came as a package deal." She grinned, trying to lighten the mood and put them at ease.

Baffled by her calm, casual attitude, Lina simply nodded before turning her focus to Cassidy. "She'll be okay." She rubbed her friend's back. "Everything is all going to be okay."

Cassidy shifted her weight and leaned against her. "I could have killed her. I almost did."

"But you didn't."

The others began quietly discussing what to do next. Lina barely registered the conversation, but something was agreed upon before Arik and Dare left the room. There was movement, laughter, and someone mentioned Thai food.

Cassidy slid away from Lina. "This is surreal," she blurted.

The others stopped and looked at her.

"We were attacked, then I ran someone over, and . . ." she lifted her arms and dropped them. "Now we're . . . we're talking about *Thai food*."

"Cassidy," Rae said, her voice instantly turning gentle, full of empathy. "Why don't you and Lina come sit over here?" She indicated a sofa and chairs positioned around a large square table. "You've both been through a lot tonight."

Cassidy followed Rae like an obedient zombie, heading straight for a high-backed ivory chair.

"She's right. Let's sit." Bryn motioned to Lina, waiting to walk with her. Side-by-side, they crossed the parlor and sat on the couch.

After a moment, Bryn spoke, addressing Willyn and Shauni who remained standing. "I guess you both know what this is like."

"We do, "Shauni replied. "We know exactly."

"Willyn and Shauni." Lina shook her head as the last of the adrenaline rush seeped away and her mind cleared. "Of course. You're part of the Savannah Coven. Bryn's told me about you."

Lina recalled a vague explanation of how they'd stopped a group who'd practiced black magick. Yet now, seeing what Willyn could do firsthand, she suspected Bryn had given her the lighter version—the fairy tale version. After the last two days, Lina understood that true evil existed.

After tonight, she knew monsters were real.

"We went through something similar," Shauni said. "None of us knew what to expect when we first arrived at the St. Germaine island, but each of us had a unique gift, a special power we'd lived with our entire lives. So we were at least acquainted with the supernatural."

"We were thrown in," Willyn added, "but not as far into the deep as all of you."

"Good analogy." Cassidy leaned back in her chair. "And I feel like someone is holding my head under."

Lina nodded slowly in agreement.

"When did you start to feel normal again?" Bryn furrowed her brow. "When did you move from accepting to functional? Because I don't think I'm there yet. I just keep bouncing back and forth between denial and anger."

Stunned, Lina turned to her friend. Bryn had been raised around witchcraft, so Lina had just assumed she'd be more comfortable being called to fight a mystical battle. Hearing her speak of her own struggle filled Lina with shame. She should have realized.

She should have known.

"I'm sorry, Bryn. This is all new for you too, and I've only been thinking of myself."

Bryn leaned closer to give her a shoulder-nudge. "I don't know about that. I seem to recall someone showing up here yesterday to check on me. With comfort food to boot." Her brown gaze locked with Lina's. "And I've known you a long, long time. You *never* think only of yourself."

The guilt she felt loosened a bit, and Lina nudged her back. "Then is it terrible that I'm glad you're here with me?"

"No. I totally get it," Bryn said. "Because I feel the same. You've been a part of every other crisis in my life. How could I face my greatest challenge without you?"

"Friendship doubles a joy . . ." Bryn began, quoting the words Lina had cross-stitched and framed for her as a high-school graduation present.

"And divides a sorrow," Lina finished, exchanging a smile with Bryn, the special one reserved for her oldest friend.

"Since I'm owning up," Lina shifted her attention to Rae, "I was harsh with you yesterday, because I blamed you. But if I'm doing the math right, you haven't had much time to adjust to this either. I know you only recently came back for a wedding, so when did you actually open the globe?"

Rae drew a breath and dropped into a seat opposite them. "Oh, last week. Though it does seem like more time has passed." She rubbed her forehead. "I didn't have a chance to think about how to react or what I should do, because that same night, Bryn—"

"Um, I haven't told her that part," Bryn broke in, casting a remorseful look to Lina. "I didn't want to scare you any more than you already were. But," she shrugged, "after what happened to you and Cassidy tonight, there's no reason to hold back."

Bryn launched into a horror story, telling of the night she'd been marked with the symbol for air.

And had been taken over by a dark entity.

Ignoring Lina's alarmed expression, she hurried on, explaining how Rae had found her in an abandoned house and, with the coven's help, had fought off demonic forces to banish the vile spirit and save Bryn.

"We should have told you all of this yesterday," Rae said, her voice flat, her stare shaded with regret. "But you'd already had your world turned upside down, your identity shaken . . . Still, I should have anticipated an attack."

Hands balled together in her lap, Rae straightened her spine and said, "I tried to protect you and ended up putting you at risk. I swear I won't make that mistake again."

"But we were attacked by men," Cassidy said. "Not demons."

"Possibly," Shauni interjected. She looked to Rae, who

nodded for her to go ahead. "Some demons can possess people and control their bodies, while others take on a human form. Either way, they blend right in."

"Well, that's just peachy," Cassidy said, her dry humor rearing its head again.

"Hopefully, we'll develop our abilities and be able to tell the difference." Rae zeroed in on the woman still sleeping on the couch. "According to the writing in the globe, our magick should be stronger now that our circle is complete."

"North, South, East, and West," Bryn said solemnly and glanced to Rae. "With you as our center."

"You've found the final Maiden." Michael spoke from where he stood by the window. Lina had almost forgotten he was there. "And if I learned anything from spending time around the coven women, it's that unity will be one of your greatest weapons. You'll need each other in more ways than you realize."

He also looked toward the couch. "When she wakes up, it will be your turn to give answers, to lead the way."

"He's right," Shauni said, joining Michael and leaning into him as he wrapped his arm around her. "I won't lie to you. I was the first to face my trial, and I was terrified. I don't think I would have found the strength to stand on my own if it hadn't been for the help of my coven. The support of my sisters," she added, exchanging a small grin with Willyn.

"We only made it through, because we did it together," Willyn said. "And so will all of you."

Arik chose that moment to breeze through the doorway holding two huge paper bags. The faint aroma of spices filled the air as he stopped long enough to throw a concerned look to the woman on the couch. "No change?"

"Not yet," Willyn answered as Dare entered with another large bag. "Where do you want these?" he asked Arik.

"Through the door there to the dining room. Thanks." Arik scanned the others. "There's plenty of food if anyone's hungry."

"I don't know—" Rae began, but a groan rose from the fainting couch and grabbed her attention. The biker lolled her head to one side, blinking slowly.

Everyone moved at once. Arik set down the bags, and Rae rose to hurry toward the woman as she roused. Lina, Bryn, and Cassidy followed suit.

Whether Michael's words had penetrated or something else guided their actions, the four women formed a circle, instinctively surrounding the fallen Maiden.

"It's all right. You're safe." Rae kneeled and spoke quietly. "You were in an accident."

"Oh. Yeah." Sliding her fingers into her auburn hair, the woman held her temple as if staving off a headache. "Where's my bike?"

Amused by her first concern, Arik smiled down at her. "It's in the garage, locked up. My name is Arik Mansur, and you're in my home. You've been examined by a nurse."

"I . . . remember." Before anyone could stop her, the woman rolled to her side, dropped her feet to the floor, and sat up. She sought out Willyn. "You did something to me, didn't you? You were leaning over me, and I felt . . ." she waved her hand over her chest, "this weird heat. It tingled."

"Yes. I helped you." Willyn didn't elaborate.

"Can I bring you anything to drink, anything for pain?" Rae asked, easing closer. "You took a hit, but you're fine now. Maybe you'd like to eat something? Or to get some more sleep? There are plenty of guest rooms, and then in the morning we can—"

"No," the woman said, her tone low but stern. "Tell me now." She hiked a single red brow and surveyed the group. "Tell me what the *nurse* did to help me."

She shifted abruptly, shaking off Rae's attempt to help her as she found her feet. "I remember taking that hit. I remember going in and out of consciousness." She rubbed her right shoulder. "I remember a lot more pain than I have now."

Going rigid, she surveyed the room full of people. "So tell me how I'm miraculously healed and here with a bunch of strangers, when I *should* be in an emergency room."

"There's a lot to explain," Lina said, surprising herself when she stepped forward. "And we'll tell you everything. Just know that you're safe here and surrounded by friends. I promise, we mean you no harm."

The woman narrowed her gaze but kept it fixed on Lina, sizing her up. "Fine," she said at last. "So explain."

Cassidy spoke, wringing her hands. "I was driving the car that hit you. It was completely my fault."

"But there were extreme circumstances," Bryn said, leaping to Cassidy's defense.

Lina couldn't help but feel a swell of warmth and affection. They were already looking out for each other.

"I'm Lina. What's your name?"

"Peyton. Peyton McKenna." She looked around to the rest of them, clearly asking for reciprocation.

Brief introductions were made, and then Bryn said, "You must be exhausted, after the accident and the healing. We could all sit and have something to eat while we talk."

Peyton slipped her hand up and rubbed her neck. "I'm not all that hungry."

Noticing the action, Rae made her way to a large mirror hanging on the wall in a gold frame. "Peyton, I need to show you something." She gestured for the other woman to join her. "There's more you need to hear, more you need to understand, but this should be first."

Frowning, Peyton took tentative steps toward Rae. "What do you want to show me?"

In reply, Rae lifted the sweep of her rich brown hair and revealed the left side of her neck. "Do you see the symbol below my ear?"

Peyton released a short laugh and pulled back. "What are

you talking about? What does this have to do with—"

"Please, just look."

Huffing, Peyton leaned forward. "Yes. I see something. Kind of flesh-colored, but it's there."

"Now look at your own neck, in the same location." Rae's expression was gentle, her voice insistent. "Please," she said when Peyton opened her mouth as if to argue.

Brushing back her own hair, Peyton angled toward the mirror.

Lina waited for an angry response, for her to demand to know what they'd done to her. Instead, Peyton simply stared, a small wrinkle on her forehead as she trailed her fingertips across the mark.

"Fire," she said.

Rae's brows shot straight up. "You recognize the sigil?"

"Not this one specifically." Peyton blew out a breath. "But I've seen elemental symbols before." She raked her hands over her face. "Damn. *Damn*. My grandmother was right."

Before anyone could ask her what she meant, a door slammed somewhere in the house, followed by clattering sounds, high-pitched yips, and a woman's voice. "Hold on. Just hold on."

The commotion drew closer, like a contained hurricane whooshing through the mansion.

A woman appeared in the doorway wearing a floral-patterned skirt of lime green, perfectly matching the scarf wrapped around her head. Cocoa skin flushed and brown eyes animated, she lifted the end of the leash she held in her hand. "We're back."

"Mahalia," Arik lifted his hands, "where have you been? You left before I went to get dinner."

"I'll tell you," she said with one bob of her head. "This picky little girl of yours made me take her all the way to Forsyth Park. She must have sniffed twenty different azaleas before she found one that would do."

She pursed her lips down at a puppy who looked like a mutt, with Labrador and Husky somewhere in her gene pool. Fur a shiny gold, the pup had clear blue eyes and a white bib on her chest.

"You gave this little girl the right name, because Lillian Poppy the Prim can turn a five-minute walk into a half-hour quest for the perfect potty spot." The woman bent down to free the dog, who barked twice, turned in a circle, and sat on the corner of the carpet with the grace of a princess.

"All right." Dropping the leash, the woman put her hands on her hips and eyeballed Peyton. "Who is this, and what did I miss?"

One hand still on her chin, Peyton looked at the woman, the dog, and the assembled group, all of them staring back at her.

She inhaled deeply and slid her attention to Rae. "You know," she said, expression blank, "I'll take that guest room after all."

12

Searenn settled into the soft leather sofa, a triumphant smile creeping across her lips. The G650 belonged to a music executive from Atlanta who'd given her full use of the luxury jet.

After she'd forced the idea into his mind, of course.

She dialed up the strength of her psychic influence, making sure he'd never wonder why he'd let a complete stranger play with his pricey toy. She'd always known people were weak and stupid, like cattle, but now she viewed them more as slugs. She could either twist them around or stomp them flat. Her choice.

Smug and satisfied, she caught the eye of the flight attendant, a sleek and attractive Latina with long, gorgeous legs. "I'll take an Old Fashioned," Searenn said before adding, "and when is dinner?"

"Whenever you'd like." The woman's tone was like a stroke of the hand, calming and subservient. She retrieved a menu card from a drawer in the long cabinet across from Searenn and handed it to her.

After a quick perusal of the laminated card, Searenn gave it back. "I'll have the steak."

"Right away. My name is Dianna, and please feel free to call on me for whatever you need." She moved to the rear of the cabin and disappeared through a door.

Picking up the remote control, Searenn got more comfortable against the ivory cushions and clicked on the television atop the cabinet. After flicking through the offered movies and shows, she chose a series that looked gritty and violent. Pimps, cartels, street gangs—some of her favorite kinds of people.

She had a long flight ahead of her and might decide to sleep, but only because she still enjoyed the all-too human activity. But she didn't need slumber, not like she used to.

Resurrection, it seemed, came with a shit ton of perks.

Either way, she'd be right at home as she traveled across the ocean, following the first clue from her family's records. The genealogy book had given her a place to start, a specific location to begin her hunt.

Huktai scribes had spread the aethyrical texts all over the world, but one thing was true of ancient rivalries. The fighters always clashed again, coming together at different points in history.

And as always, the Droehks had watched. They'd chronicled, planning for the day the chosen would return.

And now she had.

Content to relax for the duration of the flight, Searenn turned her attention to the opening scenes of the TV show. A black screen appeared with the sound of a scream, then a shot of blood streaming across a dirty cement floor.

Dianna returned with the Old Fashioned, just as a woman on screen began pleading for her life. Without so much as a glance to the attendant, Searenn savored the taste of bourbon on her tongue, while the sound of sweet terror echoed in her ears.

This was the good life and, if she did her job, she could live it forever.

As the scent of cooked meat teased her appetite, Searenn licked her smiling lips.

Let the hunt begin.

13

"Thanks, Bex. I'll check in soon." Lina ended the call on her cell phone and released a long sigh of relief. Outside Arik's kitchen window, the sun had barely begun to turn the sky pink.

Good thing Bex was an early riser. Lina had called to ask if she could cover at the café, with Bex gladly accepting the extra hours. Lina had come to depend on her, certain she could handle the responsibility and, with everything happening now, she would need to promote Bex to Manager and hire another server.

It was the right move to make. The smart thing to do.

Since Lina had some new responsibilities herself.

As she filled the coffeemaker to brew a pot, her mind raced through the steps necessary to make the changes happen quickly. Where some might be stressed or daunted, the act of clicking along in business mode actually soothed Lina. Planning and execution was a path she could walk with her eyes closed.

But curses, demons, and ancient magick? Those things created a foreign landscape—dark, dangerous, and filled with pitfalls.

Beside her, the machine gurgled and hissed, the only sounds as she waited for dawn.

She distracted herself by perusing the kitchen, a sophisticated blend of old and new. The porcelain tile floors were likely original, their white and gray palette mimicked in marble countertops.

Made of dark wood—*maybe walnut?*—the butcher block island gave a hint of vintage, as did the brushed nickel hardware and dark gray shelves. Pots hung between a stove of stainless steel and its huge matching hood above. The polished metal contrasted with an entire wall of subway tiles, their clean white brightening and modernizing all at once.

But the massive Victorian-style clock, that was Lina's favorite part. Two feet wide at least, the round face graced one wall, its Roman numerals lending a sense of history.

She was pouring a second cup of coffee when floorboards creaked overhead. She glanced up. Who else would be up at this time? Arik and Rae? Cassidy? Definitely not Bryn, she thought with amusement. Her friend claimed to need eight hours of sleep but rarely closed her eyes before midnight.

Maybe Peyton was prowling around. After all, she'd been the first to bed. Deciding to take the offered guest room, she'd sailed quietly past the brightly-garbed woman who'd come late to the gathering.

Mahalia. Arik had made introductions but had only described her as a family friend.

There was more to the story, of that Lina felt certain. There was more, period. And she intended to ask some pointed questions once they were all together. All five of the Watchtower Maidens in one room. Ready to begin.

A bump on Lina's leg drew her attention to the floor. "Hey, Remi. How you doing, my sweet boy?"

The cat meowed back up at her and purred, rubbing his cheek against her calf again.

"I've got your breakfast, and I made sure to bring your favorite."

Last night, after everyone had decided to stay at Arik's, Lina had made one request—to go home and get her cat. Leaving him all alone had been out of the question.

If those monsters or men or whatever they were had found

her and Cassidy at the bookstore, who was to say they wouldn't target their homes? So, agreeing there was safety in numbers, Lina, Cassidy, Rae, and Arik all went back to the bookstore to lock up, and then to Lina's place to pick up Remi.

Now, in the morning light, Lina wondered if she'd overreacted, even though her organized world had been dumped on its head. Everything she knew was now scattered, uncertain, and unpredictable, with only one thing clear in her mind.

Protecting the innocent.

Grabbing a packet of the cat's food and his bowl, she walked past a table for ten with a view of the courtyard. She stepped out a door and into the gardens where she filled the cat's bowl.

High brick walls surrounded the courtyard, and Remi rarely wandered, so she felt safe leaving him to eat outside. Plus, *eau d'tuna* didn't go well with coffee and breakfast.

Closing the glass-paned door behind her, she returned to the sink. By now, brighter sunrays were filtering through treetops, and Arik and Rae—with a groggy-eyed Bryn—were filtering into the kitchen.

"Wow. I do believe in magick." Lina's mouth turned up on one side. "Because that's the only thing that could get Bryn up before seven in the morning."

"It's too early for humor, even for me." Bryn ambled to the table, a classic style in distressed white paint. She sunk into a chair. "By all the blessed stars, tell me that coffee is ready."

Pivoting, Lina slid the carafe out from under the stream and caught the hot black liquid in one of the cups she'd retrieved from a cabinet. Sliding the pot back in place, she carried the cup to Bryn. "Here you go, sunshine."

Bryn grunted and lowered her head to drink.

"Thanks for starting coffee," Rae said.

"No worries. It's just what I do." Lina trailed her fingers over the shiny machine. "Plus, I've never used this particular style before and couldn't resist."

"How'd you like it?" Arik sidled over and put his hand on top where two compartments held different flavors of beans. "It's brand new. Rae suggested a bigger, better version than the one I had."

He looked at Lina. "Since we'd probably be making coffee for a lot more people."

"It's great," Lina said, shaking her head. "And again, I'm struck by the strange clashing of two worlds. Buying a new coffeemaker, which is perfectly normal. And making sure it's big enough to fuel all your witches for a supernatural war."

She closed her eyes and opened them again. "Just not something I'd ever thought I'd hear myself say."

Rae moved to Lina and gave her a quick one-armed hug. "I know." Without adding anything more, she eased away and leaned against the island. "Emma sends her love. She wanted to come over but felt guilty about leaving Dad alone again."

Lina had grown up around the whole Scott clan, including Emma—Bryn's other aunt and Rae's sister. "How is she handling this?" she asked, without need to expound on what *this* meant.

"Oh, in her usual Emma fashion. Mothering, supporting, making food, and keeping laundry clean."

"She feels guilty," Bryn piped up, stretching her arms above her head. "She thinks it should have been her instead of me."

"I can see that. She's always looked out for you." Lina glanced to Rae. "You both have."

Rae nodded, opening her mouth as if to reply, but Cassidy strolled into the room. Tossing everyone a nod in greeting, she headed straight for the table and sat opposite Bryn. "The others are right behind me, so I say we get our first council meeting underway."

"No. Uh-uh." Bryn waved an agitated hand. "Food first."

Lina and Rae shared a look and burst into smiles. "That's our Bryn," Rae said. "Good thing we prepped for this scenario."

Edging to the microwave, she opened the door and removed a box with a local grocery store's green logo.

"Arik and I went out one more time last night after you all went to bed. We have eggs and bacon, but for now . . ." She set the pastries on the table in front of Bryn, "emergency rations."

"I could have—" Lina started, but Arik held up a hand to stop her.

"We will happily accept your higher-quality croissants in the future, but we made a command decision." He put his hands on Rae's shoulders. "And that was to give all of you a small break."

Despite a pastry snobbery she wouldn't deny, Lina had to admit feeling relieved. It was nice to have someone else covering the little details. "Did Mahalia stay last night?"

"No," Arik answered. "She prefers her own cozy cottage, but she promised to be back today." He quirked his mouth to the side. "She doesn't want to miss out on anything else."

Lina would have asked more about the colorful and charming older lady, but female voices drifted through the doorway, just before Peyton entered pushing Marit in her wheelchair.

Lina tensed, tossing a glance to Bryn and Cassidy. What would the newest Maiden have to say this morning? Surely she'd spent sleepless hours tossing and turning and worrying.

It was surprising she hadn't bolted in the middle of the night.

Frowning, Lina gave her a onceover. Not only had she stayed, but she looked well-rested, having fixed her red hair in a long braid.

Laughing at something Marit said, she strolled in and called out, "Morning." And then to Arik, "Love the elevator, by the way." Eyes the deep blue of the Mediterranean crinkled when she laughed. "But I felt a wee bit like a bird in a gilded cage."

Lina's mouth fell open, as did Bryn's, while Cassidy simply looked puzzled.

Peyton showed no signs of being scared, shocked, angry, or confused. In fact, Lina mused, she was downright chipper.

Cassidy's raven brows knitted. "How are you feeling, Peyton?" She studied the newcomer like she might be an android.

"I'm . . . well, I'm okay." Peyton shrugged and crossed her arms as Marit wheeled herself to an open spot at the table.

"Please don't take this the wrong way," Lina began, trying to broach the subject gently, "but you don't seem to be . . ."

"Freaking out?" Peyton finished with a lopsided grin. "I am. I did, at least a little." She too crossed the kitchen and sat, making the table look more and more like the council meeting Cassidy had joked about.

Peyton stared at the centerpiece, a bowl of sunflowers. "You could say I have a unique family history, so I'm not as surprised as maybe I should be."

"You mentioned your grandmother last night," Lina said, sliding back a chair and easing in. Rae did the same, leaving only Arik standing. "You said something about her being right."

Still boring her gaze into the sunny flowers, Peyton chuckled and bobbed her head slowly. "My Scottish granny, still living beneath the boughs of Faskally Forest. She always told mystical tales, taught me a little green-witch magick. She claims we're descended from those who 'Knew the Oak.'"

"What does that mean?" Bryn asked.

"Druids," Cassidy answered, leaning forward with interest. "Your ancestors were Druids?"

Peyton nodded and looked up at last. "I spent a lot of my summer breaks visiting her, walking in the woods, learning about plants." Here she laughed again. "Especially mistletoe, a magickal herb for sure, according to my gran. She spoke often of the elements, and how they contained power only some could see."

Rubbing her arm, Peyton frowned. "Only some could harness. That's the word she always used. *Harness*. And whenever she spoke of it, she would call me by a pet name. Kenna."

"From McKenna," Bryn said. "Your last name."

"Yes. Except that in Gaelic," with a shiver, Peyton glanced around to the rest of them, "Kenna means 'born of fire.'"

"Whoa," Bryn whispered while the others sat quietly, absorbing the significance of a grandmother's endearment.

Finally, Peyton settled her gaze on Rae. "When you showed me the mark on my neck, I absolutely recognized the symbol. It was both scary and familiar all at once."

Rae inclined her head, saying she understood with the simple gesture.

"Well," Lina said and sighed, "you're handling this a lot better than I did. I don't come from a magickal family, but I've known the Scotts my whole life. The notion of power isn't completely foreign to me, but it's definitely not in my wheelhouse. Or it never used to be," she added.

Lina shrugged. "I just can't figure out a way to manage this."

"Nope," Cassidy said. "Me either."

"I have methods for dealing with problems or work to be done," Lina continued, "but how do I make a checklist for the supernatural? Buy magick wand. Check. Get broom repaired. Polish crystals. Check. Check. Luckily," she gave a short laugh, "I've already got a cat."

Her joke drew smiles from the others, including Marit. "This is good," the older woman said. "You need to be able to laugh. Friendship, family, love, laughter—those are the strongest of magicks."

Placing her elbows on the armrests of her wheelchair, she told Lina, "It's natural to seek control, especially in a new and intimidating situation. But like with anything else, there are steps that need to be taken."

Trailing her gaze to each of the women, she continued. "Each of you will find a way to master these new roles, these new abilities, and while not everything will be certain or predictable," she focused on Lina again, "you will gain confidence. When you're ready."

"We needed to be ready last night," Cassidy said. "We need to be ready *now*. But we don't even know if the men who attacked us last night were human or not."

"You were attacked?" Peyton paused with a croissant halfway to her mouth. "By *demons*?"

No one had a chance to answer as doorbell chimes cut through the air. All heads turned toward the front of the house.

Rae frowned and exchanged a glance with Arik. "Who could that be?"

14

Lina and the others sipped their coffee or chewed their pastries, a heavy silence in the kitchen as they waited for the surprise visitor to Arik's house. With the way things had developed the last few days, it was no wonder a layer of tension hung over their heads.

A moment later, Lina perked up, listening to footsteps drawing near.

"Da-dum. Da-dum." Bryn sang the suspenseful notes from Jaws, breaking the strain and drawing laughs from the rest of them. Even Marit chuckled into her mug.

"At least we can still laugh," Cassidy murmured, her stare fixed on the doorway.

Rae reappeared, grinning, with another woman right behind her. "Anna," Rae said, gesturing to the group, "I'd like you to meet everyone." She introduced Lina, Cassidy, and Peyton. "Ladies, this is Anna St. Germaine."

Anna wore a long sable-brown ponytail, and had a genteel elegance about her, despite her casual T-shirt and paint-splattered shorts. "Peyton," she said, "it's nice to meet you. And I've spoken with Cassidy a few times at the bookshop."

Cassidy nodded. "I remember."

"It's good to see you again. And you," Anna pointed at Lina, "I remember when you still wore two braids, and you and Bryn got into as much mischief as you could find."

"Anna and I were teenagers then and into our own brand of

trouble," Rae added in a wry tone, raising her brows at Anna.

"And I remember *that*," Bryn joked.

"Well," Anna held up a palm like a traffic cop, "no need to go into the details."

Marit folded her hands in her lap, a mischievous glint in her gaze. "I'd love to hear some of those stories."

"Marit." Anna moved to the older woman and bent over to wrap her arms around her. "You look wonderful."

Marit hugged her back. "Better every day. Other than my weakened muscles, there's no aftereffects of the curse at all."

"Curse?" Peyton piped up. "First demon attacks and now curses?" She shot a look to Arik. "Got anything stronger I can add to this coffee?"

Anna tilted her head and sent Peyton an understanding smile. "I know it's shocking at first but, believe it or not, you get used to it." She spoke to the group. "I don't know if Shauni or Willyn mentioned it last night, but Lucia and Ethan are moving into their new house today. So if you'd like to come over and meet the girls . . ."

"Yes." Bryn jumped to her feet, grabbing an apple fritter before slipping away from the table. "I've met them, of course, but I think a melding of minds is exactly what we need right now."

"Uh . . . is that a witch thing?" Cassidy asked.

Bryn waved her off with a grunt. "Just bring your food or coffee or whatever, and let's go." She nodded toward the door, prompting Anna and Rae to lead the way.

"Where are we going?" Peyton asked, the words muffled by a quick bite of croissant.

Bryn stepped out of the room but grabbed the doorjamb to lean back in. "We're going to meet the Savannah Coven."

Setting aside her cup, Lina hurried after her, eager to meet the coven witches. They'd already experienced, and triumphed over, a similar ordeal. If anyone could offer words of wisdom, it was Anna and her friends.

Marit wheeled herself to the coffeemaker. "Have fun," she called to Cassidy and Peyton, who now trailed behind Lina. The three of them walked quickly through the maze of corridors, exiting the front door to a gorgeous spring day.

Bryn tossed back a *hurry-up* glance. She was a few steps behind Rae and Anna, crossing the street at a diagonal toward a four-story house. If *house* was even the right word to describe such a palatial home.

Built of pale beige stone, the home stood tall, the top three levels boasting balconies with black wrought-iron in a swirling design. Thick, vibrant shrubs provided privacy to a large yard on one side, out of which rose one of the biggest live oak trees Lina had ever seen.

And she lived in Savannah, so that was saying something.

A moving truck sat parked out front, a variety of men and women trailing back and forth as they unloaded boxes and household furnishings. Lina stutter-stepped when she noticed a woman with white-blonde hair carrying three stacked boxes at once.

"Is that—" she began.

"Paige," Bryn said over her shoulder. "Yep. That's her."

Super-strength indeed. Lina made a sound of amazement and kept walking. She noticed Willyn and Shauni from last night, both chatting with a brunette with a killer figure.

As if sensing Lina's regard, she jerked her head toward the group strolling her way and waved an enthusiastic hand. "*Buenos dias*! I was hoping we'd see you today." She trotted down the sidewalk towards them.

Smile wide and steps lively, she rushed to Rae and gave her a hug. When she pulled back, she surveyed Lina, Cassidy, and Peyton. "So you've found your Maidens," she said softly to Rae, approval glinting in her Spanish-brown gaze.

"We all found each other," Rae said. "Or bumped into each

other," she added.

"More like crashed." Cassidy lifted a shoulder, chuckling with Peyton who continued to go with the ever-turning flow.

"Where are my manners?" the woman said, her accent just thick enough to be utterly charming. "I'm Lucia, Arik's new neighbor. Would you like a tour of the house?" She frowned as if second-guessing the offer. "Unless you're busy. I know you're getting used to a lot of new things."

"Actually, we were just discussing demons over breakfast," Peyton said. "A distraction might be nice."

"Demons over breakfast." A woman walked up, glasses perched over her gorgeous Asian eyes. "Sounds like the title of a book."

"Yeah." Cassidy nodded. "I'd read it."

Bryn grunted. "I think we're living it."

"And this is Viv," Anna said. "Don't worry if you can't remember everyone's names, because the entire village turned out to help Lucia and Ethan move in."

"Which brings us back to the tour." Bryn rubbed her hands together. "For the last fifteen years, at least, I've been dying to get a look inside the old Chadwick place. Although, now I guess we'll have to give it a new name."

Lucia put one finger to her chin. "Hmm. The Ruiz-Drake place. Drake-Ruiz." She shook her head.

"Time to get married and make things simple?" Viv slid the black glasses down her nose to peer at Lucia with a devilish gleam.

"You know, you're right, Bryn. We'll have to think on that." Lucia deftly sidestepped the wedding reference. "But for now," she waved both arms toward the house, "I'll show you around."

They all traipsed up steps rising from the sidewalk to a set of double doors on the second floor. Here they entered into an atrium, a room that whispered of wealth rather than shout. A glass dome allowed light to shine down, highlighting tile floors in a gorgeous pattern of gray and buttercream. An arched doorway led them to a set of pillars distinguishing the entryway from the rest of the home.

Awed, Lina eased inside, spinning to take in the open interior and high ceilings, illuminated by light streaming in through a wall of windows. "I can cook," Lina said, "if you need a live-in chef."

"Ha. Don't tempt me," Lucia teased. "There's not much furniture yet, but that will come in time."

"You have so much space to fill," Peyton noted, stroking the tip of her fiery braid. "You have a lot of furniture to buy."

"And that will be so much fun," Cassidy said, zeroing in on a room to the left with myriad built-in bookshelves. "Um, I can't cook, but I'm sure I can make myself useful somehow."

"That's not necessary. You are all welcome any time." Lucia moved to stand between Anna and Rae, wrapping one arm around each. "Soon we will be neighbors *and* family. A sister of my sister is my sister too."

"I think I actually got that," Bryn said, pointing at Lucia.

"Just be glad she didn't say it in her mother tongue." A younger woman with golden hair piled into a messy knot walked up. "*A hermana von mis hermana es . . . hermana.*"

Lucia shook her head as Anna cringed and said, "I think you're mixing languages, Kylie."

"It's from the traveling." Lucia gave Kylie an excuse, tugging lightly on a stray blonde curl. "Try to practice only one language for a month before mixing in another."

Kylie wobbled her head from side-to-side. "Yeah. Now that Quinn and I are staying put for a while, I'll work on my Spanish." She sidled up to Lucia and rubbed against her like a cat, "Since I have my own teacher."

Lucia pushed her away and laughed. "Go rub on your boyfriend."

"Ugh. Please." Anna held up a hand. "I don't need that

picture in my head."

"Quinn is Anna's brother," Bryn explained. "And apparently, she expects any future nieces and nephews to be dropped off by a stork."

"Nieces and nephews?" Kylie backed away waving both hands frantically. "And on that note, I'm leaving. More boxes in the truck." She snapped her fingers, spun toward the front door, and bounded out.

"Okay," Lucia said, waving at the departing Kylie with a chuckle before clapping her hands one time. "On with the tour."

She led the eager group through mostly-empty rooms, aside from stacked boxes, lamps, a couple of couches, and various household items. They sauntered through a stylish kitchen—obviously updated within the last several years—up a rear staircase to the higher floors for more touring, and finally, at the top, they all filed out to a balcony.

Lina wasn't the only one who gasped at the view. Bryn moved to the corner, surveying Arik's house and the rest of the neighborhood. "It's a whole new world from up here."

"This is one of my favorite spots." Lucia leaned on the black iron railing. "Amazing how peaceful it is up here." A bird shot from the leaves of the gigantic oak, crying out as it soared over their heads and disappeared behind the roof.

"It's incredible." Rae stood next to Bryn, enjoying the spread of Savannah's historic district for as far as she could see. Then she turned and spoke to Lucia. "Thank you for showing us around. However, this is moving day, and I'm sure you have plenty to do."

"Yes," Lucia admitted, "but with so much help, it's honestly not so bad."

As they reentered the house and walked downstairs, she pointed out a few more details of the home. Once back on the main level, another woman came over to greet them. She had a sweet look about her and hair the soft color of caramel. "How was the tour?"

"Great," Rae said. "I'd heard this place was something special, and it is. Ladies," she added, turning to Lina, Cassidy, and Peyton, "this is Hayden."

Rae introduced them to her as well, and Hayden inclined her head in greeting. "We are all so glad to meet you, and I'm sure Anna already offered, but we'll help you in any way we can."

"Thank you," Peyton said. "I only became a part of this last night, but I'm already feeling more at ease. Don't get me wrong," she said, pursing her lips, "I'm still nervous. But the support from everyone here, and across the street," she grinned at Rae, "goes a long way toward taking the edge off."

"Good." Hayden hesitated as if unsure she should say whatever was on her mind, but then she did. "Willyn and Shauni filled us in about last night, not only about finding Peyton, but also about the two of you being chased."

Lina and Cassidy shared a glance.

"That's actually what got us on the topic of demons this morning." Rae stuck her hands in the pockets of her shorts and sighed. "We've got to catch up with the bad guys. They obviously know who we are, so first on our agenda is to learn who *they* are. And to prepare for any more surprise attacks."

"I was going to talk to you about wards and other things you can all do to protect your homes," Anna said to the three newest Maidens. "We've already done some work on Arik's and the Scott family home. Just the basics for now, but we can make them more specific when we learn exactly who or what is coming after you."

Lina's chest felt suddenly lighter. "Oh, good." She blew out a breath and put a hand on her stomach. "I'll feel better with some protection. Right now, I'm too afraid to go home, or even leave my cat there by himself."

"A cat is good." Hayden nodded. "They can warn you when certain entities are present. Dogs, too."

Rae chuckled.

"What?" Anna asked.

"I'm just imagining how Poppy would react. When she gets upset or afraid, her barks are ear-piercing."

At that moment, Kylie entered the front door again with the one named Paige. Tall and leanly muscled, she strode across the tile floor with utter confidence. "All of the boxes are where you requested, General." She gave Lucia a mock salute.

"Already?" Lucia beamed. "You and Chris together could probably have just lifted the moving truck and poured everything inside."

"Sure, but then your fancy lamps would have been broken." With the teasing tone still in her voice, Paige said her hellos to Lina, Cassidy, and Peyton.

"Listen," Anna said, "since we have time for a break, why don't we take the first step toward getting prepared?" She and Rae exchanged a moment of silent communication.

"I was thinking along those same lines." Rae glanced around to the grand home and all of the boxes that still needed unpacking. "The timing may be bad but—"

"No such thing." It was Lucia who answered. "The timing is perfect. You're all here," she indicated the Maidens, "and so are we. And I just happen to have plenty of space in the yard."

Lina paused, trying to grasp their meaning. It was like they were speaking in code. "So . . . what are we going to do in the yard?"

Hayden laughed. "Like someone once said, when it comes to small boys and novice witches, it's better if they play outside."

"Um . . ." Cassidy began, quirking her head to the side.

"We should move outdoors," Rae explained, "if we're going to practice magick."

Peyton's gaze went wide. "What kind of powers do you expect us to have?"

"You might be surprised." Anna put her hand on Peyton's

shoulder. "And fireballs have a way of popping out here and there."

"Whoop!" Kylie thrust a fist into the air and pivoted in a half circle, cupping her hands around her mouth in a makeshift megaphone. "Official break time for coven witches."

"That doesn't seem fair." A man with dark hair and eyes came out from one side of the staircase. He stopped where he was and raised his voice. "Official break time for coven support crew."

"Ha ha." Lucia swaggered over to him and kissed him on the mouth. "You're so underappreciated, I know."

"Make it up to me later?" he said, kissing her back.

"And that would be Ethan," Anna said before telling him, "Sub sandwiches are in the fridge."

"You're an angel, Anna." He swooped in to peck her on the cheek. "I don't suppose you brought—"

"Beer, too." She rolled her eyes. "You know Ian and Quinn wouldn't forget that."

Lina recognized Ian as the name of Anna's new husband. So many names to remember, she thought. However, while it was nice knowing the coven ladies had their backs, it was even better knowing they came with their own army.

"Right, then." Anna spoke to Rae. "Shall we?"

"I'm up for it if all of you are." Rae searched the eyes of the Maidens, her gaze landing on Lina last.

"I don't want to feel that vulnerable again," Lina said, rubbing one arm. "I'm scared of whatever power might be inside of me, but I'm a lot more scared of what's out *there*."

"Same." Cassidy put her hands on her hips. "Those guys last night looked like body builders, and that was bad enough. But if they were more than human . . ." She shuddered. "So, yeah. Magick 101. I'm in."

"I've been ready since that foul thing crawled inside me," Bryn said, crossing her arms with a scowl. "Peyton?" she asked, giving the final vote to the newest member.

Peyton nodded slowly. "Absolutely." Then her mouth curved up on one side. "Wait until my grandmother hears about this."

15

Lina and the others stepped out into the sun, finding the rest of the coven ladies sitting on the stairs chatting. Only one of them she didn't recognize, a woman with hair as red as Peyton's who glanced up when the larger group descended to join them.

"What's up?" Viv asked, her gaze quizzical behind her glasses.

"You guys ready for some practice?" Anna asked. She didn't need to specify what they'd be practicing.

"Always," the redhead replied. Then to the newcomers, "I'm Claudia, by the way."

"We can just go in the gate," Lucia said, guiding them to a latched panel in the wrought iron fence, also black to match the balconies and streetlights styled as faux gas lamps.

Now that all of them were together in one place, Lina realized just how many women were gathering on Lucia's grass for a little Saturday witchcraft. "Do you think anyone will notice?" She glanced around to the other houses.

"We'll be fine once we're past the oak." Bryn trailed her hand along the leaves of a low branch, one of several that had grown in twisting curves toward the ground.

As soon as Lina edged around the tree, she understood. In addition to the privacy afforded by the house itself, a tall wall ran along the back of the property to block the view from behind. The massive oak full of spring leaves did the rest, sheltering them from the front and side.

Anticipation rippled through her, little waves of fear and excitement. She was about to attempt magick. *Magick!* How quickly her life had taken a hard left turn down an unknown path.

As she tried to calm her jangling nerves, her back pocket vibrated. She'd forgotten she still had her phone. She pulled it out to read the text. It was from Cade.

Lina, please call me as soon as possible.

Her muscles clenched and her chest felt hollow. Not because she didn't want to hear from him. Not because she didn't want to speak to him.

But because when she did, it would be to break things off.

She thought of all the times they'd chatted at the café, and the nervousness she'd felt fell away, swallowed up by a deep, dark pit—a sense of loss. She rubbed her thumb across the screen, lingering on his name.

Cade. A friend at first, one who'd slipped past her defenses. Then a man who'd come to mean more to her than she'd admitted to herself.

And now she had to give him up.

Being a Watchtower Maiden had already put both her and Cassidy's lives at risk, and it was clear the fight had only just begun. There was a good chance things were going to get worse and, no matter how it might hurt, she had to push Cade away. She refused to expose him to that kind of danger.

So she shoved the phone back into her pocket and shoved the sadness into a box. She was good at compartmentalizing, at locking things away. Like the feelings for Cade that she could no longer pursue.

"You okay?" Bryn wore a frown as she touched Lina's arm.

She swallowed against the sadness. "Yes. Just a little anxious."

"I know, but at least we're here together." She notched her

chin toward a few of the ladies. "And the coven. We'll all watch out for each other."

Lina faked a calm she didn't feel as the coven positioned themselves into a large circle. Rae and the Maidens then created a smaller one inside.

"You know," Kylie said, retying her locks into a more subdued ponytail, "if I hadn't matured into such a classy woman, I'd have to point out that this ever-growing posse of witches now has two fire crotches."

"Kylie!" Willyn said, smacking her forehead.

Despite herself, Lina chuckled with some of the others.

"Yeah," Cassidy added with a mischievous grin, "except ours is literal. She has the symbol and everything."

Kylie tossed her head back and gut-laughed. Peyton immediately joined in, lifting her braid in Claudia's direction as if to say "cheers."

Claudia bowed her head in return.

"Is this part of the process?" Lina asked Bryn, trying to keep a straight face. The female camaraderie felt wonderful. And somehow comforting, helping to fill that hole inside of her just a bit.

"Kind of." Bryn quirked her mouth to the side. "Rae's worked with me a little bit and, apparently, emotions can help you find the seat of your power."

"The seat of my power?"

"It's hard to explain," Bryn winked, "but you'll understand in a few minutes."

"Great. Now I'm nervous again."

"Don't be," Rae said from across the circle. "We'll take it slow." She inclined her head to Anna and, as the women began to quiet, Rae addressed the Maidens.

"When I first called on my magick, I felt it in my stomach, just below my heart." Rae pressed a fist to the place she described. "It was like a tiny pinch, followed by a sigh, as if a key had opened a lock. It came easily at the time, because I needed it to fight."

She glanced to her niece. "To help Bryn."

"I'm grateful for that," Bryn said. "But now we have to learn to do the same." She reached out to Lina, taking her hand before grasping Peyton's on her other side. Peyton stood next to Rae in the circle, so she clasped her hand while Lina took Cassidy's. Finally, Cassidy and Rae connected to complete the link.

"For now," Rae said in a soothing tone, "just focus on your connection to each other. Be open to whatever you feel."

Peyton inhaled deeply and closed her eyes. Having no idea what else to do, Lina took a breath and did the same.

At first, her concentration led to a hyper-awareness of her palms pressed to the warmth of others. Cassidy gave a quick, encouraging squeeze of her fingers, and Lina returned the gesture.

Anna's soft voice spoke from the outer ring. "Relax and let it find you."

Lina realized she'd been holding her breath, so she released it with a low *whoosh*. *Let it find me*. She breathed in slowly, and then out again. *Let the magick find me*.

Suddenly, she felt a stirring, right where Rae had said it would be. Just beneath her heart.

Remembering to breathe, she imagined the sensation growing, gaining strength from her acceptance. *I can do this. I have to do this.*

A sense of fullness flowed into her arms, warm and scintillating. She couldn't stop the laugh that burst free as she reveled in fascination.

And the thrill of *power*.

"Whoa," someone whispered. It sounded like Paige.

Still clasping her friends' hands, Lina lifted one lid for a peek. Her jaw dropped as she looked around at the other

Maidens. Each of them emitted a soft haze of color. White from Bryn, violet from Rae—like the magic she'd demonstrated in the library—red from Peyton, and blue from Cassidy.

She took a cautious glance down and saw her own light blending with the green of the grass.

"Wow." This time it was Kylie who spoke. "We have a hum when we're all together, but you guys—"

"Glow," Shauni finished, smiling proudly at their accomplishment.

"You almost sparkle," Willyn said, her expression also proud, and filled with a kind of sisterly love. "I think I'm a little jealous."

Lina, Bryn, and Peyton all laughed in response, and their combined wattage amped up, brightening the colors.

Cassidy pulled away, and the light show ended.

"Sorry. Shit." She rubbed her face. "Sorry."

"Don't be." Rae spoke with insistence. "This is a lot. It's okay to flinch while we're learning."

"Two for flinching," Peyton said, raising her fist.

"Don't you dare." Cassidy pointed at her and grinned. Then she rubbed her bicep as if remembering the hard little knuckle punches from grade school.

"I have a feeling we can use our magick for different things." Rae held up her hand and conjured the purple glow. "But even on my first night, I used it as a weapon."

"A weapon," Lina repeated, a memory jumping at her like a ghost in a haunted house. "I completely forgot." She jerked her gaze to Rae. "Last night, one of the men had a curved weapon in his hand. And it had a haze around it, a faint sparkle. Just like ours, only," her breath hitched, "it was black."

Rae's features morphed, her happy smile replaced by intense focus. "Do you think you can describe it for Arik?"

Lina summoned the vision of the man's raised hand, a blade held high, sharp and curved on both ends. She nodded to Rae.

"I can."

"Good." Rae glanced in the direction of the Mansur home, though she couldn't see it through the thick leaves of the oak. "Marit is helping him decipher his father's journals. This will be one more piece of information they know to look for."

The mood had changed slightly, a somberness stealing some of the joy they'd created.

"Can we try again?" Peyton asked. "I felt something inside of me, but when I tried to expand it or . . . I don't know, *feel* it better, I couldn't get it to go any further. Like it was uncharged or . . . I can't explain."

"Like a car when the battery is dead," Bryn said. "You keep trying but the engine won't turn over."

"Yes." Peyton thrust a hand toward Bryn. "That's exactly right."

"But it was only our first try," Lina said. Taking Bryn's hand, she pressed her lips tight. "Let's go again."

"Okay." Cassidy grabbed Lina's hand and then Rae's, having regained her enthusiasm.

"This time, choose whatever emotion you're feeling the most right now and channel it." Rae forged the last connection with Peyton. "Use your feelings to fuel your power."

Again, Lina let her lids close. She concentrated on the place in her chest, the secret spot where her magick slept. Still envisioning the rise of power, she searched her own emotions.

First a comforting sense of friendship and solidarity floated to the surface, followed by a trickle of fear when she remembered the man and his weapon.

But one feeling rose above the others, and suddenly all she saw was Cade's face. She thought of his kiss, his scent, his taste, his *eyes*.

And the loss of him crashed over her, drowning every other emotion.

Energy erupted from Lina's center, bursting through her

limbs and down to her hands. She heard Bryn's gasp and then her chuckle.

Peyton gave a short whistle. "I can feel that surge from over here."

Then a sharper sound followed, a cry of pain.

"Anna?" Kylie's voice. "Anna!"

At once, Lina and the Maidens opened their eyes. Rae pulled free, breaking the circuit as she rushed to join several of the coven witches crowded around Anna who sat on the ground, the fingers of both hands pressed to her forehead.

"What did I do?" Lina asked. "I'm so sorry. I couldn't control it."

"You knocked it out of the park," Anna croaked, but she immediately looked up to meet Lina's worried gaze. "Don't worry, it's a good thing. I just didn't expect this effect."

"Are you okay?" Kylie helped Anna stand, her face cloaked with worry.

"You had a vision." Rae rushed to her friend. "Your pupils are the size of planets."

"I did." Anna shook her head. "It came fast, hard, and painfully clear."

Lina's pocket buzzed. Still watching Anna, she pulled out her phone. An ingrained habit for any business owner who couldn't afford to miss an important message.

Another text from Cade. *I'm at the café, and Bex said you called in. I'm worried.*

Lina furrowed her brow. This wasn't like Cade at all. He wasn't the pushy type.

She'd have to get back to him, but right now her greatest concern was Anna. Lina still didn't understand what she'd done or what she'd caused.

She clenched the phone in her fingers and let it fall to her side. "Anna, I didn't mean to hurt you, and I am so, so sorry."

"It wasn't your fault, Lina and I promise, it's all right. It was actually helpful." Anna shifted her gaze to Rae. "Because now I know what the word on that piece of paper meant."

"Wait. What word?" Cassidy stepped forward. "What paper?"

Still speaking to Rae, Anna said, "The one Mahalia brought to you that night."

Rae explained to the others but kept her focus on Anna. "Mahalia's mother was trying to tell her something before she died. Mahalia finally figured out what it was and showed us what she'd discovered. On the night I opened the globe."

"But I had it wrong," Anna said. "I thought the word referred to one who has an affinity for demons."

"But it didn't?" Bryn asked, her arms folded protectively across her middle. She had to be remembering that same night and the evil force that hijacked her body.

"No. Not an affinity for demons." Anna licked her lips. "But the *mastery* of demons."

"Anna," Paige said, looking fierce, "you're not talking about another Droehk, are you?"

"Not another one." Anna stood straight and stiff. "But the *same* one."

"Oh, shit," Paige uttered, gazing up to the tree.

"But that's impossible." The red-haired Claudia held out her hands. "She's dead."

"Who's dead? What's a Droehk?" Lina tossed out the questions, ignoring the vibration of the phone in her palm.

"Dead or not, she's back," Anna said in a definitive voice. "I saw her clearly, here in Savannah, and she was reading a book. A book that mentioned the Huktai." She heaved a sigh. "And the Watchtower Maidens."

"We'll take care of her." Paige slammed one fist into the opposite palm. "We'll kill her again. She's ours to deal with."

Rae spoke softly. "Not anymore."

"No," Anna said, agreeing with Rae. "She's different now. She's no longer ours to defeat."

Anna stepped to Rae and took hold of her hands. "Our connection as friends, and now the coven to the Maidens, that's no coincidence. But this is a war we just can't fight."

"I know." Rae hugged her friend close and held on to her. "I know."

"But we can help, right?" Willyn's hands were clasped into a ball.

Anna nodded and stepped out of the embrace. "We'll do whatever we can."

The phone buzzed again, and Lina opened the screen, prepared to shoot off a text to let Cade know she was all right. He'd sent another two messages. The first one read only, *We need to talk.*

But it was the second one she zeroed in on. The one that made her stomach drop to the ground.

I know about the mark on your neck.

16

Cade pulled to the curb just as a moving van ahead of him drove away. He searched for a number on the house, making sure this was the address Lina had texted him, but then she stepped through a black metal gate wedged between tall hedges.

At the sight of her, relief washed through Cade. She looked fine but slightly on edge, her feet shifting as she looked at him, then away, and back to him again.

Exiting the car, he strode over to her. "Lina," he began, but she shook her head and tugged him back inside the gate to a sheltered lawn, leading him across the grass until they stood behind the trunk of a towering oak tree.

Once afforded the privacy, he did what he'd been imagining himself doing since he'd opened the book the previous night and confirmed his fears. Gently, he cupped her face and kissed her lips. "I was so worried."

"I'm fine," she whispered.

Moving his right hand from her cheek, he slid it down the side of her throat. "Let me see."

Grabbing both of his wrists, she pushed his arms down and glanced over her shoulder as if afraid they'd be seen.

Cade's gut tightened with instant concern and something else. The need to protect. "Are you afraid of them?"

"What?" She whipped back and frowned at him. "Of course not."

"You seem jumpy."

Her mouth moved, but no words came out. Finally, she drew a deep breath and began to rub her pendant between her fingers. "How did you know about the symbol on my neck?"

Cade paused, thrown off by the way she'd turned things around on him. "I noticed Cassidy's last night when she reached up to touch it, and then you mirrored her movement. I recognized her mark from a book I have, and it all just . . . clicked."

Lifting a shoulder, he answered the question before she could ask. "The book is from an occult phase I went through when I was younger."

"Occult," she whispered, grimacing before glancing over his shoulder.

"I used to pore over those pages, those images," Cade said. Back when books had been his only way out of a mad, mad world.

Her whole body seemed to sag. "So you know what the symbol means."

"Yes." Cade touched her arm, telling her that he was on her side, despite what he'd learned. This time, she didn't push him away.

She appeared calmer, so he reached again for her hair, easing back the thick mass of gold. And there it was. This time, it was fear clenching in his gut, roaring up to grip him around the throat.

All the way here he'd wanted to be wrong, to find out Lina wasn't involved with this kind of darkness. But here was proof he couldn't deny. He skimmed a finger across the mark, the color of flesh but lighter.

When he spoke again, his voice was quiet but firm. "You don't have to do this. You don't have to be a part of whatever they've told you."

Lina shook her head. "You keep making it sound like a cult.

Like they've done something *to* me."

"Haven't they?" He scowled at the symbol before drawing back and dropping his hands. "How did you get the symbol? It doesn't look like ink."

The slight discoloration seemed almost natural, as if it were a part of her. But Cade didn't want to accept that. He didn't want to believe the legends were true. He *couldn't*.

"If I told you how . . ." She scoffed and leaned against the rough bark of the tree.

"Whatever this is, I won't let you go through it alone." No, damn it, he wouldn't. And he wouldn't bolt, wouldn't run back to his isolated and safe little world. Population of one.

This was *Lina*. Over the months, she'd gotten to him—*really* gotten to him—and finally, he'd decided to let her in. Now, no matter what she brought with her, he wanted her to stay.

"I'm not alone, Cade. And no, I can't let you be a part of this." She hardened her jaw. "In fact, I don't want you anywhere near it."

Around people who believed in an apocalypse? And insane doctrines that would put all of them directly in harm's way? Hell no. He didn't want *her* near it either.

He'd read about these people. He'd been told they existed in Savannah. He'd been warned to steer clear.

Shouted, angry words ricocheted in his head, memories from the day his father had found one of his other books. He'd flown into a rage, accusing Cade of witchcraft . . . and far worse.

Shaking off the terrible images before they took hold, Cade was the one to draw a long, slow breath. "Lina, listen to me. I don't think you know what you've gotten into. However you got that mark and whatever they've told you, these people . . ." he gripped her arms softly and locked onto those enchanting green eyes, "they're *dangerous*."

"They aren't," she insisted. "But my life has changed, and danger may come. Which is exactly why we can't see each other again."

"No. That's not the answer."

"Cade, I have no right to expose you to this. I care—" She released a small sigh, tilting her head and gazing softly at him. "I care about what happens to you. If nothing else, I'm your friend, and I refuse to drag you into this."

"And I care about you, Lina, so there's no asking me to ignore this, to just walk away and forget about you." Making a sound like a growl low in his throat, Cade raked a hand through his hair. "I don't understand how things changed so fast. What has happened since I dropped you off at home?"

Lina shook her head. "It's better if you don't know. Making sure you aren't involved is the least I can do."

"Too late." His tone turned gruff. "I'm already involved." Moving in, he slid his palm down her arm and took her hand in his. "Lina, I know we only had last night, but this thing between us, it's been building for a long time."

"I can't let it go any further." She tried to withdraw, but he pressed his other palm to the tree, trapping her in place.

"You can't stop it. Neither can I."

"I have to." Her eyes darted in panic.

"You want to push me away because of the mark on your neck." He dropped his head closer to whisper, "But that's exactly why I won't let you." Tenderly, he rubbed his thumb across the back of her hand.

They stared at each other, still connected. Still standing close enough for him to smell her light, sweet scent. "I won't let you," he said again.

Her lips parted, her pulse thrummed in her throat. "Cade," she said softly, lifting her mouth to his.

But then she gasped and jerked free, sidestepping to put distance between them. Speechless, she held up her palms.

Both glowed green.

"Oh, my God." She held her arms out from her body. "I don't

even know how I—"

Without hesitation, Cade gripped her shoulders. "Breathe, Lina. Just breathe." He stood in front of her, capturing her gaze. The fear he saw there was a stab to his heart. "Just take deep breaths and let them level you out. You're going to be fine."

Making a show of lifting his chest with each inhalation, he paced his breathing with hers. "Just look at me. And breathe."

Gradually, the panic in her stare receded. She glanced at her palms, made a sound of relief, and leaned into him. "It's gone. It's gone."

For a moment they stood that way, her side pressed to his, her head against his chest.

"That's another reason you have to go," she said, so low he almost didn't hear. "My emotions affect my power, and when I'm with you, those emotions are all over the place."

She raised her face to look at him but didn't move away. "You make me *feel*, Cade. Because you're right, something is between us, and it's too strong for me to handle."

"But you just did. You controlled it."

This time, she did step away. "I just made green light burst from my body, and I don't even know how it really works. My own magick, and I'm still unnerved by it. How are you not?"

"It *is* unnerving, and I'm still wrapping my head around it. But like you, I grew up in Savannah. Talk of the supernatural is as common here as Spanish moss."

"But seeing it is different." She rubbed her chest. "So is experiencing it."

"I imagine so."

She made a fist and pressed it against her thigh. "You saw what just happened, and that was when I was only thinking of kissing you."

"So what were you thinking when you brought it back down?" He pressed on. "What were you *feeling*?"

She thumped her fist against her leg. "It doesn't matter."

"I think it does. How did you feel, when I was with you, when I was helping you?"

"Damn you," she said, but the words held no heat. She studied him for a second before admitting, "I felt safe."

Cade nodded. "Good. That's all I want."

"But—"

"I want to be with you, Lina. I want to stay." Cade kept his tone level, without insistence or entreaty. "But it's your choice."

Voices carried from somewhere in the house, but Cade stood his ground, praying she'd changed her mind. "So will you let me?"

17

Lina had said yes, and so he'd stayed. He'd met the group, and remained to help organize boxes and furniture and, afterwards, to eat pizza on paper plates.

And, Lina thought, casting him a glance over a slice of pepperoni, she was ridiculously happy he had.

A piece of pizza waving in front of her face grabbed her attention. "I've never seen you eat so much," Bryn said. "You want more?"

Mouth currently full, Lina swiped at her friend and forced a swallow past her own chuckle. She followed it with a sip of soda. "I don't know what's wrong with me, but I'm starved."

"It's the magick," Hayden said, tossing a caramel-hued strand out of her face. "I ate like a horse for the first week. I was always able to see and talk to spirits, but the kind of power I discovered with the coven just burned through every calorie I put in."

Beside Lina, Cade coughed to clear his throat. "Did you just say that you can see and talk to spirits?" He stared at Hayden. "You mean ghosts?"

"Aw, this really takes me back." Kylie sat on a counter wearing a sappy grin. "It's been a long time since we've seen that look on a man's face. The kind all of these guys wore when they first learned all the coven's secrets."

"Not me," Quinn said, bumping her with his shoulder. "I grew up with a sister who was always a real *witch*." The emphasis implying a rhyming word.

"Ha ha," Anna said. "Like I haven't heard that one before."

Lina turned and studied Cade, his forehead wrinkled as he took it all in. She leaned closer to him. "You still sure about sticking around? I can't promise there won't be more surprises. In fact, I can almost guarantee there will be. For me, too."

A half-cocked smile forming, Cade lowered his head so their faces were close. "I'm sticking."

Just when she thought he was about to kiss her, he sat back and winked at her before taking a bite of sausage and mushroom. He seemed remarkably at ease, and Lina couldn't help wondering how the other men here had adapted to dating a witch. Had they questioned? Balked? Or simply accepted?

She had no time to consider asking, because a knock on the front door had them all turning to look. Anna poked her head around the doorjamb and toward the front of the house. "It's Arik," she said before calling out, "Come in!"

Soon Arik appeared, droplets shining on his clothes and tawny hair. "Hey," he said, expression tense as he flexed his fingers into half-fists. Relaxed. Flexed. Relaxed. Flexed.

"Everything okay?" Rae asked.

"Yeah. Sure." As if noticing his own telltale behavior, he rubbed his palms together. "Just found some information."

"Pizza?" Lucia offered, sweeping her arm to indicate the several boxes scattered around the room.

"No, I'm fine," Arik answered automatically, but then he recanted, his stare boring a hole into a box. "Actually, I don't think I've eaten since this morning."

"You haven't," Rae said, handing him a paper plate. "And since I have a feeling we're about to get back to business, you should fuel up."

"Yeah. Thanks." He piled two slices onto the plate and devoured them without speaking, chasing down bites with a beer passed to him by Quinn.

After wiping his hands, Arik balled up his napkin on the plate and dropped them both in the open trash bag on the floor. Then he faced the group. "So Mom and I did discover some things, and there's a lot to discuss. I don't mean to seem rude but—"

"But you need to get it done." Ian, Anna's tall blond Viking of a husband, nodded slowly. "Don't worry. If anyone understands, it's the people in this room."

Arik inclined his head in acknowledgement. "I didn't want to drag my mother out in the wet, so if we could relocate?" He gestured to the others. "You're all welcome to join us, of course."

"Yes, come over," Rae said to Anna. "We could use your input."

"And Ethan." Arik locked gazes with the other man. "If you don't mind, your perspective might come in handy."

This announcement made the coven men and women exchange glances. Rae crossed her arms, and Bryn stared down at the floor.

For a moment, no one spoke, the only sound from pellets of rain growing louder outside.

"What?" Lina asked, the nape of her neck prickling. "Why did you all react to that?"

Bryn shot a look to Lina. "Ethan is a demonologist."

Lina stiffened, but she caught herself and forced her shoulders to relax. She was going to have to get used to this. Her world now held the kind of monsters she'd only ever seen in horror movies, and she couldn't play the role of the screaming, running damsel in distress.

Like it or not, she'd been cast as a heroine.

"Then let's go." She stood and moved to toss her garbage in the bag. "Knowledge is power," she said, turning back around, "and we need all we can get."

Bryn jerked her head back and studied Lina as if she didn't recognize her. But then a smile broke over her face and she hopped to her feet. "Alright, let's do it."

"I have to go by the clinic and check on the animals," Michael said, cleaning up his and Shauni's plates. "I have post-op patients, so I've got to pass."

"So do we." Trevor towered behind Hayden, staring at his cell.

Cole, Trevor's partner in the homicide department, studied his phone as well. "We just got a case." He frowned before kissing Claudia's cheek. "Check in later?"

"Will do." Claudia said. "Be safe."

With that, the group began moving and gathering trash to leave for Arik's house, except for the three men who had their own duties to fulfill.

In small clusters they filed outside before dashing across the street, doing their best to keep to the cover of trees. Lightning streaked in the sky, illuminating the door as Arik pushed inside.

Lina, Cade, and Shauni were near the back of the group and encountered Mahalia coming from the direction of the ladies' parlor. She wore another scarf and broom-skirt ensemble, this time in all white. Little Poppy danced at her heels, whining in the way excited pups do.

"Looks like everyone's here." She chuckled and gave Shauni a one-armed hug. "Y'all bringing all the cats, too?"

"Not tonight," Shauni said, grinning. "They've done their part, so now they lead lives of sunshine, treats, and long, lazy naps."

"Speaking of cats," Lina said to Mahalia, "have you seen Remi?"

"Well fed and napping in your room." She patted Lina's shoulder.

"Not anymore." Cade notched his chin, and Lina followed his gaze to see her cat trotting toward them.

"Must have heard your voice," Mahalia said. "Well, might as

well let these two come with us." She clicked her tongue to the little golden dog who answered with a yip.

Mahalia led the three of them into the maze of corridors, both animals trailing along behind. Remi kept close to Lina, his orange tail standing straight as a flagpole.

Once inside the library, the coven witches and their men spread out, leaving the seating area near Arik's desk open for the Maidens. "We're hear to listen," Anna told Rae, "to help if we can. But this is your show."

Rae gave her a look of appreciation and moved to stand with Arik near the desk. Marit was already there, parked in her chair between the globe and a side table stacked with books.

The journals, Lina realized, marveling at the apparent age of some of the books. What had those ancient pages revealed to Marit and her son? And why had whatever they'd found put Arik so on edge?

Taking a seat on the sofa, Lina scooted in to make room for Cade. He hesitated until Bryn said, "Go ahead. You're here for Lina, so you should be informed."

Dropping to a seat, Bryn leaned back casually. "And if you decide it's too much for you, we'll just put a binding spell on you before you go. To make sure you don't talk."

"Bryn," Lina scolded, "that's not funny."

But Cade gave a good natured nod. "I'd expect nothing less."

Cassidy sat on the sofa as well, taking the open space on Lina's other side.

Peyton filled the remaining chair. "Good to see he can take a joke," she said, hiking an auburn brow at Cade. "I have a feeling we're all going to need a sense of humor in the comings days."

"Among other things," Lina said and sighed. Bryn had plenty of humor. And bravery. Peyton seemed to have an open mind and magic in her veins, while Cassidy filed away knowledge like a computer.

So what did Lina have to offer? Organization skills? Bookkeeping? Making a perfect cappuccino foam?

She clamped her jaws when self-doubt tried to creep in, sliding her hand over to grip Cade's fingers.

She was here. She cared. For now, that was enough.

"I guess that's everybody." Arik spoke to the gathering, crossing his arms and leaning back against his desk. "You all know about the vision Anna had earlier today. Lina also gave us a description of her attacker's weapon. Both of these things were useful in our search."

He met his mother's eyes before reaching behind him to pick up a brown leather journal. "Unfortunately, the clues they gave us led in two different directions." His dark blond brows creased. "Toward two very different enemies."

"We'll start with Searenn." Rae inclined her head to Anna. "The coven is already familiar with who she was, but not with who, or rather *what* she is now."

"You said she was a Droehk." Cassidy crossed her legs and leaned back into the corner of the sofa. "What does that mean, and what paper were you talking about?"

Arik cleared his throat, and Rae indicated he should take over. "The Droehks were a clan dating back to the early days of civilization," he explained. "They possessed the ability to summon and control demons. Some say this is because Droehks were the result of demons mating with humans."

"Ew." Bryn wrinkled her nose. "Spare me that imagery."

"They were vilified and hunted down," Arik continued. "Supposedly, they were wiped from existence. But we know that's not true. Some of them survived and went into hiding, concealing their bodies and the tattoos that marked them as Droehks."

"Tattoos?" Lina asked.

"They had a special language . . . words and incantations used to harness the demons. They were chased from their homes, all of their possessions destroyed."

"So they inked their skin, so the language would never be forgotten or lost." Cassidy nodded in thought. "But they also had to keep it secret or be killed like the others."

"Exactly," Arik said. "Searenn was one of the coven's enemies and was killed during the final battle with the Amara. According to the journals," he looked down at the book he held, "there are creatures capable of performing resurrection, but they can only do so with a Droehk."

Marit spoke up as she rolled her chair forward. "We mentioned them before, the DoSaa preSyajana. They are the most powerful of the banished demons, living in exile in the Onderdâark. Only they had the power to send Searenn back."

Arik took a deep breath. "My father's writings mention a Droehk reborn, one that returns to life with the help of the DoSaa. One who is granted incredible powers. She's here to help them, to serve them from this side of the gate.

"They're ready to come back to our world," he said, "and Searenn's rebirth is their first big move. She'll have knowledge of the aethyrical language that created both the gate and the seal the first time around. And like us, she'll be searching for the aethyrical texts."

"Why?" Peyton toyed with the tip of her fiery braid. "If the first Watchtower Maidens were needed to lock the gate, what does she hope to do? Even if she gets all four pieces of the seal, how can she use them?"

Arik stared down at the journal. "We haven't found that answer yet. We don't know exactly how she'll do it, but she must have a plan to open the gate."

"And let all those banished demons back in." Bryn's expression looked grim at the prospect.

"So your goal is to find the texts and make sure that doesn't happen." Ethan stood near a wooden column beneath the upper walkway. With his hair and gaze both dark as night, Lina thought he looked like a man capable of dealing with demons.

"I've studied demonology most of my life," Ethan said, "and I've never heard a single mention of the Huktai or the Maidens. However, I have heard tales of an ancient portal to another realm." He frowned. "And the stories weren't good."

"Go on," Arik said, listening. They all were, every person in the room paying rapt attention to the man who specialized in vanquishing monsters.

"Those living in this other place, in the Onderdâark—they aren't like the ones who remained in this world, or at least, none that I've dealt with. From what I've been told, this other realm has a hierarchy, levels of demons, all with different shapes and talents." He paused. "And each with their own preferred methods to torment humans."

"Lovely," Cassidy murmured.

Ethan shrugged. "That's really all I know. Only a few dared to tell me anything. Most who know of the Onderdâark and its inhabitants are terrified to speak of it."

"This hierarchy," Arik said, "it fits with some of what we've deciphered. It goes without saying that we have to keep entry to our world closed off." He gestured to his mother. "But if what's in these journals is true, Searenn will be able to summon even more demons than she could before, beasts the world hasn't seen since the first battle and the first gate."

"But we can kill them?" Bryn asked, brown gaze darkened by dread. "Is that why we have the magick we do?"

"That," Rae said, homing in on her niece, "and to create another seal if necessary. If Searenn manages to succeed, we'll not only have a war on our hands, but we'll have to lock the gate again."

"Or the world as we know it will be gone." Arik's somber tone filtered through the library, leaving a heavy silence in its wake.

After a moment passed, he spoke again. "There's more. I'd

seen drawings of various weapons in my father's journals, so after hearing Lina's description of the curved blade and the black haze it produced," he exhaled, his lips thinning into a line, "I had an idea where to look.

"We believe there are others who work in support of the DoSaa preSyajana. My parents and Mahalia's mother were attacked years ago."

Marit glanced at her son. "I can only remember bits and pieces." Her jaw tensed, and she shook her head. She'd lost her husband that night and had been cursed, leaving her unable to speak or move for a decade. "But I have snapshots in my head. People standing over me. I sensed magick, but I'm certain they were human."

Arik watched his mother, concern for what she'd endured evident in the tense lines around his mouth. Then he addressed the gathering again. "According to Sylvie, a friend of the coven and ex-Amara member, Searenn was with their group in Colorado when the attack happened. She'd never been to Savannah, not until the Amara brought her here."

He placed the book he held back on the desk. "The men from last night were human, but they are still very much a threat. They're members of an ancient order known as the Scyths."

Lina and Cassidy looked at each other. "What do they want?" Lina asked. "Are they searching for the aethyrical texts, too?"

"Yes, but only to keep them from us or anyone else who might use them, like Searenn. They're warriors," he said, "descendants of the rogue group of Huktai who broke away and killed the first Maidens."

Cassidy sucked in a breath. "They still exist?"

"Yes." Rae jumped back in. "And they still think they need to murder us to save humanity."

"Screw that." Bryn crossed her well-toned arms, and had never looked more like the fighter she was.

Beside Lina, Cade tensed and made a sound of anger.

Lightning strobed through the windows, and thunder rolled soon after, sheets of rain still pouring down.

"They see us as being too powerful." Rae stepped forward, standing tall and unafraid, setting the example for the rest of them. As any good leader should. "The original thinking is that killing us will prevent the gate from ever being opened, since we're some of the only ones who can reverse the spell."

"That's crazy," Lina protested. "Why would we ever do that?" Remi leaped to her lap as if sensing her distress and butted his orange head against her arm.

"Corruption is always possible, even in the most moral of people. The Scyths don't want to take that risk and, to that end, have a singular goal—destroy anyone who can control Draconi magick."

"So they're no friends of Searenn's either," Cassidy said, tucking her raven hair behind one ear. "She came back with knowledge of the aethyrical language, and who knows what kind of power."

Cassidy stood then, tracking her gaze to each of the other Maidens before finally landing on Rae. "I agree with Lina, that knowledge is power. So where do we start?"

"Arik and Marit will continue to decrypt the journals," Rae said, "but in the meantime, I do have one idea." Her stare moved to take in the coven women who'd listened in silence. "Lucia can't tell us where the texts are, and we already tried letting Claudia look into the globe's past. It seems the aethyrical artifacts have their own protective magick."

Claudia nodded. "The globe gave me quite the psychic slap."

"What if we had something else?" Rae held out her hands toward Claudia. "Something that isn't enchanted but might tell a story and give us a clue? I know it's asking a lot for you to be involved."

"I'll help however I can," Claudia replied. "Like Anna said, it's no coincidence that we're all connected. What did you have in mind?"

Lightning cracked through the black skies again, instant thunder vibrating the house. The storm was right on top of them.

"There was something else at Bonaventure Cemetery, something linked to the medallion." Rae turned her face upward, as if she could see the rain through the ceiling. "We won't go tonight."

She returned her gaze to the red-haired witch who'd agreed to help. "But tomorrow. After the sun sets."

Claudia took two steps closer, her expression intense.

"We'll bring up the skeleton," Rae said. "The one we found beneath the crypt."

18

"Wait for me." Searenn held eye contact with the driver in the rearview mirror before opening the door of the town car herself. At the airport, she'd come across the driver waiting for a client and decided she'd commandeer the comfy ride.

As she grabbed the door handle, she paused, studying her fingers. She'd sensed subtle changes in herself since her return, and now her fingernails had grown long, thick, and black as pitch. She tested the sharp tip of one. Diamond hard.

Deeming the supernatural manicure an improvement, she opened the door, exiting into the still of night. The door closed with a soft thud behind her, and she stared up past a tall metal gate.

From the star-speckled sky, a full moon stared back.

Nocturnal sounds carried softly on the air, arising from the expansive lawn, gardens, and forest surrounding the estate.

Nighttime in France felt the same as home, maybe a bit crisper and cooler. The massive chateau, however, was like nothing she'd ever seen.

With a flick of her hand and contempt for the wealthy, she sprung the gates wide, gliding up the drive with whispering steps.

White flowers glowed against the night-dark grass, surrounding a fountain that looked centuries old. One side of the home overlooked a hill, where terraced gardens lined a slope that spread down to the woods.

Such extravagance, she thought with a scowl. The whole place reeked of affluence, of old money.

And old magick.

The woman who lived here might test Searenn's skills, but in actuality, she'd be the perfect first subject. Who better to practice on than a descendant of a Maiden? A Maiden and Huktai, to be exact.

According to the records, the woman had inherited some skill of her own, but more importantly, she'd inherited a piece of the ancient seal. An aethyrical text.

She made a move forward but stopped, her head jerking to the side. Angry growls came from the far end of the chateau. The sounds grew closer.

Two Doberman Pinschers burst from around the corner and charged across the lawn, teeth bared and black eyes focused. Defenders of the home, they locked on Searenn and raced toward their prey.

Until she lifted a hand.

Instantly the dogs slowed their charge, shaking their heads and whining in confusion.

Good. She'd wondered about animals, and now she knew. Though they'd given more psychic pushback than any human so far.

With the hounds dealt with, she followed stone steps up to double doors, again opening them wide with little more than a thought. If possible, the mansion's interior was even more ostentatious, more extravagant.

She entered onto a raised wooden dais, three steps down to the main level. Two suits of armor stood at the bottom, one on each side with ridiculous red feathers sprouting from their helmets.

Moonlight slanted through high windows and across the parquet floor, lighting her way as she strolled toward the stairs. The place smelled like flowers. A grandfather clock chimed, somewhere she could not see. Once, twice, three times. The witching hour.

Searenn sneered in the shadows. *We'll just see about that.*

Hand on the banister, she began her way upstairs. Though her footfalls were muffled by carpeted steps, the lady of the house waited for her on the landing. She'd sensed Searenn's arrival.

"Colette, your magick is stronger than I'd expected." Searenn raised her brows, acknowledging the other woman's power.

Then she stepped closer, into the glow of a hallway lamp.

Colette's eyes widened as she studied Searenn's exposed skin. Her face paled. "Droehk," she said, the word heavily accented and filled with disgust.

"Yes. I am." Searenn scoffed. "But not just any of my kind."

Colette nodded in the dim corridor. "You have been reborn."

"Points to you, madame. Strong magick *and* well-informed. Your ancestors must have passed down more than power and artifacts." Searenn cocked her head. "Is it true your great-great-great . . ." she waved a dismissive hand, "whatever great-grandmother. Was she tortured and killed during the witch trials here in France?"

The woman didn't answer.

"The point is," Searenn said, creeping ever closer, "if she couldn't beat a few determined humans, how do you ever expect to stand up to me?"

Colette shook her head. "So you've stared into that relentless darkness." She sighed. "But you are a fool. The darkness does not reason. It does not bargain. It only feeds."

She took a bold step forward. "And now it will consume you."

"Save your fancy words." Searenn smirked, but then her features turned hard. "You know why I've come. Give it to me now and save your life."

Colette stood taller but did not speak.

"Fine." Searenn shrugged as if she didn't care, but she'd

secretly hoped for the woman's resistance. She'd hoped for a fight. For some bloodshed. "Agony it is."

She thrust her arm forward, curling her fingers as if grabbing hold of a handle. And when she pulled, Colette slid across the expensive carpet.

But the witch would not go down so easily. Sending out a pulse of magick, she did not try to break Searenn's grasp but focused pressure on her eyes instead.

The very liquid in Searenn's eyes seemed to boil, and she shut her lids. But instead of releasing Colette, she clenched her hand into a fist.

A gurgling cry of pain erupted from the witch's mouth, and the burning sensation abated. Searenn cast a cruel stare to her foe before stabbing her own palm with one finger.

Colette tried to cover her stomach, but she could do nothing to stop the piercing pain in her gut.

"*Mon dieu!*" A man rushed from an open door, his hair mussed and wearing only pajama pants. "Colette!" He rushed to the witch's side, trying to support her as she crumbled.

"Husband to the rescue?" Searenn asked in an unimpressed drawl. "Good. Let's get this done." She let Colette drop to the floor and turned her attention to the man instead. Using both hands, she curled her fingers again, crushing his throat and his balls.

Eyes bulging, he fell over instantly, shuddering and moaning as if in seizure.

"*Non!*" Colette dragged in a ragged breath and tried to fight Searenn off.

But Searenn had tasted the witch's magic, and now she knew its flavor. The pulse bounced off of her own mystical shield.

"I can't believe part of the seal was entrusted to you." Searenn strode to the woman and stared down in contempt, giving an extra twist of her hands to draw a scream from the husband. "You are worthless against me." She drew her hands closed, palm to palm, and ground them together.

On the floor, the man writhed.

A sudden impact on the back of Searenn's head made her whirl around.

With fury riding her, she released the man and homed in on a young girl. Maybe fourteen or fifteen, blonde hair hanging past her shoulders, and stare burning with both fear and rage. She babbled so quickly in French, Searenn couldn't make it out.

"What do we have now? A little witchling?" Searenn crooked a finger to summon the girl.

Instead of submitting, the teenager flew at her with both arms raised, ready to defend her parents.

Searenn blinked, and the girl slammed into an invisible wall. There Searenn held her, lifting her off the floor until her pink-painted toes hovered and wriggled a foot above the carpet.

"Enough playtime." Searenn jerked her head, looking over her shoulder to Colette. "Give me the text."

Colette gulped and looked to her daughter through tears. Yet she shook her head. "Non."

Raising her hand, Searenn wiggled her fingers and the razor-sharp nails. With cruel precision, she used one to draw a line through the air.

A jagged cut opened on the daughter's neck. The girl struggled and cried out as blood oozed onto her lily-white gown.

"Non, non. Please." The husband rolled to his knees, holding out his hand to Searenn. "Please."

"Your wife can stop this. I only want the text."

The man spoke quickly to his wife, pleading in French, telling her they must save their only child.

"You know I can't!" Colette screamed at him, a sob following her refusal.

Searenn created another slice on the daughter, this time a long diagonal mark across her abdomen. The girl buckled, bending at the waist. Still floating in the air, she gagged and wheezed.

"I will tell you!" the husband shouted and gained his feet. "I will tell you."

"Martel, non!" Corinne grabbed his leg. "She will kill us all, even if you tell her. But if she gets the text, the *whole world* will die."

"Please, you can have it." Ignoring his wife's warning, the husband babbled out a name and an address. "I swear that's all I know. We were not to be told the specific hiding place, in case . . ." His words fell to silence.

Searenn laughed, the sound low and sinister. "In case I showed up one day."

Though she'd gained information, she focused once more on the witch. "Colette, I want you to die knowing that you've lost. But first . . ."

Searenn looked back at the daughter and slammed her to the floor. "We will have no more of your poisoned line. No more breeding of bothersome little witches."

"Wait!" The husband tried to stand, tried to reach Searenn in time.

Beside him Colette lifted her hands to attack.

But Searenn was faster. She was *stronger*.

She cut off the feeble attempt with a flick of her hand. Then she returned her attention to the girl.

Both Colette and her husband screamed and begged, the man crawling across the floor toward his daughter.

Shaping her hand into a claw, Searenn made a raking motion.

From throat to stomach, the girl's gown exploded red. She gurgled in pain, blood spilling from the corner of her mouth.

Her parents fell into fits of hysteria, ignoring Searenn as they scrambled over to their dying child.

For minutes, Searenn watched, absorbing their misery and

despair. And once she grew bored, the snap of their necks echoed dully in the hall.

With a pivot, Searenn sauntered toward the stairs, ready to enjoy a meal and a man. Though she'd come for the text, her search continued. At least she had a name, and a trail to be followed.

She had her hand on the banister when the scent of flowers hit her again, the smell of human indulgence stoking her hate anew. Turning back, she studied the carnage.

Three corpses on a fancy rug.

Staring hard, she lit their bodies on fire. Then she followed the steps down, went out the front door, and across the lovely lawn.

As behind her, it all burned.

19

By the next evening, the rain had stopped, and while this wasn't Lina's first visit to Bonaventure Cemetery, it was certainly the first time she'd come at night.

The wind shivered tendrils of Spanish moss, making them shiver and sway beneath the moonlight.

"Moderately creepy," Cassidy said, echoing Lina's unease over visiting a graveyard in the dark.

With the sole purpose of finding a skeleton.

Other than the heavy gates at the entrance, the fences weren't made to keep people out. Bryn found a section low enough to climb over, dropping to the grass on the other side with Lina and the other women following. Arik and Cade vaulted over last.

Once inside, Lina caught Bryn's eye. "I know we have a history of finding trouble together, but we've never snuck into a graveyard."

"I have," Peyton said, giving a quick shrug when they turned to look at her. "What? Savannah's got some of the best graveyards in the country, and I went through a Goth stage in high school."

"I want to hear more about that." Cassidy tied back her hair, the black shining with moonlit strands. "Got any pictures?"

"You wish." Peyton dropped her head back and chuckled. "Those met a fiery end a long time ago." She glanced down at her feet. "I still like biker boots, though."

"They look good," Claudia said. She surveyed the soggy grounds. "And a good choice after all the rain."

The flame-haired woman was the only one of the coven witches to join them on their mission. While it had been agreed upon that all of the Maidens should take part, keeping the group as small as possible was important. They preferred their presence to go unnoticed.

Arik put a hand on his sword, nestled in a scabbard and strapped to his waist. The reminder that he might actually need it made Lina's throat tighten.

She studied her palms, remembering that she too carried a weapon. Would she need her magick tonight? At the thought, her throat seemed to clamp down even tighter.

"This place is big enough to get lost in," she whispered to Cade, searching every shadow for danger. What might be hiding in the dark? Behind the trees, shrubs, and statues?

She didn't feel ready to face demons. She still needed practice. And they had no idea what they might find in the tombs below.

Or what might find them.

She just hoped she'd be ready, hoped she'd be brave enough if the time came to call on her power.

Rae noticed Lina's intent gaze on her open hands. "We'll be fine. We were born for this." She looped an arm around Lina's shoulder. "And most importantly, we've got each other."

"You're right." Trying to believe, trying to have faith, Lina nodded. "We've got each other."

Rae gave her an encouraging squeeze and stepped away to speak with Arik.

That was when Cade put his hand on Lina's back to whisper, "And you've also got me."

Lina grasped his hand. In the silvery moonlight, his gray eyes seemed to shine from within. "You don't have to do this," she told him. "I would understand."

"I thought we'd already had this conversation," he said,

placing a soft kiss on her lips. "I'm not leaving you."

A breath of relief flitted through her lips, releasing tension in her chest she hadn't been aware of before.

"Okay." She clasped his fingers and then let go. "I can do this."

"I have no doubt."

Together, the eight of them wound their way through a forest of headstones and monuments. Eventually, they found the perimeter road and followed the wide dirt path toward the back.

Between the tall, thick oaks, the curving river glistened beneath cloudless skies. "This way," Arik said, leading them off the road to a crypt of white marble.

As she drew closer, Lina stuttered to a halt. "Do you see that?"

Cade sucked in a breath but shook his head. "See what?"

"It's an enchantment," Rae explained. "The magick is seeping out from beneath the doors."

Blue light shone from the crack at the bottom.

"But last time, Arik and I only saw it when we were holding hands."

"You've opened the globe since then," Arik told her. "Your magick has been released, and it must have changed something. Something in me." He kneeled and cautiously slid his hand into the light. "Because I definitely see it."

"Maidens and Huktai," Peyton murmured, rubbing her face before heaving a sigh.

"You okay?" Lina asked her. "You've had to take in a lot in the last two days."

"I'm good. Just thinking about my kids."

At this, everyone stopped and stared at her. "You have children?" Rae asked.

"Yeah." Now Peyton's stiffness drained and her expression morphed to one of tenderness. "Eighteen to be exact, and they need me to show up in the morning."

Lina cocked her head when comprehension struck. "You're a teacher."

Peyton nodded. "Second grade. The more I come to accept the reality of what we're facing, the more I worry about them." She glowered and shook her head. "They don't deserve a world of evil, and I'll do whatever it takes to keep this Droehk demon-spawn from getting anywhere near them."

"So will I." Cassidy stuck her hands on her hips.

"I take it you're all ready for this then?" Arik studied the five Maidens. Each gave a nod or replied in the affirmative, with Bryn sounding out a "Hell, yeah."

Sharing a look, Arik and Cade pushed the crypt doors open and stepped inside.

A sarcophagus sat in the middle of the space, and Arik spoke to Cade across the stone effigy. "This is where we leave you and Claudia."

"What do you mean?" Cade tensed and shot a look to Lina.

She could tell he didn't want her out of his sight, and the protective gesture warmed her inside.

"Only Maidens and Huktai can go below," Arik said.

Cade wrinkled his forehead and scanned the floor of the crypt. "Below where?"

Arik pointed. "See the back wall?"

"Yeah."

"Instead of stone, we see a barrier of rippling light."

"And you went through last time?"

"Yes." Arik lifted his hands. "I don't know what would happen if you or Claudia tried to step through. You might just bounce off." Again, he studied the blue barrier. "But I can't make any guarantees, so you shouldn't risk it."

"We'll be in and out as quick as we can, and we'll bring the skeleton back up here." Rae lifted a large Army-green duffel bag.

Shifting on his feet, Cade crossed his arms. "Fine, but if it sounds like you're in trouble, I can't promise I won't try."

"Understood." Arik gave the other man a half-grin. "And I can't promise you won't just bash your head against rock."

Cade still looked unhappy about being left behind, so Lina eased to his side and kissed his cheek. "We'll be quick," she assured him. Then she eyed the illuminated wall, waves of energy coursing from top to bottom. "And honestly, I'd just as soon get this over with."

Cassidy shook her hands as if to cast off nervousness. "I can't believe I'm about to help bring a skeleton out of magick caverns beneath a cemetery. What sci-fi adventure am I living in?"

Peyton lifted a shoulder. "Just pretend you're Lara Croft. That's what I'm trying to do."

"Well, if Lara's taken, I'll just have to be Indiana Jones." Cassidy shrugged, winked, and then the two of them exchanged a fist-bump.

Noticing Bryn's smirk, Cassidy said, "Hey. Don't judge."

"Who's judging?" Bryn delivered a soft stamp kick to Cassidy's calf. "I'm channeling Bruce Lee."

Lina just shook her head as Rae rolled her eyes to the crypt ceiling.

"Okay," Rae said, "if everyone has chosen their alter ego, then let's go." She stepped into the light to show it was safe, and then one by one the others filed through—Bryn, Cassidy, Peyton.

Lina motioned for Arik to go ahead, and she went last, looking over her shoulder to meet Cade's gaze one more time.

As she passed through the sparkling light, a cold sensation swept through her core. She shivered not only from the touch of chill . . . but from not knowing what waited on the other side.

Once through, she paused to adjust to true darkness. After a moment, her vision cleared, and she scanned the cavern. The open space went on and on, endless darkness in every direction, and a bottomless chasm straight ahead.

"Do we have to cross that?" Bryn asked, her gaze locked on the abyss.

"No, the skeleton is this way." Rae turned on a flashlight, like a shot of sun into the heart of night. She jerked her head to indicate a narrow ledge. "Just keep to the wall."

"You don't have to tell me twice," Lina murmured, pressing against jagged rock the color of soot. The path—if it could be called that—curved back and forth, like a switchback road created for a mountain.

With Arik taking point, they took the thin pathway down into the gorge. Soon they came to a bridge that crossed the chasm, made of the same black stone found in the walls and barely visible in the dim light.

"Who could have built this?" Cassidy stepped onto the structure and ran her hand along the heavy, curved railing. She peeked over into the bottomless pit. And swayed.

"Whoa." Lina jumped toward her, grabbing Cassidy's arm to steady her. Without thinking, she looked over the edge, too.

She shut her eyes before the vast emptiness could make her dizzy as well. "There's no bottom." Lids still shut, she backed away from the side of the bridge. "There's nothing."

Her voice echoed in the blackness. And something answered.

A muffled whistle, then a skitter-and-scrape, like clawed feet raking across the rocks.

"We should keep going." Still on the ledge, Arik spoke softly but sternly, concern etched on his face. "We still don't know what might be down here, so let's get the bones and go."

Lina only nodded, afraid to further disturb whatever terrors lived in a place like this. Quietly, she and Cassidy stepped back onto the path and walked as stealthily as possible.

Finally, Arik and Rae stopped and kneeled down, their flashlights illuminating a human skeleton. Without speaking, Rae unfolded the duffel, and she and Arik began to transfer the bones from the ground to the bag.

Bryn dropped to a squat and started to help. With no more room around the skeleton, Lina, Cassidy, and Peyton remained standing, their backs to the three on the ground and watchful stares facing the darkness.

The hollow clinks of bone hitting bone rose from the ground, and an odor surged over Lina. She wrinkled her nose. "Is that him?" she whispered. "That smell?"

Arik froze with his hands inside the duffel. "What smell?" Then he stood abruptly.

Lina could see the moment he caught the scent. "Hurry," he told Rae and Bryn, hand on his sword.

"Do we need them all?" Bryn asked, moving at a faster pace.

Rae didn't look up from her task. "He deserves a proper burial."

Lina heard what sounded like a baseball bat swinging through the air—one short, loud *whoosh*! And what had been a slight stink grew to a foul stench.

"Guys," she said. "I think something's here."

"Done." Rae jumped to her feet, zipping the bag and looping the handles over one shoulder. "Let's go."

"You lead." Arik shone his flashlight down the ledge and then out into the gorge. "I'll take up the rear."

Rae started up with Cassidy and Peyton right behind her. Lina went next, then Bryn and Arik. Panning the light around behind them, Arik walked backwards.

The horrible smell seemed to be following them.

"It's close," Bryn said.

"I know, but I can't see anything." Arik's voice was a frustrated rasp.

The skitter sound came again, only this time, it was closer. Lina stopped walking. Slowly, she looked up. "Arik, shine the light—"

A shriek rang from overhead.

"Shit." Staring upward, Bryn stumbled into Lina. "Do you see anything?"

"No."

The beam from Arik's light bounced around the ink-black stone above.

Another mind-numbing shriek bounced off the subterranean walls, then a loud scratching noise, and *whoosh—whoosh*. Tiny pebbles hit Lina's shoulder.

"It's flying," she said. "It's coming."

Arik thrust a hand at them. "Go!"

"Stay close." Bryn's breath hitched as she jerked her head around, scanning the huge, dark space while rushing up the incline.

The awful cry came again, louder this time.

Closer.

Two giant wings and open jaws swooped down into the beam of Arik's light.

All three of them threw themselves to the ground.

The flashlight bobbled across the ground. Lina grabbed the handle before it went over and left them in darkness.

'Help!" Bryn screamed. "I can't hang on!"

Lina flashed the light around in a panic. Bryn hung from the ledge, dangling over an endless drop into nothing.

Arik flung his body toward her and latched onto her arms. "I've got you. I've got you."

"Bryn!" Rae called out from somewhere on the trail above, terror stretching her voice to a wire.

Lina couldn't answer, any sound she might have made drowned out by the angry, shrill cries of the flying monster. The thing was coming back, making another pass.

Arik still struggled to pull Bryn up. Rae and the others were too far ahead.

With a steadying breath, Lina shoved the light into her pocket.

Then she raised her palms.

Emotion. She had to channel her emotions.

And right now, she was filled with terror.

She released that sharp, cold fear, letting it run down her arms in tidal waves. Instantly, her palms began to glow, illuminating the cavern like a green bonfire.

Arik had Bryn halfway onto the ledge.

And the creature had them in its sights. It made another dive, heading straight for Bryn's dangling body.

I can do this. Lina's cold fear turned to burning fury as she targeted the beast zooming toward her friend. *This power is mine.*

She released a shout along with her magick, both striking out into the blackness. Energy coursed from her hands, sparkling lines, as if emeralds had been crushed and flowed on streams of light.

The flow of power struck the beast in the chest, knocking it off-course. It bellowed and spiraled down into the gorge.

Arik had Bryn now, and they both scrambled away from the side of the gorge.

"You did it!" Bryn gasped for breath, still on her knees but safely back on the ledge. "Lina, you did it." She gained her feet and rushed to hug Lina.

Stunned by how quickly everything had happened, Lina leaned into the embrace and exhaled. "I did it."

"I haven't fired off my magick like that yet." Bryn's smile was huge. "It was awesome. I mean, you lit this place *up.*"

"I completely agree," Arik said, "but I still want to get the hell out of here." He gave them both a gentle shove while tossing a glance over his shoulder. "For all we know, those things are like bats and a hundred more are waking up."

Bryn grimaced. "Good point."

With caution and haste, they made their way up the thin path, not slowing until they met Rae, Peyton, and Cassidy on their way back down.

"What was that thing?" Peyton asked. "We could all see it in Lina's glow." She hugged Lina while Cassidy stood holding the duffel.

Rae grabbed Bryn and pulled her in. "I saw you hanging there." Over her niece's shoulder, she reached out to touch Arik's cheek. "I saw both of you. If Lina hadn't—"

"We're fine," Arik said. "We're okay."

"That was intense," Lina whispered, wrapping her arms around herself. "I'm getting the shakes. My adrenaline must be fading."

"Let's all get back to the safety of the crypt." Cassidy made a face. "Never thought I'd say that."

She and Peyton stepped aside, allowing Lina and Bryn to step through the light first.

Inside the crypt, Claudia and Cade waited with expressions of concern, only relaxing once everyone was back safely.

Claudia released a breath. "You got it." She eyed the duffel and then motioned to the crypt doors that still stood open. "Let's take it outside. The ground will be better, so I don't get mixed signals from the things in here."

Cassidy carried the bag out, setting it on the grassy spot Claudia indicated.

The coven witch kneeled before the bag and spread it open. Watching in silence, the others gathered around.

She gently searched through the contents of the duffel, the soft clacking of bone against bone rising in the night air. At last, she pulled out the skull, yellow and spotted with age.

With care, she placed it on the ground. "All right," she said, sitting back on her heels. "Let's see what he can tell us."

Taking a deep breath, she closed her eyes and wrapped her hands around the skull.

20

Cade edged closer to Lina, needing her near to help soothe the ragged edges of worry still poking inside him. Eleven minutes. She'd only been gone eleven minutes. And it had taken every bit of his self-control to not burst through that damned magick door and go after her.

But if he had, what would have happened? Would he still be standing here beside her?

She's back, and she's safe. That's all that matters. He'd just deal with each potential pitfall as they came.

As Claudia sat quietly with the skull, he marveled at how quickly he'd gone from the regimented and normal life he'd always craved to a world on the edge of bedlam.

And he would make that trade again in a heartbeat.

He cast a sidelong glance to Lina, and something in his chest clutched. She'd reached him on a deeper level than any other woman ever had. Anyone at all, if he were honest. It was as if she looked into him, saw the heart of who he really was—and that was enough.

That kind of acceptance, that level of connection, it was something he'd never known before. He believed it was the same for her. And he would do anything to protect what they'd found in each other.

Claudia gasped, jerking Cade back to the here and now. She removed her hands from the skull and looked up at Rae. "I saw his final day," she said. "And I saw how he died."

A tiny snap carried on the night air, easy to detect in the silent resting place of the dead. Cade's instincts went on high alert, and he scanned the cemetery, his eyes already adjusted to the low light.

There. Behind a tree. Movement.

Without pausing to explain, Cade shot off into the dark, his gaze laser-focused on the spot he'd seen the motion. It had been nothing but a slide of silhouette over shadow, but he knew it was a man.

A man who'd been watching.

He heard Arik's shout behind him but kept running, vaulting over a line of shrubbery to land on a gravel and dirt road. The watcher was running now too, sprinting straight down the road, aware he'd been discovered.

Cade skidded on gravel as he made a hard turn but continued his pursuit. He had the guy in his sights. He was faster.

And he was gaining.

As if sensing Cade closing in, the man stopped abruptly and whipped around, pulling something from his belt as he pivoted.

Cade had no weapon, but he didn't stop. Whoever this was, he posed a threat. And too bad for him. Cade's bastard of a father had destroyed so much, but he'd always been right about one thing.

Cade had been born to fight.

He drew up short just as the man swung out, the curved blade swooshing in an arc a foot in front of Cade's chest. A blade engulfed in a glittery haze the color of onyx.

As soon as the other man missed, Cade moved in, grabbing his forearm. He planned to go for the nerves in his wrist and elbow, forcing him to drop the weapon.

But the man stilled, staring hard at Cade, and every bit of resistance seeped from his muscles.

"Hey," the stranger said, voice shocked and brows slammed together in confusion. "Aren't you—"

"Cade!" Arik shouted from right behind the two men frozen mid-battle.

His voice, combined with the man's odd behavior, distracted Cade. That's when the man elbowed Cade in the ribs, slipping free and sprinting down the road.

Cade went after him, but he leaped over the fence into a stand of trees. By the time he made it there, the man had disappeared into the woods bordering the cemetery.

"Damn it," Cade swore. Who the hell was that guy?

"Where is he?" Arik had his weapon out and, by the look on his face, Cade was glad he wasn't the one Arik was after.

"Forget it. He's gone." Cade stared out into the forest again. "Let's get back."

As they took a path through headstones and monuments, Arik angled his head toward Cade. "Who was that? It sounded like he recognized you."

Cade measured his words. He couldn't be certain, but he had a feeling he knew why the man had recognized him.

"Yeah, I caught that, too. Maybe he's seen my books?" Cade looked straight ahead as he walked. "The paper ran an article a couple of weeks ago, local author kind of thing. Plus, Cassidy made a display a few days ago, so my face was in the window."

Arik nodded but didn't respond.

They rejoined the women outside the crypt to find Claudia standing and all of them with expressions of curiosity and concern.

"Did you catch him?" Bryn asked, untapped energy coming off of her in waves. The guy was lucky he'd gotten away, because Bryn looked ready to tune someone up.

"Yeah," Cade admitted, "but he caught me off guard. Acted like he knew me, and . . ." He cleared his throat. "Sorry I messed up." He looked at Lina. "Especially since he had a weapon like you described."

"With the black haze?" Claudia asked, an unnatural stillness about her posture.

Cade inclined his head. "Yeah."

She gestured to the bag of bones and the skull still sitting on the grass. "I saw him on his last day. He met with a man, a friend. A good friend, I think."

She searched the gazes of the Maidens. "Before he died, he gave an aethyrical text to this man, and I got the sense it was for safekeeping." Claudia motioned with her hand as if recalling her vision. "From what I saw, I'm guessing the date to be early twentieth century."

A blank look stole over her face. "I know the house where they met. I mean, I've seen it before." She shook her head and spoke to Arik. "I can identify it, but it might take me a day."

"Of course," he said. "And whatever you need, just ask."

"There's more." Claudia glanced again to the skull. "We all know he died down there, beneath the earth, but I know who did it. Men," she said, standing straighter. "Three men. They all had weapons like Lina described."

Cade tensed. So did Lina.

Arik nodded, a grim set to his mouth. "So the Scyths have been in Savannah a long time." He met Rae's eyes beneath the moonlight. "And they're watching every move we make."

21

I shouldn't feel this way. Lina all but danced up the steps to Cade's top-floor condo, a feeling of lightning in her veins while she waited for him to open the door. She was still so . . . *charged* after using her magick, she had energy buzzing in every cell.

After the events at the cemetery, Arik and Rae had taken the bones of the Huktai, planning to give him a respectful burial, while Bryn, Cassidy, and Peyton had all gone to their respective homes to do whatever things normal life required of them.

Everyone's houses had been protected with wards and enchantments, which made going their separate ways a lot less worrisome. So when Cade had offered to make dinner at his home, she'd happily accepted.

This would be her first time seeing where he lived, but she already loved the location. Adjacent to City Market, he had quick access to shops and cafes, with only a five-minute walk to River Street. There was no elevator to take them to his top-floor apartment, but what the older building lacked in convenience, it made up for in charm.

Cade swept an arm to invite her in, and she entered a modern-looking hallway that led to an equally stylish living area. Sophisticated yet masculine furnishings paired perfectly with exposed brick walls.

In lieu of telling him how much she liked the space, she simply moved to the center of the room and did a slow turn.

"I won't lie," he said, a half-cocked grin on his handsome face. "I had help with the decorating."

"Well, they did a great job." Emboldened by the night's success, she strolled over to him, stood on her tiptoes, and gave him a slow, sweet kiss. When she pulled back, she added, "And I can still see your personality."

And she could, in the shelves and shelves of books, the game console tucked away in the entertainment center but not completely hidden, and the old film noir posters framed on one wall.

"Careful." His voice had grown husky, and he nipped her bottom lip. "You might distract me from dinner."

Her arms curled around his neck. "Would that be so bad?"

"Normally, no." Another kiss, short and chaste, and he stood back. "But from what I hear, that was some magick show you put on, and I'm betting you need to refuel."

As if in agreement, her stomach growled. "How do you know so much?" she teased, taking a seat at the table as he went to work in the kitchen. The open floor plan let one room flow right into another, allowing for views of historic downtown in two directions.

He turned to lay out the makings for a salad and tossed her a wink. "Can I get you some wine?"

She considered but asked for tea instead. "Can I do anything to help?"

"Nope. I've got it." He deftly sliced tomatoes as she watched. "This is one of the few meals I'm good at. Even if it is only pasta and salad."

"Two of my favorites." Too invigorated to stay still, she stood and wandered to a window, sipping her glass of iced tea while he worked. She took in the lights of the city before letting her gaze travel to the other room.

What kinds of books did Cade have on his shelves? Though she already had a pretty good idea. Moving to the living room, she went to the rows of hardcovers and paperbacks. She wasn't shocked to see plenty of crime novels along with a fair number of history books and two large atlases, but the works on unexplained phenomena were unexpected. A few knickknacks sat on the shelves, including a couple of pictures.

Kneeling, she studied the face of a much younger Cade, his brown hair longer and with a bit of curl at the ends. He and another boy his age had their arms slung over each other's shoulders.

"You look so happy here," she said, standing with the frame in her hand. She realized he couldn't see her, so she slipped back and held up the photo. "Who is this?"

Cade looked up. The knife hit the cutting board one more time and stopped. "That's my cousin."

His face gave away nothing, but she could hear the tension in his voice. Returning to put the picture back in its spot, she walked slowly to the table and sat, some of her energy sapped by his obvious discomfort.

"We were once very close," Cade said without prompting, "but you could say we had a parting of ways. Ryker's father and mine were brothers."

"Ryker? That's a strong name, almost . . ."

"Intimidating?" Cade scoffed. "Yeah, that was the idea. My uncle and my father were cut from the same cloth, one stitched with maniacal and violent tendencies." Cade looked at his hand clenched on the knife's hilt and slowly, deliberately, set the blade on the counter.

"Sorry." He shook his head and blew out a breath. "Sometimes it just hits me sideways."

"No, it's okay," Lina said. "I'm sorry I brought it up." She hated to spoil their night together, especially since Cade had gone to the trouble of planning a meal.

After a moment, he spoke again. "When Ryker's parents died, my father took him in and raised him as his own. We'd always been tight, but then practically became brothers."

"So he was raised in the same way as you." Lina remembered the story of the monastery and how much Cade seemed to resent his father.

"Yes, but where I pushed away, my cousin embraced the lifestyle." Staring a hole into the wall, Cade explained in a monotone. "Eventually, we grew apart. I left. He stayed."

Finally, his mask slipped, pain etching his expression as he glanced toward the living room. "I don't know why I keep that picture."

"Because he's still family, and you love him." Lina spoke the truth so plain on Cade's face. "Even if you don't always see eye-to-eye."

He nodded, inhaled deeply, and picked up the knife. When he looked at her again, his features had relaxed and the misery had faded. "Like I said, it just comes out of the blue once in a while. It frustrates me, because I always considered Ryker a rational person." He gave her a weak smile. "Until he wasn't."

Lina nodded but decided not to press it. With both of them having fallen silent, she sat and sipped her drink, taking turns watching the action outside and Cade while he worked. He added sliced tomatoes, cucumbers, and carrots to a mix of romaine and iceberg and, after retrieving cutlery and smaller salad bowls, he grabbed a bottle of beer and carried it all to the table.

"About ten minutes until the pasta's ready." He held out his bottle, and she clinked it with her glass.

"Speaking of family," he said and sat, his tone lighter, as if he'd never been upset at all. "You've found a second family, haven't you? With the Maidens and the coven?"

"I guess I have." She lifted a shoulder and poured oil and vinaigrette on her salad. "It's really a sort of sisterhood, one I never realized I would want to be part of."

"But now you do?" Cade went for ranch dressing. "You've

had a change of heart about your magick?"

"Yes. No." She laughed. "I don't know. Somehow it doesn't seem as crazy as it did. At first I kept telling myself that if I could just find some normalcy, some way to keep it all in check, that my regular life wouldn't be affected."

Cade only listened as she talked.

"But that's a lie," she said. "Everything has changed. Because *I* have changed. How could I not?"

Now she set her fork in the bowl, so she could gesture with her hands as she spoke. "My friends and I are being stalked. Hunted, actually. And tonight," she lifted her hands and let them drop, "tonight I fought off some weird underworld beast with my bare hands."

Lina angled toward him. "And you know the craziest part of all? Fighting that thing felt *right*. Almost as normal to me as rolling croissants in the morning. At first I was terrified, and then when the power flowed . . ." she paused, searching for words, "well, it just came naturally."

One side of Cade's mouth tipped up. "And you saved Bryn and Arik. They might both be dead if you hadn't found it in yourself to pull out your power." He tilted his head. "From what you've told me, you sound like you were in complete control."

He laid his hand on hers. "I knew you could handle this, Lina. And you did."

"I did, didn't I?" She couldn't stop the proud grin from bursting free. She gripped his fingers. "You've been here for me, too, just like you promised."

"I will be, as long as you let me." Cade held her gaze, his fingers warm on hers.

Something in the air suddenly shifted.

Still holding his hand, Lina simply stared, losing herself in his eyes. How could the wintry gray be so warm?

Cade's thumb rubbed lightly on her wrist, the most tender yet erotic thing she'd ever felt.

"Cade." The air caught in her lungs and her belly pulled in one long, liquid stroke. Food forgotten, she focused solely on him. "Why do I sometimes feel like we're still getting to know each other?"

His thumb stroked again, and she sucked in a breath. "But other times—"

"It's like we've always been together," he said, finishing her thought. It was quiet for a moment, his leg barely touching hers beneath the table.

Even that minor contact jolted straight to Lina's core.

They'd ignored this part of their relationship, putting it aside as if being attracted to each other was wrong in the midst of all that was happening. And Lina knew she'd have to be the first to make a move. To give permission.

She laced her fingers between his, and leaned toward him.

He met her halfway.

This time when their lips touched, the kiss was more intimate. Cade's heat reached down inside, wrapping gently around her heart.

Yes. This was right, and this was what she wanted. Cade. All of him. Because Bex had been wrong, and there *was* such a thing as the perfect man. Perfect for Lina, anyway. And here he was.

When her lips curved against his, Cade broke the kiss but kept his forehead pressed to hers. "What are you smiling at?"

"I'm happy," she said simply. "And I wasn't sure I ever would be again. Not like this." She sighed and stroked his face.

As if that one caress was his undoing, Cade stood, pulling her slowly to her feet and against his chest. He took her mouth again, urgent this time, more demanding, his hands sculpting their way down her waist to her hips.

Lina's legs melted beneath her, so she grabbed on to his shoulders. With his tongue doing wicked things to hers, all she wanted was to lie down somewhere soft, and let Cade spread his hard body all over hers.

Together, they did a kind of dance, one step moving toward the couch, and then a pause as they thought of nothing but each other—all the curves and angles to be explored.

Before she knew it, she was falling, a soft descent with Cade keeping her safe. The cool leather of his couch met her back, the wild heat of man trapping her from above.

Wrapping her leg around his hip, she held him close, gasping when he pressed himself between her thighs. She dropped her head back, and his mouth fell to her neck—kissing, discovering, taking.

And she would let him take, Lina thought with a sigh.

She would let him take *everything*.

22

Cade rocked against Lina as he kissed her neck. Her scent surrounded him, teasing and taunting, making him weak. When he heard her sigh, he pulled back, saw her green eyes had gone soft with pleasure.

Humbled by her beauty, he grazed his thumb across her bottom lip. Hers was the kind of mouth that begged to be touched, so soft and supple, parted just enough to release her sweet little sounds.

He leaned in for another taste, determined he would take his time. This was Lina, and he'd craved her for far too long to rush. He needed time for the things he wanted to do to her, for the kind of love he wanted to make.

A tiny voice in his head told him he should move her to somewhere more comfortable, but he couldn't stop exploring. His hands found her waist and squeezed before tracing their way up and over her silky skin.

Her gaze locked with his, and her lips curved. Love tore through him and left him stunned. "Lina." When his mouth found hers again, she found her way beneath his shirt, trailing her fingers up across his abs.

The air grew dense, almost hazy from the effect she had on him. He slipped his own hand inside her clothes, his hunger for her growing unbearable as he roamed upward to—

The ring of his cell phone sliced through the air. He ignored it. Nothing in the world was more important than this.

Lina laughed softly. "Should you get that?" Her breathy voice was like a siren's call.

"No. Whoever it is can wait." Kissing her again, he pulled out the band in her hair. And slid both hands through all that glorious gold.

At last, the intrusive sound vanished, allowing full focus on the woman beneath him.

He'd barely settled against her again when the strident sound returned to break the spell. With a growl, he turned to stare into the hallway. His cell sat on the entry table.

"Persistent," Lina said. Then the chime of her phone joined with his.

"It's like the whole world suddenly needs to talk to us." He frowned down at her, wanting nothing more than to stay exactly where he was.

"All things considered, we should at least see if it's important." She lifted her hips suggestively. "Then we can turn them off."

"Sounds like a plan." Cade felt cold when he stood, striding to his phone.

Lina answered hers. "Hey, Bryn."

Maiden business. Heaving a sigh, he picked up his own cell. Unknown number. Might as well see who it was.

"Hello?"

"Hello, Cade." Hearing the deep and familiar voice, Cade went rigid. His first instinct was to hang up, but something told him to wait, to stay on the line. The timing was too coincidental.

He glanced at Lina then turned away. "What the hell do you want?"

"What? I can't call to see how you are?" A low chuckle. "It's been such a long time since we talked."

Cade caught Lina's eye and held up a finger, telling her he would only be a moment. Then he slipped down the hall and into his office, closing the door behind him.

In the dark, he could just make out his desk, so he moved

to stand beside it. And pressed his fist down against the wood.

"Cut the bullshit, Ryker. What do you want?"

"Come on, Cade, we're family. I know you needed some space, but now it's time to come back and—"

"That's not going to happen. That's not my life anymore." Cade kept his voice low, making sure he wasn't overheard. "It never really was, and you know that."

"You can't escape who you are, Cade." Ryker's tone hardened in a flash. "It's in your blood." A heavy pause and then, "Does *she* know that about you?"

A cold quick stab to Cade's chest, a stab of fear. His gaze tracked to a navy-blue box on a shelf behind his desk. "Stay away from her."

"Why?" Ryker's tone held sarcasm in reaction to Cade's warning. "I can't meet the woman you're seeing? The one you've so obviously fallen for?"

Cade moved to the box and lifted the lid. Though staring at the object inside, all he saw were images from his past. Bloody, brutal, violent images. His so-called family had their own ways of dealing with betrayal. With traitors.

In his father's eyes, Cade's desertion was the worst sort of treachery.

"If you think I care about her, then you should know better than anyone to keep clear." Cade's hand tightened on the phone, knuckles burning. "I don't fight anymore, unless I have to."

"And you'd fight for her?" His words held a challenge.

Cade accepted. "Come near her and you'll find out. But Ryker," Cade said, fury forming each word, "we aren't kids anymore. If I have to put you down, I'll make sure you never get up again."

Punching the screen with his thumb, he ended the call, slamming the cell down on his desk.

"Cade?" Lina called from the living room. "Are you okay?"

Leaving the phone where it lay, he eased out and managed an easy smile for her sake. "I'm fine." He made his way down the hall, and a buzzer went off in the kitchen. The pasta was ready.

Stopping next to Lina, he pulled her in for a short, sweet kiss. "Everything is just fine."

23

Lina didn't think anything could top a boat ride to an island on a sunny day. That is, until she entered the grand hall of the St. Germaine home. Gasping, she clapped both hands to her chest and let her gaze track around the huge, open room.

Slate floors paired with mahogany wainscoting created a castle-like vibe, but comfy-sleek furniture made the space inviting. As did the mix of classic and contemporary art, with one large painting moved to the side to reveal a television.

"Welcome to witch central," Anna said. "Or at least that's what Kylie likes to call this room. It's where we used to all hang out when we needed to relax between our trials, or," she tilted her head, "when we needed to relax *during* the trials."

Lina nodded as she and the other Maidens walked farther inside. Bryn and Rae had filled them in on the individual tests the coven witches had been required to pass. Not only had they fought demons and powerful enemies led by an immortal witch, they'd also had to complete specific tasks.

The more Lina heard of what they'd really gone through, the more grateful she was for their guidance and advice.

"Speaking of Kylie," Anna continued, "she won't be here today. She, Quinn, and Hayden went with Claudia to help her search for the house from her vision. Willyn's missing out as well, since her little one is sick, and Shauni is helping at Michael's vet clinic today."

She looked at Lina then. "No Cade today?"

"He's at home writing." Lina let a brief memory of the night before sweep in and felt a tingle in her belly. Too bad her surge of magick, followed by pasta, had made her so sleepy. Cade had insisted on taking her home, and they'd never resumed their pre-phone call activities.

She pushed the erotic images out of her head and focused on the here and now. "I think he actually feels better after what happened in the cavern."

"He knows you can take care of yourself." Anna nodded and kicked up one side of her mouth. "If he's like the other men, though, he'll always be protective."

"He'll relax soon enough, especially since today we start learning to fight with what we've got." Peyton stood next to Lina in casual clothing, her red braid falling like a stream of lava down her black T-shirt. The front featured a Pug, his happy little tongue lolling. "All we need is more practice with the magick."

"Magick," Rae interjected, "and other things."

When the women looked at her quizzically, Anna took a step back. "Why don't we just show you?" She began to turn but stopped when the phone in her hand buzzed. She stared at it and frowned. "Lucia is out, too. Says she's not feeling well."

"Maybe something's going around," Rae said.

"Hope not." Anna exhaled. "Mrs. Attinger will want to make up some of her famous sick-day soup, and I'll check in on her later. Okay, ladies, right this way."

She motioned for them to come with her, and together they trooped back to a hallway, following the corridor until they came to a set of double doors.

Grabbing both handles, Anna threw them open. "Welcome to the ballroom."

This time, Lina wasn't the only one who sucked in a breath. She and the Maidens entered slowly, mouths open, gaping like kids in a fun park.

Creamy marble floors spread before them like clouds, hinting of majestic grandeur from days gone by. On the far side, a grand staircase curved up to a second level mezzanine supported by eight massive columns.

Lina could picture people waltzing here—violins and piano, black tails and glittery gowns.

"You want us to practice in *here*?" Cassidy asked, her face tilted up as she studied the mezzanine.

"It's fine." Anna waved her hand to encompass the huge room, including the shining chandeliers. "We've cast protective spells to absorb any magick you throw out, so you don't have to worry about hurting anything. You can just focus on learning to wield your power."

Lina heard voices and realized Paige and Viv were also there. They'd been told to wear exercise clothing and now, as she eyeballed the two women rolling out blue floor mats, she had a suspicion something else had been planned. "Why do I feel like we'll be doing more than magick?"

"Because you will." Dressed in what looked like an Army-issue T-shirt and black yoga pants, Paige strolled closer and stopped, crossing her arms. "You'll need more than sparkles to survive."

Beneath the other witch's scrutinous gaze, Lina automatically stood straighter. The coven's warrior made her feel like a soldier on her first day of boot camp.

"Oh, don't let her intimidate you." Viv, her hair tied back and her glasses gone, waved a hand and smirked at Paige. "She gets way too much fun out of scaring people."

Paige shrugged and smoothed back her white-blonde bangs. "What's wrong with that?" But she tossed a wink to Lina before moving to Bryn. "Okay. Since you already know how to fight, you get to help me teach."

Rubbing her hands together, Bryn sent the others a mischievous look. "I promise, the pain will be for your own good."

Lina held up a finger. "I'm sorry, but Bryn talked me into sparring with her once before. And only once." She narrowed her eyes at her friend. "I still remember flying through the air and getting the breath knocked out of me."

"You ran right into my side kick." All innocence, Bryn blinked her doe eyes. "And I told you to guard your ribs."

Groaning, Cassidy massaged her side as if feeling phantom pains.

"Thank you, Bryn." Paige plopped her hands on her hips. "Because that story is exactly why you all need to practice. Magick is only part of the fight. If you can't physically defend yourselves, you'll get taken out and won't do anyone else any good."

Now the ex-soldier put a hand on Cassidy's arm. "But I promise to teach you what you need." She grinned. "Before you know it, you'll all be kicking ass the coven way."

Cassidy wrinkled her forehead. "The coven way?"

"With deadly little one-two combos of magick and muscle, guaranteed to put anything on its ass." Now Paige's grin turned devilish. "Or its tentacles. Whatever."

She turned to Peyton then, giving a squeeze to the Scottish witch's arm. "You work out?"

"Some resistance exercises." Peyton looked down at her own bicep. "The only weight I lift is my bike, or the occasional seven-year-old."

Paige nodded and finally focused on Lina again. "How about you? You ever punch anyone before?"

Lina felt her cheeks warm. "No."

"Not true." Bryn shook her head. "Remember that girl who pushed you at that frat party?" She rocked back on her heels and hooted. "And the Jell-O pool just happened to be right behind her."

Now Lina's face rushed with heat. "I don't remember that."

"Ha. I bet you don't." Bryn mimed tossing back a drink. "You were in rare form that night."

"Is humiliation part of our training, too?" Lina pointed at her friend. "Because I have a lot more embarrassing Bryn stories than any you have on me."

Bryn's laughter dried up and she shot a glance at Rae. "You make a good point."

"Have no fear." Paige patted Lina's back and notched her chin toward the blue mats. "After you land on your butt enough times, embarrassment becomes a thing of the past. All of that, however, will have to come after."

"After?"

"After I get my turn." Anna stepped in. "You'll need to become comfortable with both the magickal and the physical, attack and defense." She made a blocking motion with her arm. "Both need to become second nature to you, so you don't even have to think about what to do in the moment."

She tossed a ball of fire into the air and, when Paige followed its path with her gaze, Anna delivered a soft kick to her stomach.

Paige released a little "Oof" and twisted her mouth to one side. "I see how it's gonna be."

Anna chuckled. "Just demonstrating."

"Here comes your target." Viv's voice drew their attention as she rolled out a mobile chalkboard with a bullseye drawn in the middle. "This has been spelled, too. You'll leave a mark but won't destroy the board."

Paige gestured to the bullseye. "Controlling your power is essential. That's why we start here before sparring."

Lina thought of the flying creature she'd blasted with her magick. Yes, she'd hit her target then, but the flow of her power had been unchecked, like water through a broken dam.

That's why she'd been so hungry after, and so exhausted.

"Can I go first?" she asked, surprising herself.

In answer, Anna stepped back and indicated the board. "Fire away."

"Last night, I just let 'er rip," Lina said, taking up a wide-legged stance and wiggling her fingers. "It did the job, but I felt depleted afterwards."

"You'll get stronger," Rae said. "I was tired at first, too. And hungry. But it's like any other kind of exercise."

"You just have to keep doing it." Bryn spoke from behind Lina and to her left. "All right, Lina. You got this."

Nervous now that everyone was watching, Lina wondered if she should let Rae demonstrate first. She glanced over her shoulder. "Maybe you should—"

"You know how to summon your strength," Rae said, sensing her hesitation. She moved closer, putting her hands on Lina shoulders and angling her back to face the board.

"Now connect with your power. The power of the earth." Rae's voice was low and soothing. "It's part of you. It's been gifted to you." Letting go, she eased back. "And only you."

Lina felt something stir in a place just beneath her heart, as if Rae's encouraging words had whispered straight to the source of Lina's magick. Rae was the Akasha, after all, the power of spirit that bound them all together.

Bolstered by her faith, Lina focused, imagining her power building inside. Warmth came first, then a small twinge in her chest. When she was ready, when she sensed a buildup of power, she raised her palms and aimed for the bullseye.

Emerald lines of magick exploded from her palms, smashing against the board on either side of the target. Startled, she jerked back instinctively and cut off the flow.

"Wait," she said before anyone else could speak. "I just need a minute."

Rae was right, calling the power wasn't her problem. She could sense the strength within her, she could summon it more easily every time.

But was she truly connected? Determined to take a different approach, Lina pictured the glistening green that had shot from her hands, a power that had come from *inside*.

Only this time, she closed her eyes and drew a deep breath. Her body relaxed. Her mind opened. She envisioned a door opening to a bright, beautiful world.

Images rushed through and filled her head—tall grass waving in the wind, verdant vines spreading, plump green leaves catching summer sun.

Basking in the warmth, she'd swear she was actually there, soaking in the sun amongst the green.

Energy flooded her chest, and a new connection formed. She opened her eyes, saw her target and, this time, she told her magick where to go.

Twin streams of power left her palms before combining into a single surge. She knocked the board back a few feet. But hit the bullseye dead center.

Cheers and claps erupted behind her.

"Yes!" Rae cried, excitement ringing in her voice.

Lina spun around with her arms wide. "Did you see that?" She put a hand to her heart. "I felt the magick, and it felt me, and we were connected, and, and . . ." She stammered to a stop. "I can't even describe what that felt like. It's like, it *knows* me. Like it's been waiting for me. For *us*."

She laughed through tears. "Like the five of us were always meant to be."

One by one, she met the gazes of her fellow Maidens. And in that moment, something clicked, as if the new link to her magick had also strengthened the bond with her friends.

Not just friends, she thought, remembering something Willyn had said. But her sisters in magick.

She looked to Rae. "That was awesome."

Rae nodded, her honey brown eyes misting up. "You felt it, didn't you? That immersion into the world where your power lives."

"I did." She grasped Rae's hand and felt a tear on her cheek. "It was like . . . coming home." Wiping at her cheeks, she and Rae turned to Cassidy, Peyton, and Bryn. "You've got to try it. It's just so—"

"Amazeballs," Rae said, then laughed at her own choice of words.

Lina nodded. "Exactly right."

"I'm next," Bryn said, before looking to Peyton and Cassidy. "Unless you guys want to go?"

Cassidy extended a hand toward the board. "Be our guest."

Bryn did a little happy wiggle. "Okay, Lina. What did you do? In your head, I mean."

"Honestly, I just let myself go and completely relaxed. It's like the power is there, ready for us." She got choked up again but cleared her throat. "But it's waiting for us to invite it in."

"Okay," Bryn said in a soft tone. Then she gave Lina a quick hug and moved into position.

"Hold on a second," Paige called as she and Viv adjusted the board. "Don't want to be a casualty of friendly fire."

Bryn waited for them to move to safety. Her arms hung at her sides, and she shook them out, pent-up energy practically rolling off her in waves. At last, she grew still, her shoulders rising slowly as she took a deep breath.

She lifted her hands, clenched her muscles, and two huge sprays of sparkling white blasted the board.

"Whoa!" Bryn stumbled back, as if stunned by her own power.

Lina knew the feeling. "That's okay. Try again," she said, hoping to give some of the same boost she'd gotten from Rae.

"Relax. Relax. Relax." Bryn mumbled to herself before calling over her shoulder. "Relaxation is not my natural state, you know."

Taking more time, she inhaled several deep breaths. The

ballroom grew eerily quiet, heavy with expectation as everyone watched. Seconds passed. Minutes.

Suddenly, the tips of Bryn's dark hair lifted, as if teased by a light breeze. "Oh," she said, her voice soft and reverent.

Then, with the grace of the fighter she was, she raised her arms in one smooth motion, sending a direct shot to the center of the target.

Again everyone whooped and cheered while Bryn jumped into the air and landed on her feet facing them. "Woohoo! That was the best thing I've ever felt! Well," she said, tilting her head, "except for Blake Milbourn that one time—"

"Too much," Cassidy said, but her protest ended on a laugh.

"Me next. Me next." Peyton rushed forward. "Okay, I can do this. My grandmother started me on meditation years ago, so the relaxation part I've got."

"Watch that first kick," Bryn said, hurrying past Peyton and giving her a slap of solidarity on the shoulder.

When she rejoined Lina and the others, she crossed her arms and watched intently.

Peyton went still and quiet. But in addition to her breathing, she spoke, the words too soft for them to hear. After a moment, she lifted her arms high, as if inviting the power in. Her palms began to glow like embers.

Easily, as if she'd done this every day of her life, Peyton fired and hit the bullseye on her first try.

"Yessssss!" Cassidy shouted while Bryn yelled, "Hell yeah!" Rae, Paige, and Viv clapped with huge smiles on their faces.

Lina jumped up and down herself, deciding in that instant she would start meditating.

"You make it look easy," Bryn told Peyton, high-fiving her when she returned to the ranks.

"I had the benefit of watching you two try first." Peyton's eyes sparkled, as if the deep sea-blue were lit from within.

"Save the best for last," Cassidy quipped, moving to take

the place of honor. "And by best I mean the best at needing multiple attempts."

"You'll do great." Peyton cheered her on and Bryn let out a sharp whistle of encouragement.

"You got this!" Lina called, reveling in the growing sense of excitement and camaraderie. She looked over and caught Paige and Viv sharing a smile. They knew what it looked like when a coven of witches found that bond.

There was only one Savannah Coven, Lina thought, nodding at Paige who nodded back.

And that was okay, Lina realized as she watched Cassidy. Because she had found a sisterhood, too.

She had magick. She had the power of earth.

She was the northern point of the Watchtower Maidens.

Cassidy held her arms far out to her sides, then she brought them forward, pressing her hands together thumb-to-thumb. She only took one great, heaving breath, and a sea-blue streak flew to the bullseye, rolling the board back several feet.

Tossing her hands up, Cassidy released a kind of war cry and spun around to run back to the others. As a group they all hugged and congratulated each other. Not only because they'd each managed to control their magick and hit the target, but because they'd tapped into something else, something deeper.

Energy swirled within the room, the whole vibe amping up even more. Their powers were spreading, reaching out to each other as they all clapped and yelled.

Lina caught flashes of wind in the trees, of ocean waves and raging flames. And amidst it all, a gentle purple mist, whispering of joined destinies. They were all joined in that other world now, in that place that was the source of their magick.

The five of them stood in a group, laughing and sharing stories of what they'd seen and felt. And they were still chattering when the double doors burst open.

Kylie, Hayden, and Claudia strolled in, their expressions of triumph quelling the chaos.

Lina and the others fell silent. They looked to the coven witch who'd had a vision in a graveyard.

"Good news, witches." With her flaming hair straight as rain down her back, Claudia beamed at the gathering of women. "We found the house."

24

"Fucking snow." Searenn stomped down the front steps of the hotel, leaving behind the classic white sideboard and old-fashioned lampposts lighting the way. She cared nothing for the cut roses in crystal vases or golden-framed pictures in every room.

Norway was a frozen hellscape.

Not only that, she thought with a sneer, this slab of ice and snow was Ronja's homeland, and she saw that flaxen-haired bitch everywhere she looked.

Two days. *Two days* she'd been trapped in this place, with its moody skies and scenic views. Spring had technically arrived over a month ago, but ten seconds outside still chilled her bones.

She'd already survived the coldest pit of the netherworld and now? Sandane, Norway.

Not much of an improvement.

Tromping through mush and snow, in badass boots that didn't keep her feet warm enough, Searenn focused on the task ahead, telling herself she was *this* close to having what she'd come for.

In her time here, she'd used her skills—and occasionally her teeth—to interrogate some locals. But none of them had recognized the name she'd given.

Until today.

She wondered if the body of the waitress had been found yet.

She wondered what the authorities would make of the damage to her flesh.

But Searenn's patience had run out, and she'd do whatever it took to have the answers she sought. If that meant trails of blood and gore down every snowy street.

At last she came to the bar, or pub or tavern, whatever they called it in this forsaken place. She opened the door to a blast of light and warmth, yellow globes lighting the long, narrow room.

In three determined strides, she stood by the counter where a bartender wiped down the gleaming wood. "Einar Pederson," she said, her tone as frigid as the night outside. "Which one is he?"

The man stopped wiping up beer and glowered. "*Hvem spør?*"

"*I'm* asking, asshole."

He drew up and opened his mouth, but Searenn stabbed into his mind before he could reply. "Point. Him. Out."

His arm raised as if pulled by a string, and his finger extended toward a skinny little man with a thick black coat and red hat with ear flaps. "Good," she told the bartender without looking at him. "Now go back to work as if you never saw me."

Like a robot, he did as instructed, a confused wrinkle on his heavy brow.

Searenn pushed her way through the throng of boisterous drinkers, her gaze locked on the man. The French witch's husband had provided a name, his last pitiful attempt to save his family.

The man had proven to be elusive, but little red cap was rumored to be some kind of go-between, interacting with anyone who desired a meeting with the big man himself.

She stopped next to the diminutive man. "Einar Pederson." It wasn't a question.

Mug in hand, he shifted toward her and leered. "Hello, pretty."

He spoke English. Probably picked up on her accent.

To make things easier, Searenn had glamoured herself for her stay in Sandane. No need making a stir before she found her mark.

"I'm told you work for Dag Gundersen."

Still with that happy drunk smile in place, he shrugged. "Don't know him. Ah . . . and who are you?"

"I'm not in the mood." Scraping his brain with her power, she added an extra dose of pain, his reward for having pissed her off. "Put down your beer and take me to him."

He shook his head, waving at his ear as if swatting at a bug. "*Hva?*"

He'd resorted to his native tongue and actually put up the smallest bit of mental resistance. *Interesting.*

So she scraped a little harder. "Take me to Gundersen."

This time, he grunted in pain, then set down the mug hard enough to splash brown liquid on the table. Without a word to her or his companions, he barreled for the door like the pub was on fire.

Her influence had certainly taken hold, because the little man practically ran down the middle of the cobbled street.

Eager to be done with this part of her quest, she followed him at a fast clip, keeping him in sight as he rushed down an alley before turning to follow a winding road uphill.

Her breaths puffed out in clouds, hot steam hitting frozen air. As the lane rose, she moved farther away from the lights of the town. But the moon shone a strange blueish white on the snow, making it easy to track his red cap.

Soon she could make out fire through the trees, then the sound of many voices.

As the thick forest gave way to a clearing, she saw a house with people milling outside with drinks in hand. Two giant bonfires burned, one in front and one out back. The little man had brought her to a party.

Clomping straight through the deep snow, he headed for a woman with blonde curls spilling from beneath a black ski hat. She looked toward the back, said something, and the man set off again.

With Searenn in pursuit.

She caught up to him at the other fire, standing next to a bear of a man with a thick beard the color of wheat. Her red-capped guide stared at her, his eyes wide with fear. Somehow, he still knew he should be afraid of her.

"Here he is. This is Dag." The English had returned.

Dag Gundersen gripped the smaller man's arm. He jerked him back and forth while speaking heatedly in his ear.

Shoving red cap so he fell to the snowy ground, Dag sent Searenn a derisive look. He turned and tromped away from the gathering, heading into the woods in back.

At first Searenn thought he expected her to follow. Then he demonstrated the unmistakable moves of a man whipping his dick out to pee.

A growl sounded low in her throat. This peasant would learn some respect.

Footsteps crunching, she walked up behind him and whispered near his head. "Put that disgusting thing away."

"Fuck off, bitch. You weren't invited."

In her anger, she'd spoken without using her influence. But maybe, she thought with a lust for violence, there was a better way. A more entertaining way.

She glanced back at the people, drunk and loud and oblivious.

Dag still had a grip on his member when she kicked him in the small of his back. He flew forward, arms flung out to catch his fall.

Picking him up by the scruff of his jacket, she dragged him several feet deeper into the cover of darkness. His curses came out as broken gasps as the ground jarred his body.

She flipped him on his back and put a boot on his stomach.

"Colette Marchand gave you something to hide." She pressed down hard on his gut. "Tell me where it is."

His only answer was to shove at her leg, as if he could actually dislodge her.

"You shouldn't make me angry." She leaned down and hissed at him. "Anger makes me get creative."

"Bitch." He wriggled in the snow and ice, still trying to get free.

His flaccid member drew her attention as it flopped to one side. And she got an idea.

Using her hands—because she still liked to use her hands—Searenn pulled his pants down to his thighs, fully revealing the organ a man held most dear.

She stood again and said, "Stay still." This time, she used her power of coercion. "Look at it."

Lifting his head, he let his gaze track down to his groin.

"Now watch."

With barely a thought, Searenn made the pale flesh change. A putrid grayish-green began at the tip and slowly spread, open red sores popping up as the decay crawled along the shaft.

He heaved breaths in and out, panic taking over.

"Don't scream," she told him, pausing the magick long enough for him to rip his stare away from his own body and look at her. "Give me what I want, or I'll rot it off. Then I'll keep going until you're basically a woman."

"*Stoppe. Stoppe.*" He held his hand up to her, pleading for mercy. He folded much faster than the woman who'd paid him to hide the artifact.

When he babbled about the location of the text, Searenn threw back her head and laughed, the malicious sound rising up through the evergreens.

"Well, that will be a challenge, won't it?" With his manhood forgotten and her task accomplished, Searenn directed him to pull up his pants and stand. "You've made things harder for me, Dag. And for that, you need to be punished."

He put both hands over his groin.

She gave him a smile that could only be called hostile.

"Tell me, Dag." She looked to her right. "What will you find if you keep walking that way?"

"A short climb, and on the other side of the ridge lies the fjord."

"Start walking and don't stop until you get to the fjord." She clamped down hard on his mind, making sure the effect would last, no matter what. "When you get to the water, I want you to swim in and dive down. Dive all the way to the bottom."

Fear tinged his stare, but he went anyway, unable to fight her commands.

Another time, she might have toyed with him a while, but all she wanted was a hot bath and a plane ride back to warmer climes.

Still, she watched a minute more, following his steps until the dark woods swallowed him whole. Wind howled through the treetops as Dag Gundersen disappeared, leaving no trace of himself behind. Nothing but footprints in the snow.

All that fucking snow.

25

"This is the house?" Peyton ran a hand down her auburn braid as she stood beneath a magnolia tree with the other Maidens, looking across Huntington Street at a home built in 1881.

Nestled in a quiet neighborhood of the historic district, the large white home was the perfect balance of sophistication and charm. Though Claudia had located the building from her vision almost right away, it had taken a couple of days to garner an invitation from the woman and her son who lived there.

The afternoon sun hung low in the sky, casting a golden glow across trees and rooftops. Lina, Peyton, and Cassidy had all come from work, the strange reality of life going on.

Lina tilted her head and gazed at the house. "Claudia says she's certain, and the Regency-Italianate style isn't that common." Lina pointed to an arched doorway. "Plus, she recognized the area on the ground level."

A metal gate protected the entryway now, but Claudia had noticed the distinctive wall fountain through the bars, confirming it was the room she'd seen.

Lina stared into the first-floor room, basically a patio enclosed by cement walls, and imagined the respite provided before the invention of air conditioning. "This is definitely the house, and that's where she saw the text changing hands."

In the cool, dark chamber, hidden away from prying eyes.

A quick burst of cool wind raised bumps on Lina's arms. She reached up and rubbed her pendant.

"Arik has also researched the family name," Rae said. "Turns out an ancestor of theirs was in business with the man whose skeleton we found beneath the crypt. He must have trusted his partner completely."

"I'll say." Cassidy sighed. "Enough to give him an artifact that could help save or destroy the world."

Her words hung in the air a moment, reminding them just how much was at stake.

Finally, Bryn stepped forward, angling her body to glance back at Rae. "And they know to expect us?"

"They do." With Rae's nod of affirmation, they all stepped off the curb to cross the street. "The son was more than happy to entertain our questions." She lowered her voice as they neared. "I get the sense he's lonely and doesn't get much company."

Two sets of staircases led up from the left and right, meeting directly in front of the door. Black shutters framed the windows, and ferns hung in baskets, adding even more of a Southern feel to the historic home.

Before Rae could ring the bell, the door swung open. A handsome man with dark brown hair stood smiling at them. "I saw you crossing the street." He stood back and gestured. "Please come in."

Lina guessed his age to be late forties, and while he seemed affable and welcoming, the circles beneath his eyes hinted at exhaustion.

"I'm Cliff Wesley," he said, focusing on Rae, "and you are . . ."

"I'm Rae Scott. We spoke on the phone." She offered her hand. "Thank you so much for agreeing to see us. I know the request was out of the blue and maybe a little strange."

He bobbed his head a little side-to-side. "Not all that strange. These old homes often draw the attention of magazine writers or students working on architecture degrees."

He slid his hands into the pockets of his khaki pants. "The specificity of your interest, however, does pique my curiosity. You'd like to know about items acquired by my family from 1908 to 1930. Items that would have been considered antiquities even in the early nineteenth century."

"Yes," Rae said. "My good friend is a historian, and she found a lead on a particular artifact. She believes it might be part of your family collection."

What she didn't tell him was that Claudia had glimpsed a Ford Model-T in her vision, a car only produced between 1908 and 1927. She'd been unable to narrow the timeline down any further, but it was a start.

In response to his inquisitiveness, Rae launched into the lie they'd prepared. Telling the real story—and the real reason they were in his home—would likely get them thrown out. "My father is a collector of this particular type of artifact, and my niece and I," she inclined her head to Bryn, "would like to find a special piece for his sixtieth birthday."

"If you're interested in selling, that is," Bryn said with a smile.

Bryn could never be accused of flirting or employing feminine wiles, but Cliff Wesley still grinned at her like a schoolboy. "Well, *if* we have the item you're looking for. That would be the better question. I'm afraid my grandfather sold many of our heirlooms around, oh . . ." he looked up as he searched his memory, "about sixty years ago."

"We're still grateful you're willing to talk to us." Rae tried to hide the flicker of disappointment, but Lina caught only the barest slip of her eager expression.

"And thank you for letting the rest of us tag along," Lina said, filling the pause. "You were right before. These historic homes are fascinating."

"Now tell me your names," he said, offering them each a congenial incline of his head as they introduced themselves.

"I'm happy to meet you all, and I'm just going to have to give you the full treatment." With that, Cliff led them through the foyer, over floors inlaid with what looked like mahogany and pine, creating a gorgeous pattern of dark and light wood.

He stopped at a door and indicated they enter. "Make yourselves at home, and I'll prepare tea."

"You don't have to go to all that trouble," Rae told him.

"No trouble at all." He turned to look towards the back of the house. "My mother is in the sunroom, but I'm not sure if she'll join us or not." His mouth turned down briefly, and then he disappeared.

While they took seats and waited, Lina cast an admiring eye around the parlor. The sofas and antique fireplace were the same dove gray set against furniture of honey-toned wood and ancient-looking artwork. Potted orchids provided pops of color around the room.

"Tasteful," Rae said, rubbing her hand across the gray velvet.

Cassidy hiked a raven brow. "Yet the wealth here is impossible to hide."

They didn't have to wait long for Cliff to return. He pushed a cart holding a teapot, cups, plates, and a three-tiered silver tray exploding with small sandwiches and pastries. "I know it's a little late, but who doesn't enjoy a true teatime?"

"It's wonderful," Lina said, appreciative of the offering he'd prepared, including the shell-shaped mini sponge cakes. "And you have madeleines."

"Why, yes. I didn't expect anyone to know what they were." He squinted and studied her. Then he brightened. "Oh, I know you. Your family owns the French café on Factors Row."

"Yes." Lina accepted the cup of tea he poured for her.

"I just love that place. Such amazing food and inviting atmosphere." He made a *tsk* sound. "So many cafes and restaurants just don't understand the importance of ambience."

"Thank you. The design was all my mother's work."

"Well, it's lovely." He continued to hand out tea as the women took some of the delicate food items on plates. Though still playing the part of gracious host, his features seemed more tense than before, his mask failing to disguise some sort of emotional turbulence.

"Hey!" The single word carried through the house, the voice thin and tremulous.

Cliff flinched but quickly brought back a smile. "In the parlor, Mom." He rubbed his hands together and glanced around at the Maidens. "I should tell you, my mother's not quite herself anymore."

He worried his bottom lip as if deciding how much to say. "It's Alzheimer's, early onset."

Lina felt a pang of sympathy and now understood the darkness beneath his eyes. He was her caretaker. "I'm sorry. I know that's difficult. My grandfather," she said, no need to explain further. "Do you have any help?"

He nodded. "A nurse comes in several times a week, and sometimes a nurse's aide. I've only been living here full-time for about six months, but . . . it's challenging."

"I'm sure it is," Rae said, soft with compassion.

"My sister was here before, and I was going through a divorce." He waved a hand as if he felt he were talking too much and wanted to hurry himself up. "Well, then she was killed in a car accident, and my wife and I were separated, so," he lifted both hands and sighed, "it just all pointed to my moving back home."

"She's lucky to have you," Cassidy said.

"I'm grateful to have the time with her, such as it is." He cocked his head to the sound of shuffling footsteps before looking back to his guests. "I'm sorry. You don't need to hear all of this. I just wanted to let you know beforehand."

Rae stared down into her tea, contemplating. "If this is a bad time—"

"Oh, no. It's as good a time as any." He inclined his head. "And I would really love some conversation."

Rae's shoulders relaxed. "All right."

"So tell me—"

"Hey." Though she didn't yell, the older woman standing in the doorway looked none too pleased to find her parlor filled with strangers.

"Hey, Mom." Cliff stood and introduced the women.

As soon as he got to Peyton, his mother's glare glued to her face. She thrust a gnarled finger in her direction. "Oll igger."

Cliff chuckled nervously. "I'm so sorry. She has aphasia, trouble speaking and with words in general."

She continued to stare hard at Peyton. "Oll igger.'

"Mom, this isn't Melanie. Her name is Peyton, and she's come to visit with her friends."

He blushed when he told Peyton, "My ex-wife had red hair like you. Mom always said she was a gold digger."

"Oll igger." Mrs. Wesley shook her head and walked to a chair to sit.

"It's fine," Peyton said, her lips turned up to let him know she understood.

"Now where were we?" Cliff rubbed his thighs again and sat. "Yes. I was asking you to tell me what you were specifically interested in finding."

Taking her cue, Rae set down her teacup. "We have reason to believe the item we're looking for came into your great grandfather's possession in the early part of the last century. If you don't still own it, we were hoping your family kept some sort of records."

"No." He rubbed his chin. "No records that I know of, and as I said before, my grandfather sold off many of our most valuable items. You said this piece was very old?"

"Yes, it wouldn't have looked expensive, but its value comes from its history. A piece of stone, rough at the edges." Rae made a triangle shape with her hands. "There may have been writing etched into the flat surface, some type of symbols."

"Hey!" Mrs. Wesley sounded off so suddenly, they all jumped.

"It's okay, Mom."

The older woman pointed her finger at Rae, eyes wide. "Hey," she said again, softly. She stood, never taking her gaze from Rae as she shuffled to Cassidy and placed a hand on her shoulder. "Susset. Susset."

She looked down at Cassidy who nodded, though her baffled expression said she didn't understand. None of them did.

"Do you know what she means?" Bryn asked Cliff.

"No idea. I've never heard this one before."

Blowing out a breath in frustration, the woman moved to Lina next. "Susset. Muhsunnasine."

"I'm sorry," Lina said, unsure what to do.

The woman clapped her hands together, growing more and more agitated. "Susset. Muhsunnasine."

"Mom. It's okay." He gently took hold of her arm, but she shook it off.

"Hey!" She jabbed her finger at him and then at Lina, her teeth grinding so hard they made a creaking sound.

"I'm sorry," Cliff said. "Sundowners hits early sometimes."

Something clicked for Lina. "Wait. Sunset?"

"And sunshine," Peyton threw in, catching Lina's lead.

The woman looked at Peyton and blew a raspberry with her tongue. "Oll igger."

"Is that right?" Lina asked the woman gently, hoping they'd hit the answer. "Sunset and sunshine?"

Mrs. Wesley nodded, blinking. "Muhsusset." She wavered on her feet.

Lina jumped up and put her arms around her. "I've got you."

Cliff immediately intervened. "It's all right. She just wore herself out."

"We should go." Rae stood, saving him from having to ask

them to leave. "I'm sorry we upset you," she told Mrs. Wesley.

"Susset," she whispered, reaching for Rae.

Rae looked past her to Cliff. "Do you have any idea what she's trying to say?"

"No, I don't. And I apologize for all of this. I hate that we didn't get to talk more."

"You've been very kind, and if we can do anything to help . . ."

"No, no. A little nap and all will reset." Cliff helped his mother hobble to the doorway. "Do you mind seeing yourselves out? I'll need to take her back to her bedroom."

"Of course," Rae said. "And again, thank you."

"You know," he said, pausing for a moment in the hallway, "I can tell you that my grandfather used to be *in* with the other old families of Savannah. Someone else with ties that go that far back might be able to tell you who he would have sold the items to."

Cliff made a *tsk*ing sound. "He definitely would have wanted to get the very best price, so maybe he used a well-known auction or a specialist of some kind."

"Thank you." Rae lifted a hand in farewell. "You've been very helpful."

Once he'd gone back to helping his mother, she watched him for another few seconds, her mind churning. They'd deciphered the poor woman's garbled words, but "sunset" and "sunshine" didn't give them much to go on.

Frustrated and sensing they'd been close to a discovery, Rae sighed and turned away, following her friends out the door.

26

Two days later, Lina waited outside an imposing black gate, along with the other Maidens and Claudia. The road stretched in both directions away from where they'd parked, each side lined by forest in the peaceful countryside location.

Claudia and Anna had described the mansion hidden far behind the locked gates, but all Lina could see was a curving driveway and landscaped lawns.

Soon though, a low whirring noise filled the air, just before a man in full butler attire drove a golf cart into view. His white teeth gleamed like the Cheshire Cat's when he saw Claudia. After performing a quick turn on the other side of the gate, he stopped and held up a remote.

The gates slowly opened.

"Miss Claudia," the man said through the moving bars. "It's so nice to see you again."

"Hi, Charles. It's good to see you, too." Claudia indicated the others. "And these are my friends."

"Ladies, lovely to meet you." He bowed his head. "I can fit you all in if three squeeze into the back."

"We can squeeze," Bryn said, tugging Lina to sit with her and Peyton on the rear-facing seat. Once they were all settled, the cart took off. Manicured gardens spread left and right, with giant live oaks and azalea bushes scattered around.

Now Lina could hardly wait to see inside the home.

After their visit with Cliff Wesley and his mother, the

Maidens had filled Arik in about what they'd learned. He'd immediately come up with the name Clermont, known to be a reclusive and discerning man in the world of antiquities.

Luckily, Claudia had scored them an invitation. Clermont had helped Claudia during her trial, and in return, she'd used her special gift to examine some of his collection, items which had colorful stories to tell.

And now he adored the history-loving witch.

Apparently, he wasn't the only one, as Charles hadn't stopped chatting with her since they'd pulled away from the gates.

"Wow," Bryn muttered next to Lina, pointing at the stately brick home rising up before them. Verandas lined the upper floor with outdoor seating areas. "How many square feet, do you think?"

Lina shook her head. "I can't imagine." The cart rolled to the sweeping front staircase, and they all climbed out.

Charles hurried up the steps, opened the door, and welcomed them all inside. They followed the butler past myriad rooms and passageways, and Lina sent Bryn a sly, sidelong glance.

One perk of being a Watchtower Maiden was the exposure to so many amazing places. Bryn had been right, too. The layout seemed to go on forever. Eventually, they came to an enormous metal door, bolts lining the edges and a seam splitting down the middle.

Charles hit a button and the doors slid open to reveal an industrial-size elevator. They all stepped inside, the seven of them fitting comfortably with plenty of elbow room.

"Time to go underground," Claudia said, wiggling her ginger brows. "Just wait, you're going to love it. And Cassidy," she added, "Mr. Clermont has a library you could get lost in."

At that, Cassidy's crystal-blue eyes perked up. She blew out through pursed lips as if trying to manage her excitement.

The elevator touched down, and the soundless slide of doors

opened to reveal a long tunnel. Rounded at the top, the channel was clearly manmade, with cement stained a regal brown that shone beneath the recessed lights.

Charles remained in the elevator. "Have fun," he said. "I'll see you soon." And waved as the doors closed once again.

Busts and statues lined both sides of the wide tunnel, yet there was still room enough for three of them to walk shoulder-to-shoulder. The chamber at the end of the passage opened up to much higher ceilings. Girders reinforced cement walls, but wooden beams added some style. As did the two rows of support columns. They'd been painted the color of wine and accented the history-themed space nicely.

Lina stopped near some old barrels along one side. Had they held whiskey? Or gunpowder for the cannon balls stacked in a pile?

A wall cordoned off another section, and Lina and the others filed in behind Claudia. It was like stepping into a luxurious museum built for comfort.

Here the smaller items were exhibited, treasures and artifacts that seemed right at home amongst the lush carpets, golden lanterns, and lighted display cases. There was even a chandelier in the middle of the room.

Lina grinned to herself. A chandelier. Underground.

"Claudia." A man rose from a reclining chair in the center of the room. Other chairs sat nearby, encircling a massive coffee table in the shape of a giant tortoise. Several large books sat atop the shiny wood.

Lina tried to watch politely as Claudia and Mr. Clermont exchanged a hug and greetings, but she couldn't stop staring at the amazing antiquities—an Asian screen of carved wood, medieval weapons and full suits of armor, two ancient globes, one of the earth and the other featuring constellations.

"Well," the man boomed in his deep voice, turning to study the others, "this is a larger group than I normally allow." He cleared his throat. "Especially strangers. But you know the saying—any friends of Claudia Grant's are certainly friends of mine."

Mr. Clermont had a glorious accent, one that rolled carelessly in a charming, Old-South kind of way. A little like Foghorn Leghorn.

"Before we get started, would anyone like a drink?" He gestured to a well-stocked bar in one corner of the room.

"Thank you, but I'd be too afraid to drink anything in here." Peyton laughed lightly, her hands clasped behind her back as if afraid to touch anything either.

"Nonsense." Mr. Clermont winked at her. "It's all insured." He chuckled. "No, we'll be drinking here at the table, a place I consider a safety zone. But," he added, lifting a finger, "if you change your mind, I also have tea, soda, water, and coffee."

The older man indicated a square panel beside the bar, a modern dumbwaiter. Clermont clearly enjoyed his collection room enough to keep comfort items on hand.

"If you'll join me at the table?" He waved an arm and waited for the ladies to take their seats before he finally sat himself.

He smacked a hand on the top of the books. "I have accounts going as far back as 1890. I'm afraid a fire destroyed my family's earliest records. We recorded many transactions, anything of interest, sold or bartered."

Leaning back in his seat, he propped one ankle on the opposite knee. "You see, my father, and his father before him— and so on and so on—have always been collectors. It's how I accumulated so many wonderful things. But we also keep track of other sales. It's the only way to know when a piece we want is available in an estate sale or auction."

Claudia gazed at the books before sliding one closer. "Maybe we'll get lucky."

"Maybe," Mr. Clermont echoed with a hopeful expression. He picked up another book from somewhere next to his chair and offered it to Rae. "Here, this makes one for each of us. I thought we'd start with the earliest dates and work back from there."

"I'm sorry," Bryn said, her gaze tracking over the old covers. "These each represent a single year, but they're so thick. All of these were sales of antiques in Savannah?"

"Oh, no." Mr. Clermont gave that deep chuckle again. "In fact, that's one reason I agreed to so many people. And so many sets of eyes." He shrugged. "With the help of auction houses and clerks, we've kept track of transactions occurring throughout the South, much of the North, and certain places in Europe."

At this, Lina couldn't help but gape at him. "How did you acquire so much information?"

"Well, back in the early days, it was all handwritten, and my family has always maintained reliable connections."

Claudia jumped in. "The world of collectors is almost a secret society of its own." She grinned at the older man. "Which is why I needed someone to vouch for me before I was allowed entry to the palace."

The older man put a hand over his heart. "And now you have a standing invitation." He dropped his foot back to the floor and clapped his hands on his knees. "If you'll tell me what we're looking for, I'll be happy to help."

Claudia filled him in on the Wesley family, and he nodded. "Nice people," he said. "Well, let's get started then." He reached back into the box for his own copy to peruse.

As each of them settled in with a book to search, Rae glanced over her shoulder and scrunched up her mouth. "Mr. Clermont, I hate to ask."

"Nonsense."

Rae wrinkled her nose in apology. "Is it too late to ask for coffee?"

Chortling, the man stood. "I had a feeling you might change your mind when you saw the workload. We can also get some food sent down."

After coffee was made and handed out, the room fell quiet as all of them scoured the old records, deciphering scrawls made on paper over a century before. This offered its own challenge, so the going was slow and hard on the eyesight. As they completed a search, the book was placed in a separate pile.

After three books, two coffees, and one major headache, Lina sat back and rubbed her closed lids. "I think I need a break. Mr. Clermont, do you have a restroom on this level?"

"Certainly. Back through the door there and—"

"Wesley!" Cassidy cried, her finger planted in the book she held in her lap. "I found them!"

Mr. Clermont wiggled his fingers in a give-it-to-me gesture, so she handed the tome over for inspection.

Two fingers pressed to his lips, he read the lines of entry. "Bulk sale," he muttered before looking up to the women. "Some items were sold by a James Wesley in March of 1858 to Theodore Pelham."

"That fits," Claudia said, looking to Rae.

"Yes." Rae edged forward on the leather seat. "Cliff Wesley told us his grandfather sold a lot of their treasures near that time."

"Unfortunately," Mr. Clermont continued, "they were sold en masse with only the most valuable pieces listed here. I'm afraid there's no mention of a tablet or anything described as stone."

A collective shoulder-drop went around the table.

"Now wait," Mr. Clermont said. "That doesn't mean your relic wasn't included, just that some of the items didn't warrant a write-up by my ancestor." He closed the book with a *whump*. "And there is some good news."

"We could use some," Bryn said, staring down at the book still open in her lap.

"I happen to be good friends with Marjory Pelham, the heir

to this family's estate and an avid collector in her own right." He frowned. "I can't guarantee she'll part with anything, as she's as protective of her finds as I am, but you can at least meet with her. Ask her about this stone you need."

Rae set her cup on the table. "You can arrange this meeting?"

"I can. Not only is Marjory a very kind person, but she owes me a favor." He stood and rubbed his hands together. "Time to cash it in."

"Thank you," Lina and Rae said at the same time.

They waited nervously and quietly as he made the call. Lina's heart plummeted when he said, "I'm sorry to hear that." Then rebounded at his, "That would be wonderful."

When he hung up, they all trailed his steps back to the table.

"Marjory will be out of town this weekend, but she can see you on Tuesday. How does that sound?"

"That sounds perfect." Rae stood and reached out to shake his hand. "I can't tell you how much this means to us."

Clermont slid his eyes to Claudia. "Considering this one's handy little gift, I imagine whatever you're up to is quite imperative."

"It is," Claudia assured him and gave him a hug of gratitude. "Thank you."

"You are most welcome, my dear." He beamed at her. "Most welcome."

"Can we help you put the books back where they belong?" Cassidy stepped away from the table, waiting for his response.

"No, no. That can wait until later." He pointed at her. "But Claudia did tell me you might be interested in seeing my library."

Cassidy actually shivered. "I'd love to."

"Right this way, madame." Offering Cassidy his arm, Mr. Clermont led the way back to the elevator. Rae and Peyton fell in behind them with Lina, Bryn, and Claudia in back.

Bryn let out a huge sigh, as if a five-ton weight had been

lifted. "One more step in the right direction."

Lina nodded. "We're getting there."

"Yep. We've followed the trail from place to place, we've made some progress, and we did exercises that tested our magick and bruised our butts." Bryn threw a small punch in the air. "Now I'm ready to blow off some steam."

Lina brought up her work schedule in her head. "It *is* Saturday, and Bex is opening the café tomorrow."

"There you go." Bryn looked past her to Claudia. "How about you? Are you in?"

A slow smile spread over Claudia's face. "I think I can round up a few coven ladies. And," she added, "I know a great bar where we can get things started."

"All right. Then it's official." Bryn clapped her hands and did a twirl. "Watch out, Savannah. Tonight the witches are coming out."

27

With her arm slung around Cade's waist, Lina walked down the sidewalk on Whitaker Street. The spring night was warm and sweet, the air rich with the scent of flowers and a big white moon shining down.

A car with music pounding passed by, and Cade took the opportunity to drag her beneath the awning of a closed boutique. "Before we go in," he said, pulling her close in the shadows.

With his hands on her hips, he held her in place and dropped his mouth to hers. The kiss was soft, slow, and all the more arousing because of his gentle touch. The kind of kiss that would linger in her system for hours.

When he pulled back, she didn't want to let go. "That was unfair." She stood on her tiptoes to nip his bottom lip. "Kissing me like that when I can't follow up on it."

His only answer was a teasing grin. "Oh, we'll follow up." He cupped the side of her face. "Later. And in private."

Her belly tingled and an ache spread. A good ache. A delicious ache. "Later," she whispered, taking his hand as they caught up with the others and poured inside the bar.

Pub, she reminded herself, which seemed to be the term used most often in Savannah. Viv's boyfriend Nick owned the establishment, and as soon as Lina stepped inside, she spotted the Asian witch behind the bar chatting up a couple sitting on stools.

"It's like a time capsule," Cade said, looking up at the tin ceiling. "I have to use this place in a book."

Lina nodded. "A time capsule with modern-day flair. My mother and I have had many a lunch here." The dark wood and historic design never failed to charm, and they always chose one of the more private tables behind the tall panels.

"Hey, hey, hey!" The happy call came from Kylie, her long blonde curls bouncing as she hurried to greet the newcomers. "Come on, we have plenty of space on the other side. Nick made sure to set us up."

"And we needed it, for sure." Quinn came up behind Kylie. He put his hands on her shoulders, and she leaned back into his chest. "Everyone is coming tonight," he said. "Everyone. Even doc Michael and the detectives, who always seem to be working."

"I knew this would be a good night." Bryn appeared with Rae and Arik, having just come in the front door themselves. "Cassidy and Peyton are right behind us." Waving to someone she knew, Bryn eased through the crowd in snug jeans and a sleeveless black top that showed off her karate-toned arms.

Going where Kylie directed, they found several tables grouped together in the back section, a semi-private room. The walls were exposed brick, painted ivory maybe a hundred years before. Wooden beams spanned the ceiling, and one wall featured an arched window of stained glass—rich yellow, red, and cobalt blue.

Plenty of chairs and tables had been provided, while still leaving space for them to roam and socialize. Music rolled in from the bar but not so loud that they'd have to shout.

From what Lina could see, everyone else had already arrived. Pitchers and mugs of beer littered the tables, competing for real estate with an array of appetizers.

A general cry went up when everyone spied the new arrivals. Claudia was there, cozied up to Cole in one corner, with the sweet Hayden and her boyfriend Trevor next to them.

Quinn was right. Even the two homicide detectives looked relaxed and ready for a good time.

"What'll you have to drink?"

Lina turned to find Ian at her shoulder. Anna's tall, golden Viking of a man clapped a hand on Cade's shoulder as he leaned in to hear their answer.

Cade notched his chin toward the tables. "I'll just take a mug for those pitchers."

"Same," Arik said.

Lina tried to think. "I guess I'll have—"

"An appletini!" Kylie interjected and laughed. "Do you like sweet drinks?" she asked Lina. "If you do, you'll love this one."

For some reason, an appletini sounded tempting. "Sure. Can I help?"

"Nope." Kylie shook her head as Peyton and Cassidy walked up. "Tonight, we're your hosts, and you guys," she swung a pointed finger in an arc to indicate the Maidens and the two men, "are just here to have fun."

After Peyton and Bryn said they'd have beer, Cassidy and Rae jumped on the appletini train. "Why the hell not?" Cassidy said, shoulder-bumping Lina as she leaned closer to say, "This was a good idea. I didn't realize how tightly-wound I've been lately."

She grimaced and added, "Yesterday I snapped at Dan. He actually told me to chill."

"Bex and Manny keep giving me funny looks when I'm at the café. They know something's changed but have no idea what's going on."

"I know, right?" Cassidy ran her fingers through her black hair. "Can we ever tell them? Shouldn't they be . . . I don't know, warned?"

"I've thought about that." Lina furrowed her brow. "I also don't want to lose good employees, because they'll think I've lost my mind talking about ancient demons and magick gates."

"Tomorrow," Cassidy said and gave a firm nod. "We'll talk about this tomorrow, when the smell of chicken wings isn't distracting me."

"Agreed." Lina laughed and went with her to find seats.

Bryn was already eating a cheese stick while Rae and Peyton dipped some sort of fried triangle into a sauce. Soon food and conversation replaced the thought of any forthcoming trouble, and Lina decided she'd follow Cassidy's lead.

Tomorrow was soon enough to resume preparations, and they'd already planned to meet at Arik's for practice.

Kylie and Quinn returned then. He held a tray while she unloaded drinks to hand them out.

Lina took one sip of her appletini and said, "Yum."

"I know." Kylie wiggled her brows.

Lina took a bigger drink. "It's like an adult version of a Laffy Taffy."

"Exactly." Kylie's gaze darted over Lina's shoulder. "There you are. I was getting worried." She spoke to Lucia as the woman returned to her chair.

Lucia sat and exchanged a glance with Ethan, such a stunning couple with their dark good looks.

"You were gone forever," Kylie said, setting a martini glass with green liquid in front of her friend. "You okay?"

Lucia nodded and gave a wan smile. "Definitely. Sort of." She looked around the table. "Is everyone here?"

"We are now." Nick and Viv chose that moment to join the group. "I've got things covered for the rest of the night. Barring any unforeseen insanity."

"Which is likely on a Saturday night in Savannah." This from Paige before she wiped a spot of something off of Chris's chin. The two ex-soldiers were blonde, and Lina imagined them as the day to Ethan and Lucia's night.

"Sorry, Kylie." Lucia pushed the martini glass toward her

friend. "You'll have to drink this for me."

Confusion marred Kylie's expression. "Why? Are you sick?"

"Not sick," Ethan said. Then he gave a huge grin.

"Oh, my Gosh!" Willyn was the first to make the connection. "You're pregnant!"

At Lucia's nod, the group rang out with congratulations followed by a lot of hugs and happy tears.

"Thank goodness for smoke-free bars," Michael said, the blond veterinarian thinking instantly of health concerns.

"*Si*. But this morning sickness is *muy malo*." Lucia flopped her arm into the air and back to the table. "So bad. And poorly named, too. It's not even morning, and I can't stay out of the bathroom."

"Aw, honey." Willyn squatted next to her friend's chair. "I've got some good tricks you can use. For starters . . ." She put two fingers to the center of Lucia's chest.

"Hmm. Better." Lucia gave a little groan. "Thank you."

Willyn kissed her temple. "Now why don't I get you a nice, cold ginger ale?"

When Lucia nodded, Nick said, "I've got it," and made his way back towards the room with the bar.

"And I'm sorry to say there won't be a wedding to attend." Ethan turned to Lucia and rubbed circles on her back, his gaze full of adoration. "We did that a couple of days ago when we were in St. Augustine. The beaches, the history."

"It felt a little like home," Lucia said, jumping in. "I hope you all understand. It was spur of the moment. And I'm traditional, so . . ." She looked down at her belly.

"Of course we understand." Anna stood with Shauni, their arms around each other, eyes brimming with unshed tears.

"We were already talking dates," Ethan said. "Then it all just fell into place."

"Ethan, the next time we play poker, I'll bring the cigars." Dare raised his glass in salute as Willyn took her seat next to him again and put her head on his shoulder.

With the joyful mood infecting everyone, Lina spun in Cade's arms. "Isn't that wonder—" She broke off when she saw his expression. He glowered at something toward the front of the bar.

She followed his line of sight to a man standing near the windows. A fist of worry punched her in the stomach. "Is that Ryker?"

Cade drew a deep breath before giving her a weak smile. "Don't worry. It's all good. But he's seen me now, so I should go speak to him."

With that, he slipped away, crossing the bar before she could say anything else.

"Who's that?" Bryn asked, appearing at Lina's side.

"Cade's cousin."

Bryn sipped her beer. "I see hotness runs in the family."

Lina's tone turned grim. "That's not all that runs in their family."

"What?"

Finally angling toward Bryn, she shook her head. "Nothing. Just some bad blood there." She grabbed Bryn's mug and took a slug herself. "Nothing to worry about."

~~~

Using every bit of restraint he possessed, Cade strode to where Ryker stood. His cousin leaned casually against the wall and wore a cat-stalking-the-canary smirk.

"Unbelievable," Cade growled, moving right up to his cousin's face. "You're following me? Doesn't that strike you as a little psychotic?"

Ryker lifted a shoulder, nonchalant as he held Cade's glare. "If you ever came to visit your family, I wouldn't have to track you down."

"Visit?" Cade made a sound of disgust. "And give you and my father a chance to drag me back into your cult? Fuck that." Cade leaned in closer, mere inches from his cousin. "I have a normal life now, and I won't allow your sickness to infect me or anything that's mine."

Still calm, Ryker gestured with a tall glass of what looked like Guinness. "You mean her? The pretty blonde?" He chuckled, but the sound held no mirth. "She looks too sweet for you, Cade."

This time when Ryker looked at Lina, an unsettling glint entered his stare. "Where did you find her?"

Cade shoved a hand into the other man's chest, spilling some of the dark brew so it foamed down the side of Ryker's glass. "I told you to stay clear of her. Don't look at her. Don't even think about her."

With a swift jerk of his arm, Ryker grabbed Cade's wrist and twisted. "If she's going to be in your life, Cade, then she's damned well going to have my attention."

Cade had forgotten how strong Ryker's grip could be. But they weren't kids anymore, and no one was there to call the fight. If Ryker and Cade's insane-as-hell father wanted to come for him, then they'd see a side of Cade they'd never seen before.

He had more to protect now than bruised ribs or a bruised ego. Lina had entered Ryker's fucked-up field of vision, and Cade would beat his cousin blind if that's what it took to keep her safe.

Forgetting his plan to stay in control, he gripped Ryker's shirt and yanked. "Outside. Now."

"Hey, Cade." Friendly yet firm hands fell on his shoulders. "Let's not bust up my bar your first time here."

Rage still simmered at the edges of his brain, but Cade remembered where he was and quickly tamped it down. "Sure," he said, releasing Ryker as his cousin did the same. The two men stepped back from each other.

"All good." Ryker's taunting grin was back.

Cade wanted to rip it off his face.

"No harm done." The grin dropped away. "Not yet, anyway. Stay safe, cousin." Setting his beer on the windowsill, Ryker pushed between Cade and Nick before exiting through the closest door.

Cade watched his back until he stalked down the sidewalk and out of his sight. Only then did he release the breath burning hot in his lungs.

"You okay, man?" Nick remained at his side, arms crossed, still a mixture of amiable and ready-to-throw-his-ass-out if needed.

"Yeah. Sorry about that." Cade pressed his lips together. "Family trouble."

"Ah. Well, thanks for cooling it down." Nick seemed ready to forget the whole thing. "Need a drink?"

"I'm good. Got one at the table." Cade offered his hand. "Again. My apologies."

Nick shook it and gave Cade a clap on the arm. "You didn't break anything. Or anyone." He laughed. "So it's not a problem."

"Right." Relaxing his features, Cade nodded.

But inside, he still raged, his cousin's words pounding in his head. *No harm done.* Cade clenched his hands into fists. *Not yet.*

His cousin's obsession was becoming an issue. He'd clearly fixated on Lina, and she had a right to know.

Ryker was getting closer and closer all the time, and she needed to know the whole truth, to know what being with Cade really meant.

He dreaded having this conversation, but Ryker had left him no choice. So tonight, he and Lina would talk. No more omission, no more half-truths.

Tonight, he would tell her everything.

28

Lina entered the townhome and moved to the side table to drop her purse and keys, then pivoted, expecting to find Cade right behind her.

Instead, he stood in the doorway, scanning the hallway as if unsure of what to do.

She'd worn the red dress with a wrap-around belt, hoping for a blend of playful and eye-catching. On their walk home from Nick's pub, she'd had every intention of dragging him up to her bedroom where she'd summon the courage provided by those cute little appletinis.

Now she wondered if she'd misread his mood.

When his gaze tracked to the living room and the big comfy couch, she cooled her desire to be in his arms and settled on offering comfort instead.

"You're upset about seeing your cousin," she said simply.

But then he swung that gray gaze up to hers. And what she saw there wasn't sadness or anger.

"I was earlier," he said, holding her gaze until the breath stilled in her chest. "But I stopped being influenced by him a long time ago." He stepped inside, closed the door, and threw the lock. "I'm sure as hell not letting him ruin this night."

One corner of his mouth lifted.

And Lina melted inside.

She was glad of her recent mani-pedi, poppy red to match the dress. She felt polished and feminine from head-to-toe, shielded by a little extra female armor.

I can do this. I'm a grown woman, and Cade is the man I ...
She cut her own thought off before it finished, telling herself it
was too soon to have those feelings. Especially *that* particular
feeling.

A stable relationship needed time to grow, to discover all
the angles and curves each person was made of. This is what
she told herself as he moved toward her, as her heart gave one
hard kick in her chest.

He closed in until only an arm's length separated them,
then he reached out and traced his thumb along her jaw, then
down to circle one finger around her pendant. "You look pretty
with your hair all windblown. With these wisps coming free to
trail down your cheeks."

She shuddered, closed her eyes, and felt that long, liquid
pull in her belly.

Looking at him again, she took his hand, tugged him close,
and made the leap. "I want you to stay with me."

His gray gaze turned stormy with desire, his breath stopping
short before drawing deep again. "To protect you," he teased,
skirting his palms downward as if memorizing her shape.

"No." She ran her hands over him in response, across his
shoulders, down his deliciously hard back, and under the edge
of his black button-up shirt. "So I can protect you."

Something in his deep chuckle danced over her skin. A
purely male sound, satisfied yet still wanting.

Easing around to the front, she trailed up his stomach,
fingers dragging over him in a light, sensuous tease. Then back
down where she slipped just inside the waist of his jeans.

Cade groaned, his lids shutting briefly.

Stepping away from him, she walked up three steps and
paused.

His stare traveled up and down, lingering on her bare legs.
And she knew the dress had been the right choice.

"I didn't want to date you at first," she told him, jerking his hungry gaze back to her face. A grin blossomed over her lips. "I didn't think it was a good idea."

"Glad you changed your mind."

Unfazed, she took a few more steps toward the second floor, toward her bedroom. "I thought you were too broody." When he would have objected, she held up a finger. "I know. You're a writer. You're supposed to have deep thoughts that take you far away."

"If I'm being honest," she dared one more step, "it's actually pretty sexy. The way your expression gets tense, and you focus on something no one else can see. All those pictures in your head."

The smile that broke over his face was devastating, and Lina put a hand to her stomach to still the effect he had on her.

"You think I'm sexy when I write?" Voice gruff with desire, he took two steps at a time until he towered over her. Button by button, he opened his shirt.

Lina nearly swooned.

He leaned in, and she put her hands up. Not to ward him off, but to feel his taut abs flex beneath her palms.

This amazing man, she thought with a thrill—intelligent, caring, considerate—yet willing to race across a cemetery in pursuit of a threat. He was part of her life now, a life that had been upended and had gone insane. Yet somehow, it was all starting to fit.

She'd taken a chance on love, putting her trust in a man when she was unsure of so many things. But they balanced each other, this man capable of seeing what might be, and her, a woman grounded in the here and now.

First friends, now lovers, and always . . . Cade.

He lowered his head, caught the breath from her lips, and lifted her off of her feet.

Cade couldn't wait a minute longer. When Lina wrapped

her arms around his neck, an arousing scent came with her. Sweet, floral, musky—a perfume that was uniquely Lina. His brain fogged over but his awareness lasered, focusing only on the seductive woman in his arms.

Reaching out with one hand, she pushed open her bedroom door.

Needing no further prompting, he strode inside. The moon provided a pale blue shine, so he didn't bother turning on the light.

His mouth slanted over hers, moving lip to lip before probing deeper. She tasted sweet yet mysterious, layers and layers to be discovered.

Lina moaned and wrenched away, heavy-lidded eyes burning green. "I want you, Cade."

He made a growling sound in his chest, a wildness in him that he'd never known. He'd never thought to have a woman like her. She was too good, too pure. He wondered if he even deserved her.

She'd been thrown into an obligation not of her own making, and she faced it boldly, forcing herself to charge ahead, even when she was afraid.

How could he not love a woman like that? A woman dancing on the edge of chaos, and the one person he couldn't live without. His own life went on, but everything else paled against the driving need to keep Lina safe.

Let the demons she fought come right to his door. He'd travel to death and back if that's what it took, ripping those cursed bastards to pieces as he went. But nothing—Droehk, Scyth, or spawn of Hell—nothing was going to touch this woman.

Slowly, he let her body glide over his until her feet touched the floor. Her heat burned through the clothes they still wore, and his blood surged in response, turning the careful man into a mindless beast.

Her mouth found his neck then, and she nipped his flesh

before suckling in the hollow below his jaw.

"Damn, Lina." His rough voice told her how much he liked what she was doing, and she moaned in response.

"You've got to get this off." He tugged on the knotted tie at her hip.

When he had no luck with the knot, he changed plans, turning to deposit her on the bed. Against the white quilt, her hair fanned out in streams of gold.

Gently now, he gripped outside her ankles, holding her in place when she would have moved. "What are you..." she began, but Cade shook his head and grinned.

Her skin was satin as he felt his way up the curve of her calves and then dipped to the back side of her thighs. The bottom of her short dress caught on his forearms, rising with him as he explored his way up.

When he made it to the sides of her breasts, she gasped and let her head loll to the side. Lips parted, breaths rasping. He teased her there for a moment before continuing up and lifting her arms with his hands under them, caressing and cherishing until the red dress slid free.

All that remained was a silk triangle, siren red like the dress.

When he flicked the button on his jeans, she made a low noise in her throat, squirming farther onto the bed.

He had to have her, had to feel every inch of his skin pressed to hers. Right now.

He took her mouth again, and the world became a blur of straining bodies and whispered promises. Stroking a hand over her hip, he grabbed the back of her thigh and hiked her leg up. He settled himself against her heat and waited . . . just there.

Lina bowed her back as pleasure flared between her thighs. She couldn't stop. She couldn't think.

And she didn't care.

In a flash, the rest of their clothes were gone, and all she could feel, see, or smell was Cade. His palm roamed up and over one hip, making her dizzy with desire.

She started to let her head fall back, but she wanted to see his eyes when he took her, wanted to lose herself in winter's gray. Overtaken by the powerful man who held her in his arms.

One of her hands gripped his hair while the other curled around his strong arm. When she offered him a devilish smile and lifted her body, he answered her by driving deep, filling her as only a true lover could.

Cade held himself still and rasped out a breath before moving within her, long slow strokes that made her crazy with need. Every time he came back was another thrilling burst of pleasure, pushing every nerve in her body to a tingling edge.

This time, she did let her head fall back, and Cade used that wicked mouth on her neck, then scalded a trail up to her lips again. She could hear him whispering but couldn't make out the words, blinded by the passion his kisses aroused.

Waves of pleasure began to build and broke over her in a shattering climax.

Cade arched his back, releasing a roar as he followed.

They lay entwined together as their heartbeats slowed, touching and kissing gently, tracing each other's bodies as if they couldn't get enough. Eventually, Cade rolled to his back with Lina captured by his arm.

She lay on his shoulder, eyes closed, lips slightly parted, and moonlight falling on her beautiful face.

In the stillness and quiet, Cade simply watched. For so long, he'd been running away from his past, but now he was running toward a future. Toward a life built around her.

He leaned down and kissed her ear. "Lina?"

Snuggling closer, she gave a tired little whimper.

"Lina," he tried again. He waited a moment but only heard the sound of breaths, slowing, deepening.

She'd fallen asleep, her cheek on his shoulder, her hand on his chest. Trailing his free hand down her silken arm, he leaned down to breathe in her scent.

Then he released a sigh and settled against her. He had things to tell her. Things he needed to say.

"But tomorrow will be soon enough," he said, kissing the top of her head and holding her tight. "We can talk tomorrow."

29

"You ready to go?" Lina walked up to the bookstore counter where Cassidy stood opening a box.

"Mm-hm, just one sec." With a sound of delight, Cassidy held up a shimmery bookmark with a scene depicting fairies. "Isn't it pretty? We just got in a whole line of them. And look." She rotated the bookmark side to side, so the fairies' wings fluttered.

"I think I need one," Lina said.

"We'll have them on display by tomorrow. Easier to see the different pictures that way."

"Sold."

"Please, girl. It's on the house."

"I might want five."

"In that case," Cassidy patted her chest, "you make my merchant's heart flutter." She turned and spoke to Daniel who stood nearby. "I'm heading out. You good?"

"All good," he said with a huge smile.

Once they were outside, Lina said, "He seemed extra chipper."

"As he should." Cassidy nodded back toward the store. "I followed your lead and made him the manager. He's full-time now."

"It's a big bite. I know." Lina pursed her lips. "I have to say, though, once I did that with Bex, I not only had the time I needed for Maiden business, but I'm getting so much more drudge work done at the café."

"Yeah. I definitely needed more time to work on advertising and events and just general running of the store, and now . . ."

"You wonder why you didn't do it sooner."

"Exactly." Cassidy reached into her purse for her car keys. "So what's this new discovery Arik's made? Any idea?"

"Nope." Lina stepped carefully down the cement steps leading to the alley below. "Just that he's found something important."

"Maybe it's a lead on one of the texts. There are four out there, after all."

"Let's hope." Lina lifted her face to the afternoon breeze, the air thick with the scent of magnolias. As she walked with Cassidy down the cobblestone drive, a couple was coming uphill from the other direction.

When they drew near, she smiled at them. They looked like twins, both dressed in similar black clothing and with pitch-black hair, except for the pure white framing their faces.

The man glowered straight ahead, but the woman stared at Cassidy, tracking her with her dark eyes as they passed. With her gaze still locked on Cassidy, she wiggled her fingers.

Lina would swear she heard the sound of bells. Tiny bells. Faerie-size bells.

Glancing over, she noticed the woman wore silver rings on both hands, but could they be the source of the sound?

Once far enough away, Cassidy and Lina exchanged a look. "Weird, huh?" Cassidy said. "Did you hear a tinkling noise?"

"Yeah." Lina laughed as Cassidy clicked the fob to unlock the car doors. "But this is Savannah, and you never know what you'll see with the art students."

"True." Cassidy climbed in and fastened her seat belt. She pushed the button to start the car but paused, angling her head to the side and shaking as if she had water in her ear.

"You okay?"

"Yeah. Just a weird tickle." She rubbed the offending ear for a moment, and then backed out of the parking space.

The ride to Arik's house took about ten minutes, typical for this time of day with all the downtown workers trying to get out of the city. When they pulled up to park, Lina spotted Cade's vehicle already at the curb.

They exited Cassidy's car and Lina met Cade at the sidewalk, going up on her toes for a quick kiss.

"I missed that this morning," he said. "You slipped out on me."

"Bakery prep time comes early, and I didn't want to wake you." She took his hand. "You need sleep for that creative mind of yours."

His only answer was another kiss, one that lingered a second or two longer than the first.

"Hey, Cade," Cassidy said, walking toward the house.

"Hey." He put his hand on the small of Lina's back as they followed. "By the way, I fed Remi this morning. He seemed pretty hungry."

Lina scoffed. "I bet he did."

"What do you mean?"

Cassidy rang the lion's-head doorbell as they waited.

"What I mean," Lina explained, "is that you got taken. I fed him before I left."

"So I guess I didn't need to give him treats or one of those little milk-in-a-cup things either."

Lina released a mocking laugh. "Taken for the whole ride." She sent Cade a sidelong glance. "I see we need a primer on the sneaky ways of cats."

"Might be a good idea." He squeezed her around the waist. "Since I plan on being around for a long time."

Lina rubbed her cheek on his shoulder just as the door opened with Bryn on the other side. "Hey, come in." Arik's puppy stuck her golden head through Bryn's ankles and barked at them.

"Hey, Poppy," Cassidy said, rubbing the dog between its ears before easing in and taking the glass of tea from Bryn's hand. She took a sip and sent her a mischievous grin. "Thanks. You should have a drink yourself."

"I thought I was." One hand on her hip, Bryn raised her brows at Cassidy.

Cassidy offered the glass back, but Bryn side-stepped away. "I don't want your cooties." With that she darted toward the parlor, chortling as Cassidy followed at a brisk pace but careful not to spill the tea. The puppy shot off like a streak, high-pitched yips echoing as she joined the fun.

Rae appeared from the opposite corridor. "Hi, guys. You can go on back to the library. You want a drink or anything?"

Lina looked at Cade before saying, "We're fine."

"Okay. I think I'll get some coffee." She crossed the vestibule, tossing back, "See you in a minute."

Lina and Cade headed in the other direction. By now Lina knew her way around the house, taking each twist and turn through paneled halls. Soon, she caught a clean ocean-breeze scent and knew Marit had lit some candles.

The double doors of the library stood open, revealing Peyton, Arik, and Marit gathered around the large desk near the fireplace.

"Marit," Lina said, surprised and pleased. "You're standing." Arik's mother had both hands on the desk for support but was up on her own two feet.

"As of this morning," she said with a smile. "Although, I can only manage a few minutes at a time. Speaking of which." She tapped Arik's forearm, and he rolled the wheelchair close enough for her to sit.

"They've found something good." Peyton's expression brimmed with excitement. She tapped her finger on a large book sitting in the middle of Arik's desk. "But they won't tell me what."

"You'll learn everything soon enough." Arik put his hand on the cover when she tried to lift it. "See?" he added when the other Maidens filed into the library followed by Mahalia. "Everyone's here, so we can start."

"I never said patience was a particular virtue of mine." Peyton winked at Lina as she walked out from behind the desk.

Leaning against a column, Bryn crossed her arms. "Don't feel bad. They wouldn't tell me anything, either."

"We just thought you should all hear this at once, as a team."

"Good thinking, coach." Cassidy teased Arik as she chose a chair and angled toward him and Marit.

Lina glanced at her friend to share in the joke but frowned when she saw Cassidy bend her head forward and shake it again, as if her ear still bothered her.

Hands rubbing, Arik waited for the others to gather around, Rae and Mahalia taking seats while Peyton and Bryn remained standing. Lina pulled Cade to the sofa to sit, so Arik could begin.

She sensed a particular energy in the room, a buzz of anticipation. Even little Poppy danced and yipped until Rae patted her leg and called the pup over.

Arik took up an orator's stance and picked up a journal. "So this, as you know, is part of my father's collection. This morning, my mother translated a large segment that covered a specific language, a very old language."

"The oldest," Marit said, rolling herself to the side of the desk where she could be clearly seen. "It's known as the Dark Speak."

"The Dark Speak," Bryn repeated, brow furrowed. "That doesn't sound good."

"It sounds like exactly what it is." Arik paused, scratching his chin as he chose his words. "The Dark Speak was used to make the seal that locked the original gate. It's a language created by blending mystical words used by the first Maidens," he took a deep breath, "and those of the world's oldest demons."

Lina and Cade shared a glance, and Peyton shuffled her weight from one foot to the other. But no one spoke.

Arik turned and picked up a different book, this one much larger and with symbols embossed on its black cover. "The journal had instructions on where to find this. I had to dig up a spot in the back yard where it's been hidden in an airtight box for over a century."

"My late husband's grandfather buried the book for safekeeping," Marit explained. "So we'd have it when the time came." She looked at them but with a faraway gaze. "My husband never even told me."

"That's how valuable this book is." Arik held it up for them to see. He needed both hands to heft the ancient tome. "It holds the language and all the spells created by the original Maidens and Huktai."

"The Huktai made spells?" Cassidy asked, tugging on her earlobe.

"Yes. My ancestors have always been scholars and scribes, and only later did they become warriors." Arik set the heavy book on the desk. "Over the years, they had researched and recorded various incantations. When the time came, they reworked the spells for the Maidens. You see," he drew a long breath, "the Dark Speak can only be used by certain people. Those descended from the Huktai, and the Maidens themselves."

"And demons?" Bryn asked.

Arik inclined his head. "I'm afraid so."

Tapping her foot on the tile floor, Bryn studied the book, the encyclopedia of demon-magick. "Can I see?"

"Of course. It's meant for all of you." Arik stepped to the side, allowing her to ease into the chair behind the desk.

"Can we hear a word or two?" Lina asked, sitting forward on the sofa.

Bryn looked at Arik and his mother for permission. Marit pressed her lips together in thought, and then she nodded. "Just a few. This language was destined to be yours, yours to master and control," she said, "but we should proceed carefully."

"We understand," Rae said, catching Bryn's eye. "Not too much."

"Right." Using both hands, Bryn tucked her dark hair behind her ears, opened the book, and cleared her throat. "*Throak mava oso nesh.*"

She stopped abruptly and scooted back from the desk. "I don't . . ." She motioned for Arik to step back in. "Can you close that? I feel . . . I don't know. *Something.*"

Cade leaned forward, his body rigid. Lina grabbed his hand. "It's okay," she whispered, unsettled by his reaction.

"This is to be expected." Voice calm and soothing, Marit cast her steady gaze to each of them. "Every word has power. Bryn only read a few and felt their strength."

"And I'm not sure I liked it." Bryn strode to stand next to Peyton, halfway across the room from the book.

"To unlock the full potential of your magick, you will all need to learn this language." Arik closed the black cover. "Without it, you'll never defeat Searenn or the horde of beasts she'll summon. But these are strong incantations. They incorporate the darkest of magicks, and you can never forget that."

"*Throak mava oso nesh.*" Cassidy spoke in a harsh whisper, drawing everyone's attention.

Bryn rubbed her arms as if chilled. "I wouldn't do too much of that."

As if she hadn't heard the warning, Cassidy began to rock back and forth in her seat. "*Throak mava oso nesh.*"

"Cassidy?" Peyton moved in from behind and touched her friend's shoulder.

Jolted, Cassidy leapt to her feet and turned, ramming her leg into the arm of her chair as she stumbled toward the bookshelves. "Stop it!" she screamed, clapping a hand over her ear.

"Stop what?" Peyton froze in a hands-up position.

"Oh, no." Lina stood, watching as Cassidy rubbed the side of her head. An image of the strange woman outside the bookstore filled her vision. "That girl."

"What girl?" Cade asked from beside her.

Lina shook out her hands and turned to Rae. "There were two people outside of the bookstore when Cassidy and I left to come here. I didn't think anything of it, but she wore some sort of rings on her fingers . . . maybe with bells or chimes."

Lina flinched when Cassidy sank to the floor. "Cassidy's ear has been bothering her ever since."

"Sound can be a conduit," Mahalia said, standing with a swish of her colorful skirt. "That girl could have placed some sort of hex or spell on her."

"But Cassidy didn't freak out until I used the Dark Speak." Bryn looked to Marit. "Could those words have done something to her?"

"They shouldn't have." Marit shook her head vigorously. "But if this woman cast an enchantment on Cassidy . . . I just don't know." She waved her hands. "Arik, give me the book."

Cassidy groaned as if tormented by something none of them could see.

Marit stared at the open book. "Damn it. We shouldn't have been so careless." Flipping a page, she began reading, mouthing the words to herself.

Seeing the normally serene Marit so upset shook Lina to her core. "I should have realized. I should have known when she kept trying to shake something away."

"It's not your fault." Cade took her shoulders and forced her to look at him. "You didn't do this."

Cassidy rose to her feet again, gripping random books on the shelves and screaming against the rows of covers. *"Throak mava oso nesh."*

"Cassidy, stop." Peyton rushed over and put a hand on her back.

Whirling around, Cassidy knocked Peyton's arm away, but then latched on to her wrist. *"Throak mava oso nesh!"* Her features were a hard mask of fury, her pupils dilated so that barely any of the crystal-blue remained.

She looked possessed.

"No," Bryn murmured, shaking her head. "Not again."

Poppy howled and scurried under a footstool.

"Cassidy, let go." Peyton tried to pull away, her boots shoving against the tiles, but Cassidy had clamped on like a vise.

Leaning back, Peyton tried to free herself. "I feel strange. I'm starting to get angry, and I don't know why." Clearly afraid, she looked at them for help. "Rae?"

"Cassidy, stop." Rae lifted her hands, the violet of her Akasha power lighting her palms. "Maybe I can bring her back."

But then Cassidy's hands started to glow, the bright blue of water. *"Meskahna,"* she croaked. A new and unknown word.

"Is she speaking the language?" Bryn asked, her head whipping back and forth between Arik and Marit. "What do we do?"

"Get off!" Peyton grimaced and shut her eyes. "Somebody stop her!"

Rae surged forward, but Arik blocked her and held her back. "No. We can't risk all of you going under."

"Try this." Marit's hands shook. She swallowed hard and said, *"Mera mivahn soya."*

"Mera Mivahn—" Rae began.

"That won't work." Cade cut her off, his voice hard.

Stunned, Lina turned to him, his expression tense, his muscles rigid. "What are you talking about?"

Without answering, Cade strode across the room to Cassidy and Peyton, both still locked together by Cassidy's death grip.

As the others watched in shock, Cade moved in close and grabbed Cassidy's head, pressing the heels of his palms to the bottom of her skull. Leaning in, he spoke in her ear. "*Revteresk nazgha orvis.*"

Releasing Peyton, Cassidy dropped her arms instantly to her sides. She leaned back against Cade as if drained of energy.

"*Revteresk nazgha orvis,*" he said again, guiding her gently to the floor.

"How did you know to do that?" Rae gaped at him, relieved but confused. They all were.

Bryn hurried over and kneeled by Cassidy.

But Lina simply stood there, her head filling with the sound of denial. Static drowned everything out, as if she didn't want to think. As if she didn't want to understand what had just happened.

"Yes, how *did* you know?" Arik repeated Rae's question in a harsh voice. His entire persona changed and, for the first time, Lina saw the warrior emerge.

Arik scowled at Cade. "We just discovered this language today, yet somehow you're fluent?"

"I can explain." Cade left Cassidy with her head in Bryn's lap. He looked only at Lina. "I promise you, it's not what you think."

Arik clenched his jaw. "You son of a bitch."

"Lina, please." Cade held out his hands.

"No. It's not possible." Lina's head pounded, refusal roared through her veins. But she couldn't stop the truth from breaking through.

She stared at Cade, and her heart gave a hard kick. "You're a Scyth."

30

The world shuddered beneath Lina's feet. She studied Cade like she'd never seen him before. "But you can't be. You can't be one of them."

"I'm not." Still reaching out, he took a step toward her.

Lina took a step back. Her stomach dropped and her throat constricted. Everything she'd known of him now carried a shadow, a darker version of the truth she thought she'd known.

"You used me." She put a hand to her stomach as the weightless feeling twisted, changing to a throb in her chest. An ache in her heart. "You used me to get close to the Watchtower Maidens."

"A goddamned spy," Arik seethed, his shoulders tensing and eyes black with rage.

"Arik," Marit called out, "stay calm."

Mahalia now stood next to the wheelchair, ready to guard the other woman.

"No. I swear." Cade held out placating arms. "Just think back, Lina. I'd been coming to the café for months, and I asked you out before you got your symbol. *Before* you were a Maiden."

"That doesn't mean anything." Still on the floor, Bryn's voice was quiet, her body still. But betrayal roiled behind the cool demeanor. "You could have known about Arik for years. For all we know, you followed him to Rae and then to me. Lina is my best friend, so you started up with her."

Easing out from under Cassidy, Bryn rose to stand. "You

just got lucky when she became a Maiden, too."

"You wormed your way right in," Arik said, brows clashing. "And now you know everything we know."

"I can't believe this." Lina dropped her head and rubbed her sternum, trying to ease the sting. Emotions crashed over her in an avalanche—pain, loss, anger. But disillusionment was somehow worst of all.

She'd fallen in love.

She'd fallen for a lie.

I must have been so easy. Stars in my eyes and my heart for the taking. She'd finally found the perfect man for her perfect life, choosing to overlook the shadows in his stare.

Now she could see them all too clearly.

"Your cousin," she said with a scoffing laugh. "Ryker's a Scyth, too." She clapped her palms to her temples. "I'm such an idiot."

"Lina, no," Cade said sternly. "Don't you think that."

"You've had time to tell her." Peyton flanked Bryn to stand with her in front of the still unconscious Cassidy.

Lina's mind raced to make sense of what everyone was saying, but the aggressive posture made the situation clear. Between the Maidens and Arik, there were six of them to his one. Not to mention whatever Voodoo tricks Mahalia might whip out.

But Cade was a Scyth. He'd trained and fought his entire life. And his single mission was to destroy the Maidens.

"She's right." Lina spoke softly but pierced Cade with her glare. "You had time to tell me the truth. But you didn't."

"Because he's a murderous Scyth," Arik said, his neck corded with tension.

"I'm not, damn it." Cade started to move toward her, but everyone shifted in response. They would put themselves between him and Lina to protect her.

Because they knew she was already injured.

And I'm the one who did that, Cade thought. *I'm the one who hurt her.*

Now I'm going to lose her.

"Lina, I've told the truth, just not the whole truth." Cade leaned forward slightly but stayed where he was. "I wanted you to know me for who I am, and everything I said about my family was true. I just left out specifics."

"You think?" Bryn said with a snarl.

Cade stayed focused on Lina. He wouldn't stop. He wouldn't give up. "Lina, you know how I feel about my father. I want nothing to do with his lifestyle."

"Lifestyle?" Arik thundered, waving his arm to encompass the women around him. "You mean the part about killing them? That's a lifestyle choice?" He raised his fist. "Get the fuck out of my house. No, better yet. You're not going anywhere."

Arik shook off Rae's arm where it still rested on his and strode to a panel between bookcases. He touched the side, and the whole section of wall rotated, revealing his sword hanging on the wood with several other weapons.

"Arik, don't." Rae walked to the center of the group, placing herself nearest Cade. "This stops now. Cade, you need to go."

"I won't leave. I can help."

"By putting a blade in their hearts?" Arik held a sword in his hand and death in his eyes.

Cade ignored him. Nothing scared him more than the thought of a life without Lina. He couldn't let her face this without him by her side. If she died, a part of him would, too.

"Lina, tell me about the bells and the people you saw."

"What?" She whirled away, thrusting a hand in his direction. "I can't do this now."

"The Scyths aren't your only enemies." Cade kept speaking, determined to make her listen. To make any of them listen. "There are other magicks out there, and I've spent most of my life being educated on the history of the Maidens and the

Droehks. But I left all that behind years ago. Hell, I didn't even believe most of it."

He gestured harshly toward Arik and his sword. "I know it's all true now, and the past I tried to leave behind has returned, threatening everything that's important to me. *You* are important to me, Lina."

Exasperated, Cade ran a hand through his hair. He turned to Arik. "If Huktai defected all those years ago to become Scyths, why isn't it possible that I have my own beliefs? That I want nothing to do with my family?" He held the other man's angry stare. "Because I think they're murderers, too."

Arik never wavered, still holding his sword at the ready. "I can't take that risk."

"I handled this all wrong, and I'm sorry," Cade said. "I am so damned sorry. But I needed to earn your trust first. All of you. I needed you to *know* me. What would any of you have said if I'd told you before?"

Arik's tone was low with menace. "You know what would have happened."

Bryn walked around Cade then, putting her fingers on the blade Arik held and pushing the tip toward the floor.

After holding Arik's gaze, she spun around to Cade. "No matter what you say right now, you know you have to leave. Put yourself in our position."

"Bryn," Cade began, but she sliced upward with one hand.

"You've done enough damage, and you'd be smart to go before we change our minds. Before we decide not to *let* you go."

Cade studied Bryn and Arik. He saw the resistance in the way they stood, their loathing for his deception. He wouldn't get anywhere with them right now.

Hoping for one more try, he retreated from the two of them and faced Lina.

She stood there, arms crossed, refusing to even look at him.

Her anger ripped at Cade's heart.

He should have woken her up last night and told her when it was just the two of them. He should have held her in his arms, looked into her eyes, and explained.

He should have told her that he loved her.

As he slowly made his way across the room, Lina angled toward him. Hope flared briefly in his chest, and then she spoke.

"Get out," she said, her tone flat and empty. "And don't come near me again."

31

Searenn ended the call and shoved the phone in her back pocket, furious with the darkheart twins. Especially that little bitch Dacia.

Even the warm sun on Searenn's face couldn't lift her mood.

The twins had acted against the Maidens without her permission. Even if their little spell worked, they needed to understand who was in charge, and what would happen to them if they pissed her off.

She imagined the demon she would conjure when she got back home, a perverse little creature who inflicted pain in the most imaginative and sadistic ways. Yes, that would make good entertainment for her homecoming.

She might even fuck the brother while his sister screamed.

Unfortunately, that pleasure would have to wait, because the text was the priority now.

Heat pulsed off the old stone walls, forged centuries ago to protect everything within. Around her people pointed, laughed, and took endless pictures. The sheer number of them made Searenn want to lash out and slice a few noisy throats.

She preferred the dark, when more than wind stirred in the shadows. So she'd go tonight, avoiding the sweaty tourists packed in like cattle.

With a sniff of disdain for all the *humans*, she surveyed her surroundings again, the ancient city where her quest would end.

A piece of the seal was hidden inside. She could feel it calling from behind the walls.

And nothing on earth would keep her out.

32

"Two cappuccinos, one mocha latte, and an Americano." Bex set the last drinks down for Lina, Bryn, Rae, and Cassidy as they sat at one of the café tables. "And let's not forget," Bex said, placing a white tray on the table with macarons displayed in a perfect rainbow of colors.

"Bex, I love this," Lina crooned.

"Well, as my favorite boss of all time once told me, presentation matters."

Lina beamed up at her. "Why, yes, it does."

A small bell rang out in the kitchen. "Oops. Order up." With that, Bex pivoted and scurried away.

Cassidy lifted her nose in the air and got a dreamy look on her face. "*Mmm*. I don't know what Manny's making back there, but it smells divine."

"Would you like something else?" Lina asked.

"No, I'm stuffed." Cassidy rubbed her belly. "And now I remember why I can only come in here once a month. But if Peyton isn't here in five minutes, I might grab another croissant."

Bryn paused with a lavender macaron halfway to her mouth. "Everything really is great."

"I agree," Rae said, licking foam from her lips and grinning. "We should make this our second official hangout." She raised a brow at Lina. "But you have to let us pay."

Lina waved the comment away. "Family always eats for

free." And wasn't that what these women had become? Her extended family. Her sisters.

She caught Cassidy's grimace, and so did Rae, who reached out and touched Cassidy's shoulder. "Hey, you okay?"

Cassidy nodded and patted her stomach. "Too full for comfort," she joked. "But I know what you mean, and I'm fine. I'm better than fine, so you can all stop worrying. I haven't had any strange feelings or the desire to attack anyone. Whatever Cade said to me really worked."

She cringed and shot her gaze to Lina. "I'm sorry. I shouldn't have brought him up."

"Don't be sorry." Lina sipped her own cappuccino, hoping to cover the quick stab of hurt she felt at the mention of his name. Like a tiny dart hitting the bullseye of her heart.

"It's been three days," she said with a forced tranquility. "I've had time to cry, eat ice cream, binge-watch the Gilmore Girls." She grabbed another macaron, in solidarity with the junk food queens of television. "And cry some more."

Cassidy rubbed her arm in a show of sympathy and support. "Have you heard from him?"

"A couple of missed calls." Lina shrugged in the silence that fell. "I think I'll have to talk to him at some point."

Bryn set her coffee down with a *clunk*. "Why?"

"Because he was right about one thing." Lina sat back in her chair and sighed. "He's spent his life studying the history of the Watchtower Maidens."

"So he knows how to kill us."

"Exactly." Lina met her friend's irritated stare. "He understands things from the perspective of a Scyth. Things that might help us."

"But—"

"Lina's right," Rae said, drawing a stunned expression from her niece. "Now that we know about his past, and we're not as emotionally charged, we should consider talking to him." She turned to Lina. "But all of us. Together."

"Safety in numbers," Cassidy murmured.

Lina bobbed her head as that dart pulled free and left a sting. She had a hard time thinking of Cade as dangerous. A man capable of hurting her? Of ripping out her heart? Yes.

But as an actual physical threat? No. Neither her heart nor her mind could go there. Despite what he'd done, she had to believe he was a good and decent man.

Just a liar with ties to an organization determined to kill her.

The hurried sound of someone's approach pulled Lina from her troubling thoughts.

"Sorry. Sorry." Peyton seemed out of breath. "My parent-teacher meeting ran late." She grabbed a couple of macarons. "But I'm ready when you are."

"Here you go." Bex appeared with a carry-out cup in her hand. "A macchiato, right? That's your drink?"

"Yes, thanks." Peyton took the cup and sipped. "Oh, that's good. You're an angel, Bex. A coffee angel."

"Hey, I like that." Bex toyed with a green streak of her hair. "Maybe we should make T-shirts."

Peyton swallowed the macaron in her mouth and said, "I'd buy one."

"Cool." Bex looked them over. "Anyone else need a drink for the road?"

Lina and the others declined, having already had at least one refill each.

"Then let's head out." Bryn stood.

"I'll check in later," Lina told Bex before strolling out with the others. They took the nearest staircase to the alley below where Rae had parked. She'd only recently purchased the hybrid SUV, a pearlescent white with a sleek body. And, of course, room enough to seat five.

After turning on to Whitaker, it was a straight shot to

Forsyth Park. There, Rae eased the car into an empty spot in front of the house, a lovely gingerbread the color of buttercream with ivy grown over the front of each step.

On the long wooden porch, Lina rang the bell. They didn't have to wait long before a tall woman with a blonde pageboy opened the door. "Ladies, hello, and please come in." She stepped aside and motioned for Rae and the others to enter.

After introductions were made all around, Mrs. Pelham clasped her hands and said, "I'm so sorry, but I'm afraid we'll have to cut this short. My daughter won't be able to pick up my grandson from soccer practice today, and I'm her emergency backup." She pressed her lips together. "I'd planned to offer you drinks and have a nice visit. You're welcome to come back tomorrow if you'd like, or we can get down to business now."

"Now would be better," Rae said. "If you're sure that's all right."

"Absolutely. I don't need to leave for another twenty minutes or so. I just feel like such a bad hostess."

"Not at all." Lina could see the woman was embarrassed that she had to leave earlier than planned. "It's kind of you to meet with us and let us view your collection."

She gave Lina a grateful smile. "I've printed a copy of the list as well. It's in my office. This way."

With brisk steps, she guided them down the center hallway to a door at the end. "And here we are."

As soon as she stepped inside, Lina could see a difference between Mrs. Pelham's collection and that of Mr. Clermont. The chamber stretching before them featured more artistic pieces created for beauty and fewer of the military items the older man preferred.

Paintings adorned every wall, and glass-enclosed shelves or cases displayed delicate items. Lina recognized a Royal Bann hand-painted vase on a stand in one corner and a hand-carved cuckoo clock on the fireplace mantle.

As she and the other Maidens studied the beautiful antiques, Mrs. Pelham disappeared into a room near the back. She returned with a piece of paper in her hand and offered it to Rae. "You're welcome to have a look around, although I must tell you, I don't have anything similar to what Mr. Clermont said you were interested in seeing."

Each of the women turned to her with disheartened expressions.

"No stone tablet or fragment of any kind?" Cassidy asked, doing her best to hide her disappointment.

"I'm sorry, no. There *are* some things that have been in storage for over a decade. I don't remember seeing the item you describe, but the list names everything sold to my grandfather by Mr. Wesley."

"Thank you," Rae said. "I'll look it over."

"All right. Since we don't have much time, I'll just let you look around. I'll be in my office if you need anything." Mrs. Pelham returned to the adjoining room, leaving them to peruse at their leisure.

Bryn, Cassidy, and Peyton spread out to search every shelf and sideboard in the event the text had been overlooked somehow. But in the clean and organized space, Lina didn't hold out much hope.

She stayed behind, watching as Rae scrutinized the list from top to bottom, and then did it again. She looked no less defeated after the second pass.

"Nothing?" Lina asked.

Rae shook her head.

Hearing their exchange, Bryn came over from the glass case she'd been examining. "So what do we do now?"

"I don't know." Rae dropped her arms, the paper still in one hand. "I just don't know."

"Guys," Peyton called out but not too loudly. She stood stock-still, gazing at the wall at the other end of the room. A large cabinet blocked them from seeing whatever she was gaping at.

As one, the four of them joined her to find a large oil painting hung on the wall. Muted tones depicted a landscape, a small country church and forest in the background. Bright morning light rose up from behind the trees.

"Oh," Bryn uttered as they all simply stared.

A cemetery was in the forefront of the picture, with a singular headstone large enough to read.

Moira Wesley
1896-1947

Though my sun has set,
remember my sunshine

"My sun has set," Peyton whispered.

Lina blew out gently. "My sunshine." She recalled the afternoon tea service with the older woman who'd seemed so confused. "That's what Cliff Wesley's mother was trying to tell us. She understood. She knew who we were and what we were looking for."

"She just couldn't say the words." Cassidy sounded sad.

"Look at the dates." Rae pointed. "Maybe this was Mrs. Wesley's grandmother. She must have hidden the text to keep it safe. Or, well, *someone* did."

Bryn leaned in closer and asked in a low voice, "So . . . does this mean what I think it means?"

"Yes." Rae crossed her arms as she stared at the painting. "Another trip to a graveyard."

33

They waited until dark. As the last of the gloaming's purple light faded, Lina and the Maidens stood with Arik in a gravel lot. The moon hung low in the sky as spring peepers serenaded with their sweet, froggy song.

"Pine Rest Baptist Church." Rae studied the small clapboard building, erected in 1908 but still in almost pristine condition. Lovingly attended by its flock for years.

"Good thing there's only one, or we might have had trouble finding it." Arik notched his head toward the wooden sign with the church's name, and then moved to the trunk of the car where he retrieved three shovels and his sword in its scabbard.

"Let me help," Lina said, taking one of the tools. They'd decided the more diggers working, the faster the job would be done. Graveyards were no place to spend time, not in the dark when both man and monster might be on the prowl.

"I feel bad digging up someone's grave," Peyton said, "but I have to believe this is what she'd intended all along."

"Moira Wesley?" Cassidy asked, her steps gliding in a silky rustle across the grass. "I think she must have. And her children probably had a hand in burying the text, because someone in the family obviously passed the secret down."

"Cliff clearly didn't know anything about it," Bryn said, "but I'm willing to bet his sister did."

"That's right." Lina nodded and turned aside to her friend as they walked. "The sister that was killed unexpectedly in a car accident. Before she ever told Cliff."

"She didn't trust her own brother?"

Peyton chuckled lightly. "No, it wasn't her brother she didn't trust. It was the gold digger he was married to."

A light round of laughter trickled through them as they remembered Cliff's mother and her abhorrence of her daughter-in-law.

Rae stopped and gestured to the gravestone sitting farthest away, close to the tree line. "I think that's it." The forest had grown since the picture had been painted, and oaks now shrouded the cemetery with their long, crooked limbs.

Arik dropped one of the shovels he carried beside the grave and paused. "I hope this is what you wanted," he said to the marker, "and I hope you'll forgive us."

"That was nice," Cassidy whispered to Lina.

"It was." Lina stepped closer, still holding her shovel. She positioned herself in what she estimated to be the center of the burial mound while Arik remained near the headstone.

"I have a feeling." Bryn took the last shovel to start near the feet. "I think it's here."

Lina drew a deep breath, because she knew exactly what Bryn meant. A light pulse emanated from beneath the earth. The text. It was sending out a signal only they could hear.

"We'll keep watch," Rae said, glancing to Peyton and Cassidy. Her tone seemed suddenly ominous as clouds covered the moon and sank them all into darkness.

Without another word, they began to dig.

~~~

Searenn's boots scudded softly on the rough stone, the streets silent and empty in the middle of the night. High walls rose before her, but she passed them by, heading straight for the huge carved entrance and doors tucked within.

The letters MVSEI VATICI were etched in the stone above. Vatican Museum. Even she had to admit it was an ingenious place to hide the text. The whole of Vatican City had a fortress quality, meant to protect the treasures within. But those safeguards had been created for mere mortals.

Not a resurrected queen of the damned.

The doors opened for her with a heavy swing, and she entered to gleaming floors polished to a sheen. A spiraling walkway circled up, but she had no interest in museum exhibits. Sarcophagi and frescos were for all to see, but what she sought lay far away. Far below.

Now that she was so close, the ancient piece of stone pulsed, summoning her like a heartbeat. All she had to do was follow its call.

She discovered a service stairwell soon enough, but a nighttime guard exited the door before she could open it. Based on his uniform, he was a member of the Gendarmerie Corps of Vatican City.

"Go about your business," Searenn said, reaching deep into his mind. "You did not see me."

He blinked twice beneath black, bushy brows and veered around her without comment.

Slipping inside, Searenn took the stairwell down two floors until she spied a hallway through a door's square window. The pull of the text was strong here.

The design down below was plain and clean, only for utility purposes. She strolled the maze of hallways, finally reaching a set of metal doors with key-card access. A wave of her hand, and she was through.

The increase in security was immediately apparent, with every door locked and cameras scanning every corridor. Two more guards sat at a station at the far end of one hall—younger, stronger, and sterner than the one she'd seen before.

She'd found an entrance to the Vatican archives.

They stood quickly when they saw her. "*Fermari. Tu chi sei?*" one of them barked, his hand settling on the gun at his hip.

"*Mi scusi*," Searenn said with a sharp smile. Before drilling her power into their brains.

Both men dropped to the floor, blood oozing from every orifice. Though humans posed little threat, she'd rather be certain they couldn't raise an alarm. Not when she was this close.

The cameras, however, were another issue. She covered herself with a cloaking spell and hoped the dead guards weren't noticed any time soon.

With a casual stride, she pushed through the doors and found herself in a clean storage area. Rows and rows of white cabinets stood on each side, each with thin drawers for housing rarities.

The pulse of the text drew her forward, through the storeroom to a second large chamber. Here, paintings hung on rows of metal racks, all kept safe behind hermetically sealed glass.

She kept going from space to space, past tapestries and sculptures and other large items. Finally, she entered an area that looked more like a warehouse, a vast chamber filled with crates and boxes.

Huge metal shelves lined the room, but many containers sat bunched in groups on the cement floor. A section near the back drew Searenn's attention. She crossed the room stiffly, anticipation thrumming in every cell.

Her gaze landed on a small crate. No markings. No tags. No stickers. Nothing to declare what was inside.

But Searenn knew.

This was it. Her quest complete. She eased closer, eagerly rubbing fingers against palms.

She'd found the first aethyrical text.

34

They'd cleared almost three feet of soil when Arik's shovel struck with a metallic *whunk*! Lina and Bryn stopped digging. "You hit something," Bryn said.

"And it didn't sound like a coffin." Rae edged in closer and kneeled, tugging on gardening gloves she'd pulled from a pocket. Using her hands, she scraped dirt away from the spot where Arik had made contact.

It took her a couple of minutes but, at last, she uncovered one corner of an old metal box. Arik then slid the point of his shovel beneath the container, using leverage to free it completely.

"It has to be," Cassidy whispered. "It has to be the text. Right?" she added, catching Lina's eye.

"Only one way to find out." Lina squatted next to Rae. "Go ahead and open it." The others gathered around to watch. It felt as if the whole world held its breath.

The lid resisted at first, likely rusted from decades of rain and caked-on dirt. But when it opened, the interior was surprisingly clean. A second metal box sat within, nestled by layers of burlap for cushioning.

To Lina, it looked to be about ten by ten inches in width and length, and several inches deep.

This time, the lid slid off easily, revealing more burlap. Rae gently lifted the material, only to discover it was a bag folded around itself. "It's heavy," she said, her voice wavering, from excitement or nervousness, Lina couldn't tell.

Clouds shifted in the sky again, this time showering them with silvery moonlight. And beneath that light, Rae reached in the bag.

She pulled out a jagged piece of stone.

Lina sucked in a breath. So did Bryn and Cassidy.

"It's beautiful," Peyton said, leaning down to trace her finger along the broken edge.

"And powerful." Arik put his hand on Rae's shoulder. "Even I can sense the residual magick."

For a moment, they all stared in silence. The breeze died down and the frogs grew quiet.

Rae touched a reverent hand to one of the symbols. "This is you, Bryn. It's the symbol for Air." Rae looked up at her niece, and then met the gazes of her friends. "We did it. We found a text."

"Looks like we're kind of getting our shit together," Bryn said, planting her hands on her hips as she grinned. "But now that we've got it . . ."

"Let's get it somewhere safe." Arik gave another stroke to Rae's shoulder before he started moving soil back to refill the hole. As he did, Rae folded the text back up in its bag and slid it into the backpack they'd brought along.

"I'll do this part," Cassidy said, picking up a shovel.

Peyton grabbed the other one. "Me, too. I just hope—" She stopped midsentence and turned.

They all whirled around at the sound of footsteps. Someone was running toward them.

Someone Lina recognized.

"Cade?"

Arik swung around, wielding his shovel, but Cade came to an abrupt halt, his hands raised. "They followed you, and they're coming." He shifted his gray gaze to Lina. "The Scyths are coming."

The wind kicked up and rattled the trees. Bryn stepped

forward, as if to confront Cade, but then she stared past him to lights on the road. "Looks like they're already here."

~~~

Searenn approached the crate, reaching forward with greedy hands. She used her power to loosen the lid, but grabbed the wooden edge with her fingers.

This was a crucial moment on the road to her victory. She wanted to feel the lid as it lifted away, and the rough stone texture as she grasped the text.

Using both hands, she gripped the front corners, flipping the cover off the crate.

And a scorching blast of powder erupted in her face. Roaring in pain, she stumbled back, wiping and scratching at her cheeks, her eyes, her mouth.

Grit coated her tongue. No, not grit. It tasted like . . . *ash*.

Channeling her power, she envisioned her skin healing and the pain diminishing. She waited, but relief didn't come. "What the *fuck*?"

"You didn't think it would be easy, did you?"

Searenn spun on her heel, squinting through watery eyes, and found a man in the center of the room. His dark looks were enhanced by black attire, and he walked closer, confronting her without fear.

Movement to the right drew Searenn's gaze as a second man emerged from behind a large gray container. He too wore black from head to toe.

It was then she noticed the blade in his hand.

Huktai. They had to be. But with access to the Vatican?

"You're Swiss Guard," she said. A small army trained to protect the Pope and Vatican City. The fighting elite.

Searenn narrowed her eyes, shifting her attention between her two enemies. "But you're Huktai, too."

The dark-haired man nodded. "We uphold two oaths, though one dates much farther back in time."

Older than the Catholic Church, she thought, and before a hint of a man who'd be known as "Pope."

"So what now?" she sneered. "You don't have any magick, and I'm still standing after whatever little trick you had in there." She flung a hand at the crate. The text still throbbed inside, and she wasn't leaving empty-handed.

"You can just fuck right off, because I'm taking what's rightfully mine." Summoning her hatred for those who would defend the Watchtower Maidens, Searenn drove every bit of it into the man's head. She willed his insides to turn to sludge, just as she'd done to the last two who'd stood in her way.

Seconds passed, and he was still on his feet. Not a red drop of blood in sight.

Then he smiled and pulled a star-shaped object from behind his back. As he did, the second man closed in.

"I'm taking it," she said again, forcing bravado into her voice. What was going on? Why hadn't he responded to her power? Why the hell wasn't he dead?

Reaching behind her and into the crate, she grabbed the bag inside.

Her hand lit up like fire and, this time, she shrieked from the pain. Pain mixed with an unholy rage.

"What is this?" she yelled, holding her wrist while the palm above it burned, the flesh bubbling as she watched.

"Ashes," the second man said. "From the original Maidens. Engineered into a special blend, a poison made just for you." He lifted the wicked blade in his hand. "And when this cuts your head off, you won't be coming back from the dead. Not again."

Searenn's hand was in agony and her face still burned, but she'd come here for an aethyrical text. And that's what she'd be leaving with.

An idea struck, and she whirled around, grabbing the crate itself with both hands. The one palm exploded with pain, but only from the damage she'd sustained from the bag. The crate itself was clean of that hell-forsaken ash.

She lunged to the side, ready to run for it, but a fresh burning streaked through her arm. Startled, she dropped the crate, the wood crashing to the floor and the bag spilling out.

Jerking her head toward the dark-eyed bastard, she realized he'd thrown that fucking little star at her. Probably coated in more of the powder, the dust left over from five long-dead bitches.

She stood too long wondering what to do. Another piece of fire sliced across her back, this time from Huktai number two.

Warmth streamed down her spine, and Searenn went cold. She was bleeding. *Bleeding!* For the first time since she'd returned to the world, fear squeezed her heart in its icy grip. If they could spill her blood . . .

Without hesitation, she threw herself behind a box, landing hard on her knees before gaining her feet and bolting toward a side door. She shoved her way out and raced down the hallway.

She hadn't expected this. She was unprepared. Though her pride screamed for her to fight, another voice whispered instead. A soft rasp of dire warning.

Stay, and you die.

She had no choice. She had to get out. So she could live and learn about this special breed of Huktai, the ones who had weapons she'd known nothing about.

The door banged open far behind her, so she cloaked herself and kept running. As fast as she moved, she couldn't escape one terrifying truth.

She wasn't immortal after all.

35

"Did you bring them here?" Arik demanded, glaring at the weapon slung over Cade's shoulder. He put himself between Cade and the women, anger and distrust rioting behind his eyes.

But Cade saw something else inside the man he'd come to know as a friend. Confusion. Arik was struggling to decide if he could trust him or not, and they only had minutes until the Scyths arrived.

Cade knew how they operated. They'd wreck the whole castle to kill one person inside. Ryker would be leading the men, and Cade expected a small army.

"Let me help you, Arik. I know how they fight." He glanced back as cars pulled into the lot in front of the church. "I know every tactic, every ploy. If I hadn't left, then I'd be the one leading them tonight. Most of them have known me since childhood, and I might be able to talk them down."

"But that's unlikely," Arik said, a little of the heat gone from his voice.

"Very," Cade admitted. "But I can try."

"If you turn on these women—" Arik began.

Cade held up a hand to stop him. "I'd sooner fall on my sword."

"Or mine," Arik said, assessing Cade one more time before he looked to Lina. "This should be your decision."

With his heart leaping into his throat, Cade followed Arik's gaze. Lina's unwavering stare met his.

"You lied to me," she said, releasing a breath heavy with inner conflict.

"I did, and I can never take that back."

"They're coming." Bryn moved forward to flank Arik and Rae. Cassidy and Peyton joined the frontline as well, everyone positioned several feet apart. Ready to fight.

"Lina," Cade tried, pleading with his eyes. He had so much to say, but now wasn't the time.

Lina shook her head. "I won't stop you from helping." Saying nothing more, she stepped up and joined the others.

Some of the cars in the lot had their headlights on, silhouetting trees and headstones.

And the line of men marching across the field.

Cade judged there to be about twenty Scyths, which meant another twenty lay in wait somewhere nearby.

Taking the sheath off his shoulder, he pulled out his weapon, one he'd retrieved from the navy-blue box in his office. A vicious-looking S-shaped blade, the zaquar had been gifted to him on his twelfth birthday. And was the one token he'd kept from his former life.

Now he would use it against those he'd known before, fighting a past he just couldn't outrun.

He brought the sharp edge close to his lips. Whispered a single word. And black haze swirled out from the enchanted metal.

He took up position in front of Lina, ignoring her huff of insult. The soldiers stalking their way through the graveyard would kill her without hesitation.

But not while Cade still drew breath. He would stand with Arik, he would stand with the Maidens, and he would give his life to protect Lina's.

Whether she wanted him to or not.

He couldn't stop the half-cocked smile from forming when

he heard her move up beside him, his pride flaring to see the warrior she'd become.

Turning his attention back to the approaching men, he singled out Ryker. Leading the pack, as expected. Fury twisted his features as he stopped, holding up one fist. The men following him halted as well.

Ryker studied Cade, his eyes narrowed in disgust. "Your leaving was one thing," he said in a scathing tone, "but I never thought I'd see the day you would align yourself with *them*." He almost spat the last word.

Curling his lip, he cut a sharp look to Lina, as if she shouldered the blame for Cade's defection. "Or that you'd be taken in by a demon's whore."

Cade let the offense slide right over him. He'd been playing this game longer than his cousin and knew better than to let anger take control.

"You're making a mistake, Ryker." Cade shared a glance with Arik before edging forward in time with the other man. Huktai existed to protect Watchtower Maidens, and Scyths had once been a part of the Huktai. As far as Cade was concerned, he was still part of that original brotherhood.

And like any good Huktai, he would defend his Maiden.

Ryker released a scoffing laugh. "I can't believe you would betray us." His jaw hardened as he gestured to Arik. "Betray us and plot with our enemies!"

Ryker's words were a growl as he closed in, coming face to face with Cade. "This is your last chance, your last warning." Slowly, he pulled his own curved weapon from the sheath on his back. "Fight with us, or die with them."

Cade felt a twinge of sadness that he and Ryker had come to this. "Do you really think I'll stand aside and let you cut her down?"

"You *have* to. You've prepared for this moment since you were born." Pain flashed on Ryker's face but disappeared just as quickly. "Damn you, Cade. You know the danger the Maidens pose."

"No, that's not true. Most of what we've been taught is a lie." Cade took a breath and eyed his cousin. "Killing them means destroying the only chance humanity has. The Droehk has returned, Ryker, and without the Maidens to stop her, she will open the gate. If she does that, the world will become an endless night."

"A night of horror ruled by monsters," Arik said. He lifted his shoulders. "Why would you ever fight against the Maidens?"

"Because their power comes from the DoSaa preSyajana." Ryker shifted his focus to Rae and gave her a derisive look. "They lie with demons to strengthen their magick."

"Wow." This from Cassidy as she shook her head. "Sounds like you've been given some bad information."

"You joke about this?" Ryker tensed, his muscles bulging and fingers tightening on his blade.

Cade angled himself between Ryker and Cassidy, forcing his cousin to look only at him. "Don't do this, Ryker. We can talk, just you and me. We can meet. You need to hear the truth."

His cousin's only response was another hand signal. Behind him, the Scyths took up fighting stances and pulled their weapons, blades hissing over leather like a mass of serpents.

"Ryker, don't." Cade held his livid glare, feeling the loss of his cousin like a kick to the stomach. He couldn't stop this, and his choice had been made. "I love her."

Ryker took two deep breaths, his chest heaving. Then he bellowed his rage and lifted his own zaquar.

But Cade wasn't his target.

Lunging toward Lina, Ryker swung the blade in an arc, aiming for her neck.

Cade leaped in and blocked, the clash of metal on metal ringing through the night.

With their zaquars locked together, Ryker widened his eyes.

"You would use your sacred blade to defend one of *them*?"

Cade kicked his cousin in the gut, shoving him away, and readied for the next attack. "My vow was to protect the innocent."

"Idiot." Ryker shook his head, his hard gaze tinged with regret. "Have it your way."

He raised one hand and gave the signal. Shouts erupted as the Scyths charged, twenty battle-trained men storming in for the kill.

"Don't hold back!" Cade called to the Maidens and Arik, and with weapon held high, he crouched to defend.

36

With her face and hands still stinging, Searenn stumbled from the cobbled street into a dark alley. All around her the smells of the city assaulted, the stench of humans, heat, and food. Raucous laughter rolled from three men passing by, so she sunk deeper into the gloom.

How could this have happened? How could she be vulnerable to the Huktai in any way?

She needed to return home and find the answers. She needed to heal. Defeated and anguished, she slid her back down the wall, hunching in the darkness.

And the darkness began to whisper.

Rasping voices called from beyond, turning the shadows corporeal to caress her body. They spoke of her power. They beguiled with their worship. They begged for release.

"Yes, it is time." Aroused and emboldened, she stood in one long, languid motion and raised her hands. "*Noth rakee gûl.*" An arctic wind cut through the heat as she called to the creatures of the night.

"*Maî sharat thraki-yayn.* Rise and obey." The ground quaked, as it had when she'd performed the ritual in the pit. "Rise, malkora! *Du bish šlaga neî må!*"

All around her, the blackness writhed. "Go," she ordered. "Go and find the Watchtower Maidens." Ravenous moans grew to a frenzy. The beasts had starved for far too long.

"Hunt those bitches down!" she yelled, the wind blasting as

it shrieked through the alley. "Hunt them down and feast!"

37

Lina's head reeled as chaos broke out all around her. She'd barely recovered from hearing Cade say he loved her when Ryker had attacked. With every intent to kill.

Now the entire horde of Scyths were rushing forward.

Fear brought an instant green glow of power to her palms—fear for herself, for her friends, and for Cade.

What had Ryker meant when he'd said the Maidens laid with demons? What did the Scyths think she and her friends were?

Their faction had existed for thousands of years, centuries spent dwelling on lies. While they developed a bone-deep hatred for the Maidens.

But they had it all wrong.

A giant of a man battled with Arik while Cade and Ryker still clashed with their strange, curved blades.

Lina looked to her friends. Bryn had already engaged with a Scyth, combining her martial arts with the occasional burst of magick. Rae had called her Akasha power, sending the force of her violet-hued magick at the encroaching Scyths.

"We can do this!" Lina called out to Peyton and Cassidy. The three of them had less experience with fighting for their lives than Bryn and Rae, but now they *had* to fight. They had to survive. More was at stake than the lives of the people in this cemetery. If Searenn triumphed, she would raise the Onderdâark and destroy the world.

Only the Watchtower Maidens could stop her.

Raising her hands, Lina zeroed in on a man heading straight for her. Streaks of emerald fired from her hands, hitting him in the left thigh.

Injured, the Scyth tumbled across the grass, landing hard against a headstone.

Cassidy let out a frustrated yell, charging forward to defend Rae's back. She hurled twin blasts, both the color of the deepest sea, taking down two men with their weapons raised.

From every direction, the men closed in. For every Scyth that fell to a Maiden's strike, two more poured in to take his place.

Peyton had somehow worked her way to one side, ducking and spinning to avoid assault. A Scyth came at her from the front, his blade-thrusts relentless as he evaded her shots. And with her full attention on the frontal attack, she didn't realize another Scyth had homed in.

But Lina saw him. And she had to act fast. Releasing a surge of magick, she sent out a jagged line of green. The bolt struck his weapon, and it clunked to the ground.

Holding his hand as if injured, the Scyth zeroed in on Lina. He called out a name, drawing another man's notice, then he jerked his head toward her. Together, the two men charged.

Until white and blue explosions came from both sides. Then Bryn and Cassidy spun back into action, as Lina and Peyton both did the same.

Men grunted, magick fired, and the once-peaceful country scene devolved to bedlam.

The moon's rays combined with headlights to cast the graveyard in an eerie glow. More Scyths emerged from the forest on both sides, and Lina's stomach clenched. There were so many. At least forty to their seven.

With Cade and Arik, the Maidens had been holding the enemy back. But now the number of their attackers had doubled. At some point, a Scyth's blade would land.

A blade coated in black mist.

She'd dropped another man when Arik stumbled beneath the onslaught of two Scyths.

"Arik!" Rae screamed, but she couldn't get to him. With Arik in trouble, the Scyths seemed to start coordinating, moving in when they saw a break in the line. More of them advanced, hateful eyes fixed on Rae.

They would destroy the Maidens in one bold strike.

By killing their Akasha.

"No!" Lina sent a surge of magick, fending off a man who'd come from behind her. She whirled and ducked, trying to get a clean shot to help Rae.

Arik yelled in fury, still blocking the blows from the Scyths surrounding him. He couldn't get to Rae either.

Suddenly Peyton was there, shooting power with the bright color of fire. She blasted the men fighting Arik.

But four Scyths were still coming for Rae, their weapons raised.

Bryn threw a roundhouse and left one man on the ground, but she was off to the side of the cemetery, far from Rae.

But then Bryn thrust her arms forward, her furious war cry a thing of terror. She loosed a mighty gush of wind on Rae's attackers, the blast flinging the Scyths through the air. Each of them landed with an audible *thud*.

As one, the other Maidens looked at Bryn, who'd called more than the sparkling white power of air. She'd summoned the element itself.

Many of the Scyths seemed taken aback. They glanced at each other and then back to Bryn, as if they too had been surprised.

Lina considered her friend, flashing back to that day in the library. The day Bryn had spoken the Dark Speak. She'd uttered only a few words, but could they have unlocked a new level of power? Is that how she'd tapped more deeply into her magick?

Lina's mind was still racing as she watched Bryn study her own palms. She stood in the shadow of a thick tree limb and, as Lina stared, she swore the shadow moved.

She blinked twice to clear her head, then jerked around when Cade shouted her name. Another pack of Scyths were approaching from the side. With everyone focused on the frontal assault, these men were slipping in like assassins.

Lina turned to face them. And that's when she saw another group creeping up from the woods in back. Only a few men in each cluster, but their stealth had given them an advantage.

Glancing at Cade, Lina saw him thrust his blade against Ryker's before they both exchanged heated words. She looked back to the furtive Scyths, danger closing in on two new fronts.

She could do this. She could fend them off while the others held back the bulk of Ryker's forces. Beside her, a headstone cast a long shadow. Like before, the dark throbbed, distorting as it grew longer.

Now certain she wasn't imagining things, Lina expelled a startled breath. But she tore her eyes from the ominous shadow, focusing on the men, the immediate threat.

Before they could advance farther, she tossed quick spurts of magick at the nearest group, but took out only one Scyth. *Calm down. Concentrate.* Five more men crept out from the trees.

How many soldiers had Ryker brought?

Lina's heart banged and her hands shook. She fired again, holding the brilliant emerald stream longer, making sure she made contact.

But they were running now. Coming for her.

She'd never be able to stop them all.

"Lina!" Cade called her name, but she didn't dare look back.

Pounding footsteps drew closer, and Cade threw himself in front of her. Just as the first of them came near enough to swing their blades. He blocked one and then another, cutting into one man's leg to drop him.

But a single man sprinted in, slicing Cade across his back.

Lina screamed and pumped her hands—left, right, left, right—shooting her power at any Scyth who threatened to advance.

A large shape barreled past her. *Ryker.* He was headed for Cade.

Summoning a blast, Lina took aim. But Ryker stopped with his legs apart, straddling Cade's prone form. He stood over him, barking at any Scyth who came too close. He was guarding his cousin.

Lina made a move to go, desperate to check on Cade. He'd taken a hard blow, and blood seeped through the back of his shirt.

Beside him, on the grass, a shadow moved, stretching and growing before it began to rise. As the dark solidified, a figure took shape.

A horrific blend of rot and sinew.

Horns emerged, long, strong limbs, and heavy-hooved feet. And with it came the stench of decay.

The creature stood well above Ryker, who was at least six feet tall. As he spoke to Cade, Ryker's head was down. He didn't see the demon at his back.

A distant scream of pain echoed in the night, just as the beast opened its jaw, revealing wickedly sharp fangs. The demon spread its arms above Ryker, a depthless black stare locked on its prey.

Lina flashed to the picture of Cade and Ryker, young and happy, their arms around each other.

Using both hands, she heaved a ball of magick at the monster. It's head disintegrated in a cloud of green.

Ryker twisted to look back, just in time to see the beast dissolve into a soot-colored pool. He stared, stunned, before bringing his gaze back to Lina.

More men started yelling and screaming. The battle turned to pandemonium as shadows rose all around, morphing into hideous fiends. Attacking, biting, devouring—any human within range.

The Scyths' weapons were useless against the foul creatures, slicing through decayed flesh with no effect.

At once, the Maidens locked in on the new opponents, lighting the cemetery with flashes of white, red, green, blue, and purple. Their ancient magick the only defense against this threat.

Scyths clustered together, standing back to back, confusion and shock marring their faces.

The creatures killed swiftly, clamping their jaws on soft, mortal necks. Though the Scyths fought to save their brothers, the beasts dragged several men away, their fearful cries fading as they were swallowed by shadow.

Lina and her friends continued fighting. The demons they didn't kill simply disappeared, blending again into the darkness.

Ryker called a Scyth over, speaking sternly to him as he gestured with one hand. Once the other man nodded and walked off, Ryker kneeled next to Cade.

Lina hurried to him as well, dropping to examine his wound as he lay on his side.

When Ryker picked up his weapon, Lina reared back. But he only used one sharp tip to slice away Cade's shirt. "The cut went deep. Had to have gotten his kidney." He cut more of the fabric, bunching it up and pressing it to the laceration.

Cade grunted and cursed.

"I know," Ryker muttered to Cade. Then more softly. "I know."

With Ryker giving aid, Lina moved around to face Cade, gripping his hand in hers.

Rae walked up behind Ryker with Arik at her side, still

scanning the graveyard for possible danger. "We know someone who can help," Rae told Ryker. Then to Lina, "Bryn is already on the phone with Willyn."

"Good." Relief flooded through her. She studied Ryker, his hands still pushing the balled-up shirt to Cade's back. "Our friend can heal the physical damage, but what will that black haze on your weapons do to him?"

At first Ryker didn't speak, but after a moment, he made a low, disgruntled sound in his throat and shook his head.

"Nothing," Cade croaked. "I'm . . . immune."

Ryker huffed, clearly disgusted with his cousin's need to tell all.

"And what would it do to us?" Rae asked.

Ryker only peered past her and Arik, taking stock of his men. Many bore wounds, and several had vanished.

"I have to go." He inclined his head to Cade, indicating Lina should take over holding pressure.

"I'll do that." Cassidy dropped to her knees beside Ryker so Lina could stay where she was and talk to him.

Cassidy pushed hard on the wound, drawing a surprised, "Ow," from Cade.

Flinching at his pain, Lina bent to place a kiss on his forehead.

When Ryker stood abruptly, Lina glanced up. His eyes traveled over her face, but then his glare returned, and veins bulged in his neck. "Just take care of Cade."

"Ryker." Cade reached out and grabbed his cousin's leg. "Think about what I said."

This time, Ryker didn't reply at all, only turned and stalked away, issuing orders to the remaining Scyths.

"Willyn will be here soon," Bryn reported, her phone still clutched in her hand. "She said to apply pressure and stay here if it's safe. She and Dare live on this side of Savannah, so it shouldn't take her long."

Concern brought a wrinkle to her brow as she looked down. "Hang in there, Cade."

"Thanks," Cade said, holding Bryn's stare as an unspoken apology passed between them.

Bryn nodded.

"Don't worry." Lina sat, cradling his head and stroking his hair. "Willyn will take care of you." She kissed his lips. "You asshole."

Cade chuckled and then grimaced. "I deserve that." Reaching up, he touched her face. "I'm sorry I lied. I should have trusted you enough to—"

"*Shhh*. I know. We don't have to talk about that now."

Shuddering, Lina shifted so she could meet his eyes. "You could have been killed out here."

"So could you. And that's why I had to be here." His hand slid to her throat, caressing her symbol before cupping the back of her neck. "That's why I'll always be wherever you are. You're *my* Maiden to protect."

Tugging her down, he pressed his mouth to hers. "And so much more."

She laid her cheek to his and whispered, "Did you mean what you said to Ryker?"

He got that cocky half-smile that she loved so much. "Which part?"

"You know which part."

"I meant it," he said, his tone turning solemn.

She nuzzled a little, teasing his ear with her breath. "You know I'll expect you to say it again." Later, in the dark, when it was just the two of them.

"And you?" he teased.

"Oh, I think I'll make you wait for a while." Pulling away, she placed a gentle hand on his chest, and let her eyes tell him what he needed to know. Yes, she loved him, so much it hurt.

Cade had been raised as a Scyth, but that didn't alter the

truth. He loved her, enough to risk his life for her. And that went a long way toward cleaning the slate.

With a squeeze to his fingers, Lina regarded the man in her arms. And then the circle of friends surrounding them both.

Her life might not be the version she'd imagined, but all in all, it was its own kind of perfect.

When Cade's upper body relaxed and his lids fluttered, Lina shook his shoulder. "Don't close your eyes," she said, worry thick in her voice, love bright in her heart.

Blinking, Cade looked steadily up at her, his gray gaze tired but clear. "Then I guess you'd better kiss me again."

Tiny frogs began to sing as moonlight fell softly. And with Arik and the Maidens standing guard, that's exactly what she did.

EPILOGUE

The Saturday following the Scyth battle had been declared an official day of rest. The whole crew had gathered to kick back and enjoy some down time—pizza, drinks, and large-screen television included.

Stately would describe the library at Arik's, while the ladies' parlor oozed elegance. The den, however, was all about comfort.

A trio of cushy sofas sat in the shape of a U, with a square coffee table in the center. Lina and Cade relaxed together in the corner of one couch, his injuries healed and a beer in his hand.

With only mild resistance, Cassidy had traded in her current book for the movie Rae and Peyton had picked, while Bryn and Arik glowered at the chess board between them, each trying to trounce the other for the best two out of three.

Little Poppy was there too, her tongue hanging out as she stared up at a sleeping Remi, the cat unreachable on a tall credenza.

Lina hadn't been able to leave Remi at the townhouse, especially since he always seemed to know when she was coming over here. The Victorian mansion was like his second home. Or at least he seemed to think so.

Reaching a dramatic moment, the film's music crescendoed, and the doorbell suddenly chimed in the distance.

"Don't cheat while I'm gone." Arik wagged a finger at Bryn as he stood from the chess table, leaving to go and answer the door.

"Did we order more pizza?" Rae paused the movie, her head cocked as she listened.

Lina and Cade shared a look. He hadn't heard anything from Ryker, but surely his cousin wouldn't show up at Arik's. The air between them hadn't been cleared, still thick with a fog of distrust on both sides.

It wasn't long before Arik returned, his demeanor sober, expression unreadable. From the doorway he said, "We have visitors."

Stepping inside, he led the way for two other men, one with hair and eyes as dark as pitch, the other fair-haired with scruff on his jaw as if he'd recently stopped shaving. Both strangers had a military bearing and the physiques to match.

"Hellooo," Cassidy said under her breath.

Lina reached over and thumped her.

The blond man held a black box in his hands and, for the space of several beats, they all just stared at each other. The one with black hair finally broke the stillness. "My name is Andrew."

The other corrected, "But everyone calls him Bishop." After a sidelong look from his friend, he added, "And I'm Killian."

Arik inclined his head to the men, then spoke to the Maidens and Cade. "They've traveled from Europe."

"Welcome." Rae smiled, waiting for more explanation.

Arik was the one to give it. "They're Huktai."

"Oh," she said, rising from the sofa.

"The Droehk came," Bishop said, "so we knew it was time."

"Time?" Bryn piped up, her eyes narrowed in speculation.

He nodded at her before turning back to assess Rae. "You are the Akasha?"

"I am," she replied, her voice strong and true.

At her affirmative answer, the one called Killian crossed the room to where she stood. He opened the shiny black box, revealing a broken fragment of stone inside. An almost identical piece to the one they'd dug from the graveyard.

Another aethyrical text.

Jaws dropped and breaths hitched. In the stunned silence, he held the box out to Rae. "Then this is for you."

ACKNOWLEDGEMENTS

An author is the beginning of a book, but the final product wouldn't exist without the help of others. My heartfelt thanks goes to Mandi Cranson, Dorothy, Beecher, Stella Racicot, Sharyn Cerniglia, and Donna Wood for their continued hard work. Editing isn't just about commas but also involves cheerleading, counseling, and a boatload of patience! Thank you all for taking part in the crazy!

Finally, I have to thank my husband, David. The last few years have seen huge changes in our personal life, and I am so glad to have had such a caring man by my side through all the ups and downs. Living abroad is full of excitement and challenges, and still being able to visit my favorite witches in Savannah makes it feel a little bit more like home.

And lastly, to all the members of the Reader Hangout and the Midnight in the Garden Readers Group, it has been so much fun, and I hope it continues. Thank you!

Suza Kates writes both paranormal romance and romantic suspense. She lives in Europe with her family and two ridiculously spoiled cats.

For more on Suza and her books visit

www.suzakates.com

SAVANNAH

COVEN

CHARACTERS

Anna St. Germaine
Hair: Long, straight, sable brown
Eyes: Sapphire blue
Color: Sapphire blue
Cat: "Ivy" gray female with lime green eyes

Anna sees visions of past, present, and future. She is the coven's head witch and is a descendant of the three women who originally banished the demon Bastraal three centuries ago. Her ancestral home is on an island off the coast of Savannah, Georgia and now serves as coven central.

Claudia Grant
Hair: Straight, long, flaming red
Eyes: River green
Color: Coral
Cat: "Rowan Von Ashbi" coloring of an American Wirehair with yellow eyes

Claudia is a history professor who only needs to touch an object to sense its past and previous surroundings.

Hayden Wells
Hair: Brownish red "caramel"
Eyes: Golden brown
Color: Pale pink
Cat: "Daisy" black tortoiseshell with yellow eyes

Hayden is a medium from San Francisco who sees and talks to spirits/ghosts.

Kylie Worthington
Hair: Long, wavy golden-blonde
Eyes: Hazel
Color: Yellow
Cat: Sassafras "Sassy" also a long-haired blonde but with bright yellow eyes

Kylie is a college student who's "on a break" to do her part for the coven and is able to control electricity in any form.

Lucia Ruiz
Hair: Long, wavy deep brown
Eyes: Brown
Color: Red
Cat: "Iris" black Persian with blue eyes

Lucia was born to privileged wealth in Spain and has the ability to find anything that is lost. She is an adventurer, world-traveler, and renowned relic-hunter.

Paige Reilley
Hair: Shoulder-length, white-blonde with ragged bangs
Eyes: Turquoise blue
Color: Turquoise
Cat: Tiger Lily "Tiger" brown and gray with white chest and belly, bright green eyes

Recently discharged from the military, Paige is a soldier in every way with the added abilities of super-strength and speed.

Shauni Miller
Hair: Long, straight, black
Eyes: Emerald green
Color: Green
Cat: "Cuileann" black short-hair with green eyes

Shauni is a nature-loving biologist from Colorado and communicates with animals telepathically.

Viv Sakurai
Hair: Shoulder-length, black, angled bangs
Eyes: Gray
Color: Purple
Cat: Kikoku "Kiko" orange tabby with yellow-green eyes and a grumpy disposition.

Relocated from Chicago, Viv is a physicist searching for an explanation for her own special power of telekinesis.

Willyn Brousseau
Hair: Wavy, shoulder-length, light blonde
Eyes: Pale blue
Color: White/cream
Cat: "Snowball" pure white with golden eyes

Willyn is a nurse, a mother, and a Christian. Raised in Alabama, she uses her healing powers to help those in need. She came to Savannah with an additional package, her young son, Tadd.

THE GUYS

Dr. Michael Black   *Whisper of a Witch*

This tall handsome veterinarian fell in love with Shauni in the first book of the series. He has dark blonde hair and gray eyes and is able to read a person's aura. He's a pretty calm guy until someone messes with his witch.

Dare Forster   *Conviction of a Witch*

Dark and handsome with deep blue eyes, this male witch came to the coven's island with his own plan. He wanted to partner with one of the women, but he never expected to fall in love. Especially with a gentle, Christian soul like Willyn. Now married, the two have made a family with Willyn's small son, Tadd.

Nick Reagan   *Binding of a Witch*

The coven likes to hang out in their favorite pub, and the owner of the bar always liked looking at Viv. His eyes are the color of the whiskey he sells, and his past is one of struggle. One night Nick finally got the nerve to approach the Asian beauty, but he got a lot more than he bargained for. The demon Bastraal had been destroyed once before, and his remains had been buried. Beneath Nick's very own pub.

Trevor Roch   *Haunting of a Witch*

One of Savannah's finest, this homicide detective clashes hard with the coven's ghost whisperer, convinced she's a con artist. Hayden has no choice but to work with the annoying man and find a serial killer who's working with the Amara. Staying true to form and following the coven's pattern, the two fall for each other. Against their better judgment.

Ethan Drake   *Possession of a Witch*

This demon hunter is well-acquainted with evil and has been chasing his own monster since childhood. When he offers to help the coven with their demon infestation, he has no idea he's about to be taken on the adventure of a lifetime. Lucia Ruiz is hard to resist, and is the one woman who might be able to save him.

Cole Lonergan   *Deception of a Witch*

As Trevor's police partner, Cole has been introduced to the coven and all of their secrets. While he admires the women and considers them all good friends, he never expects to feel anything more. But Claudia Grant is a long-legged-wicked-smart witch, and much like his favorite candies, Cole finds himself wanting to take a bite.

Quinn St. Germaine   *Suffering of a Witch*

Quinn is the younger brother of the coven's head witch, Anna. With sable hair and cobalt eyes, he is the masculine and handsome version of the siblings. His knowledge runs to occult history and magickal languages. He assists the coven in all things, and though he has his eye on a particular witch, he does his best to deny it.

Chris Decker   *Vengeance of a Witch*

An Army Ranger recently discharged, Chris was first introduced to the coven and their demon issues during a bachelor party gone wrong in the e-novella "Boys' Night out." Blonde-haired and blue-eyed, he's pretty laid back and easy going. Which is a good thing, since he's blessed with super-strength and speed, and has fallen in love with a rather temperamental witch.

Ian Keller   *Sacrifice of a Witch*

A tall, blonde, hot "Viking," Ian is the reincarnation of Ronja's long-dead brother Vanir. As lawyer for Ronja, he was introduced to the coven in previous books. Once he started to fall for Anna, Ian began to look to the future. While a dark past and vengeful "sister" wanted to drag him back to the dark side.